THE SISTERS of MADELAINE STREET

YVONNE ERWIN

Paperback-Press
Springfield, Missouri
e-book press publishing - an imprint of A & S Publishing,
A & S Holmes, Inc.

ISBN-10: 1-945669-01-2
ISBN-13: 978-1-945669-01-9

DEDICATION

For M. and Z.

ACKNOWLEDGMENTS

Whenever a writer completes a project, there are always people to be thanked. No man is an island, as someone wise once said, and we don't get here on our own.

So, I'd like to thank the following people for their instrumental help in the creation of this book:

Thank you to Paperback-Press, my publisher, and my cheerleader. Thank you for all the hours you put into making this book come to fruition.

Thank you Emily Truscott, my editor, who made this book come alive.

Thank you, Niki Bradley-Fowler, my cover artist. I am your biggest fan.

Thank you to Michael and Zachary, who always encouraged me, and told me not to give up on my dreams.

CHAPTER ONE

India

Greg's hand dropped to the sterile white sheet with a small thud. India scrambled to pick it back up, the plastic hospital band on Greg's wrist scratching her fingers.

So cold. India massaged Greg's hand, wrist, arm, not finding any warmth in his skin. Gazing down at the peppered, papyrus-thin flesh was painful.

How could it fall like that? There's nothing to him anymore.

Outside the hospital window, drizzle schlepped down the windows, sliding like a slug, leaving trails and small crystal drops in its wake.

April arrived, humid, unkempt, wet. Not the usual pastel-colored budding season in New York City.

The machines surrounding Greg's bed beeped and oscillated to the sound of some imaginary drummer, a salute to the dying.

India shuddered, watching the end of a life.

Greg's breathing was so slow, sometimes it was as

if he might not suck in another breath, but so far, inevitably, another rasp would form in the back of his throat, and a noisy, crackling bark would slip out. India knew it was called the "snore," the death rattle, a sound like no other in the world. She could only imagine Greg walking down a long, dark corridor alone with no one and nothing to guide him, only darkness and moist cool walls, and a light somewhere in the far distance.

A matter of time. That's what all the doctors told her, these last two weeks. *It's a matter of time now, India. Make each moment count, because each moment could be the last one. I'm sorry for your loss. Remember the good times. Remember him like he was. There is nothing more we can do.*

The sun rose and the sun set, splitting the sky with indescribable colors, every day a new gift.

India held on. Held on to Greg's paper-thin hand, watching, waiting, watching the minutes slip by. *Breath in, breath out, this is his day. Breathe, India. Look at his face, so beautiful, kiss his forehead, hold his hand, whisper in his ear that you're here and you always will be.*

The radio.

Someone must have turned it off earlier. India reached over with her left hand and switched the radio back on to Greg's favorite station.

He has to have music. Why would anyone turn this off?

A nurse in dark blue came into focus.

"He's doing well," she said, studying her computer monitor. "It won't be long now."

The nurse adjusted the monitor settings, pushed the contraption back into a corner and left, her thick soled shoes squeaking on the linoleum floor.

India nodded, her throat closed. *It won't be long now. But how do you say he's doing well when he's fucking dying? It's not a competition.*

Greg pushed another awful sound out. And then the stench. India pressed for a nurse.

"I can't believe he put out that big of a bowel movement," said the same nurse as before. "I'll get him cleaned up and then you can come back in. Can I get you some coffee, anything?"

No. Nothing.

What does that mean, a big bowel movement? Could he return to life, could he be healthy once again? No, India. Stop. Greg is dying, there's no hope left, nothing. Today is his day. Like his birth, that day was his day, and now, today is his day.

India looked around the room. Hospitals are supposed to be sterile, right? Clean, well kept? So why is Greg's dirty laundry hugging the baseboard? Why did the nurse kick it aside instead of picking it up and taking it away?

And the noise, the nonstop noise. It was excruciating, driving on the mind like a Mack truck. Twenty-four hours a day, pinging, binging, beeping, doors slamming, footsteps, cackling from the nurses' station, conversations outside the door. India thought her brain would explode all over Greg's bed, ruining the white sheets and the beige blanket, covering each surface with grey matter.

How can I give him the respect he deserves under these circumstances?

India leaned against the hallway wall for what seemed like hours, waiting for the nurse to clean up Greg and put him in a clean gown. Too tired to think, too tired to know she was hungry or thirsty, too tired to know anything outside that room.

So this is how it ends? In a fog of cocktail medications, raspy breath slowing with every second, this is how it ends? He's staying for me, and he shouldn't do that.

Greg was still breathing when India returned.

She leaned in, whispering.

"Greg, it's alright to go. I love you."

And then she climbed onto the bed with him, hearing it clink, gathering the extra blankets around her, reaching out, wrapping her arms around the wraith in the bed, her lips to his temple.

"India, are you okay? You look like you haven't been sleeping. What's wrong?"

Greg, whole and healthy, walked across the kitchen floor in their apartment, barefoot, whiskered jeans and unbuttoned shirt. He looked amazing, and India smiled.

"You're here. I mean, you're really here."

She was perched on one of the counter stools, hoping Greg would be making biscuits for breakfast.

Greg paused, just short of the refrigerator.

"Of course I'm here. Look, India, I'm really doing well. I mean, I'm fine, and don't worry about me. I'm in a good place, really. Hey India, I love you. I do. Sorry, love, no biscuits."

The sudden, unbidden silence jolted her awake. Lights, but no blinking, chiming machines. That nurse from earlier stood in India's space in her dark blue scrubs, a sharp light from the hall behind her.

India jumped and pawed Greg's chest, his face, his bony arms. *One more breath. One more. Please.* "Greg?" Immobile. *I don't know how I fell asleep.* Gone.

Greg's breathing was so slow, sometimes it was as if he might not suck in another breath, but so far, inevitably, another rasp would form in the back of his throat, and a noisy, crackling bark would slip out. India knew it was called the "snore," the death rattle, a sound like no other in the world. She could only imagine Greg walking down a long, dark corridor alone with no one and nothing to guide him, only darkness and moist cool walls, and a light somewhere in the far distance.

A matter of time. That's what all the doctors told her, these last two weeks. *It's a matter of time now, India. Make each moment count, because each moment could be the last one. I'm sorry for your loss. Remember the good times. Remember him like he was. There is nothing more we can do.*

The sun rose and the sun set, splitting the sky with indescribable colors, every day a new gift.

India held on. Held on to Greg's paper-thin hand, watching, waiting, watching the minutes slip by. *Breath in, breath out, this is his day. Breathe, India. Look at his face, so beautiful, kiss his forehead, hold his hand, whisper in his ear that you're here and you always will be.*

The radio.

Someone must have turned it off earlier. India reached over with her left hand and switched the radio back on to Greg's favorite station.

He has to have music. Why would anyone turn this off?

A nurse in dark blue came into focus.

"He's doing well," she said, studying her computer monitor. "It won't be long now."

The nurse adjusted the monitor settings, pushed the contraption back into a corner and left, her thick soled shoes squeaking on the linoleum floor.

India nodded, her throat closed. *It won't be long now. But how do you say he's doing well when he's fucking dying? It's not a competition.*

Greg pushed another awful sound out.

And then the stench.

India pressed for a nurse.

"I can't believe he put out that big of a bowel movement," said the same nurse as before. "I'll get him cleaned up and then you can come back in. Can I get you some coffee, anything?"

No. Nothing.

What does that mean, a big bowel movement? Could he return to life, could he be healthy once again? No, India. Stop. Greg is dying, there's no hope left, nothing. Today is his day. Like his birth, that day was his day, and now, today is his day.

India looked around the room. Hospitals are supposed to be sterile, right? Clean, well kept? So why is Greg's dirty laundry hugging the baseboard? Why did the nurse kick it aside instead of picking it up and taking it away?

And the noise, the nonstop noise. It was excruciating, driving on the mind like a Mack truck. Twenty-four hours a day, pinging, binging, beeping, doors slamming, footsteps, cackling from the nurses' station, conversations outside the door. India thought her brain would explode all over Greg's bed, ruining the white sheets and the beige blanket, covering each surface with grey matter.

How can I give him the respect he deserves under these circumstances?

India leaned against the hallway wall for what seemed like hours, waiting for the nurse to clean up Greg and put him in a clean gown. Too tired to think, too tired to know she was hungry or thirsty, too tired to know anything outside that room.

So this is how it ends? In a fog of cocktail medications, raspy breath slowing with every second, this is how it ends? He's staying for me, and he shouldn't do that.

Greg was still breathing when India returned.

She leaned in, whispering.

"Greg, it's alright to go. I love you."

And then she climbed onto the bed with him, hearing it clink, gathering the extra blankets around her, reaching out, wrapping her arms around the wraith in the bed, her lips to his temple.

"India, are you okay? You look like you haven't been sleeping. What's wrong?"

Greg, whole and healthy, walked across the kitchen floor in their apartment, barefoot, whiskered jeans and unbuttoned shirt. He looked amazing, and India smiled.

"You're here. I mean, you're really here."

She was perched on one of the counter stools, hoping Greg would be making biscuits for breakfast.

Greg paused, just short of the refrigerator.

"Of course I'm here. Look, India, I'm really doing well. I mean, I'm fine, and don't worry about me. I'm in a good place, really. Hey India, I love you. I do. Sorry, love, no biscuits."

The sudden, unbidden silence jolted her awake. Lights, but no blinking, chiming machines. That nurse from earlier stood in India's space in her dark blue scrubs, a sharp light from the hall behind her.

India jumped and pawed Greg's chest, his face, his bony arms.

One more breath. One more. Please.

"Greg?"

Immobile.

I don't know how I fell asleep.

Gone.

CHAPTER TWO

India
Before

What a good looking guy, and so interesting.

India watched Greg Allison making conversation with his friends at the next table. At the last minute, after a particularly hard day at work, India decided to go for a drink before heading home, and with that, she wound up at Brice's, a bar in the basement of a hotel on 41st Street. Brice's was a comfortable place away from the mainstream, loudness, lights, the whole New York style. India liked it because it was subdued, but with an electric vibe.

This guy, the one in the brown leather jacket, the jeans hanging just so, the attitude of "so...and who are you?"

India kept watching and listening to him speak with his group. He was so attractive and funny, and smart, and sensuous, like the best-fitting leather glove, comfortable in his own skin. This guy was everything

India would go for. She could almost smell his confidence and his smartness. Being good-looking was definitely a plus. It didn't hurt him looking damn good in those jeans. India surveyed him up and down.

She soon learned by eavesdropping on the conversation, he and she worked together, or at least for the same network, and once she figured that out, India knew she had to meet him.

Here's a conversation starter, thank God because I'd hate to have to seduce him with silly humor. Or not. Regardless, I'm going in.

And so India ingratiated herself on the neighboring table, soon learning this good-looking guy, Greg, was single, and holy shit, so was she. And they shared a love of music, and he was a photographer for the network she worked for, and, after they talked for hours, over scrambled eggs and toast in a corner diner, India and Greg fell completely in love.

Two years of a great love affair, breakfast with biscuits, snuggling in the big chair in the apartment, antiquing in Pennsylvania, snorkeling in Florida, candles on the birthday cake (his birthday, mostly), plays on Broadway, whispering in the dark, fights in the open and incredible lovemaking. And then the unexplained weight loss, the underlying pain, and the fatigue. Questions. "You're pale, do you feel okay?" "I feel like shit; I feel sick." And a whole other bunch of ugly, unforgiving stuff, and then the array of doctors and the x-rays and scans and medicine and prognosis and the supposed cures and more hocus pocus until the moment when Greg breathed his last breath.

India blew up the internet looking for information, searching for facts, cures, anything to help, to keep Greg alive.

In her wildest dreams, India never imagined the days of tossing daisies and running through fields into each other's arms would come to the point where India banged keystrokes spelling out "CANCER" on her laptop, peering, searching for The Cure, something to buy time, to alleviate his pain and discomfort, to help her help him through this time. It was never supposed to happen that way. Never.

CHAPTER THREE

Shelby

*D*amn, Shelby thought as she pulled out of Phillip's driveway. She glanced at the gas gauge and wondered how much money was in her purse.

First stop, gas station, but I gotta get to work on time. Shelby pushed her sunglasses up her nose and pulled into the first convenience store she could see. *Gotta make tracks. Can't be late.*

A greasy ball formed in her stomach. Sure, she just got out of bed with Phillip. Having sex should have relaxed her, made her feel calm, but deep down inside, she felt as if a hundred ants were swarming all over her gut.

Damn.

Her wallet yielded $108.75, which would have been good except her car insurance bill came in the mail that morning, and she owed on the cable TV.

Shelby owned no bank accounts, the number one reason being she was terrible with money and regularly overdrew her checking account when she had one. But the other reason was, without a bank account, there was nothing for creditors to seize. That happened once.

Now, Shelby flew with cash. Money orders were a pain in the butt to get, but she did so when she had to; everything else was paid for in dollars and cents.

Shelby pumped $20 in gas into her car and drove to the nearest McDonald's. Nothing else was going to get her pumped for a long shift at the nursing home but some McNuggets and an extra-large Coke.

She announced her order and pulled up to the window. Oh, who would be working the window at the McDonald's today but that girl, Brittany or Bethany or Bobohead. Whoever. The girl Phillip started seeing after, or maybe before, Shelby kicked him out.

What are you, all of eighteen? Shelby wondered, watching the girl fumble and recover and hand her order out the window. *I know your family; I tended to your grandparents before they passed. They had a farm; they owned their lives. You don't seem to measure up.*

"Thank you very much," Shelby said and drove away.

Good God, what would she think if she knew I was with him a half hour ago? Maybe I should have told her.

Shelby eased her old Buick sedan onto the highway and gunned it.

Maybe not. Let her worry and wonder the way I did. Nah, she's too stupid to wonder.

After she pulled her car into the River Oaks Manor parking lot, Shelby pulled her cell phone out again and texted Phillip.

"Just met up with your girlfriend. Working hard at McDs. But you know that."

Minutes later, a text came back. "Not my gf. Just a friend."

"Right," Shelby texted back. "That's why I saw her

undies hanging over the tub. Because friends do that."

"What u come by 4 if ur gonna fight?"

"Damned if I know. Won't happen again."

Shelby clicked her phone off and walked into the manor house ready to work.

Resolution gave over to defeat as she passed meds, wrote stats on charts, called doctors and generally wandered the halls of the nursing home.

Her urges weren't satisfied, and she didn't feel fulfilled even though the sex was like it always was, and that was good. No, she felt like dirt.

Shelby texted Quinn to find out whether Quinn was at home and if she was okay.

A text came back in the affirmative, and so Shelby called Gwen to make sure Quinn was telling the truth. Gwen answered in the affirmative too.

Hours left on her shift, and Shelby was bored, unnerved, having trouble concentrating. Her favorite patient, John, was sleeping, so no interesting conversation from him. Shelby paced, sat at the nurse's station, wrote charts, gave orders, and sighed. The episode with Phillip left her mind. Some other ethereal fingers poked into her subconscious.

I'd rather be home. I don't feel right.

The TV was on in the common room. Shelby was used to seeing the residents and staff watch the news, particularly the channel India appeared on. Shelby didn't watch the news all that much, but it did seem strange when the broadcast opened without her sister's voice and face coming out.

Shelby shuddered involuntarily and resumed her work.

Something's up. God, is my shift ever going to end?

The heavy feeling sat on Shelby's shoulders all the way home.

After checking on Quinn and pouring a glass of

chocolate milk, Shelby opened up the closet in the hall where she kept the family photo albums. The uncomfortable feeling persisted.

Something's up with India, I know it.

Dragging two or three of the dusty missives out of the closet, she sat down on the floor and opened the first one. She felt the need to go through the grimy old books, searching for the reason for her concern.

There we are, aww, look at us, Shelby thought, finding a photo of her and her sister, India, as children. India was probably twelve, Shelby younger, seven or eight. India's brown hair was pulled back in a ponytail, and she was wearing a plaid dress. Shelby, on the other hand, looked sweaty and busy, crinkled shorts, her top pulled up over her stomach, blond wisps of hair waving every which way. Their mother stood behind them, an eager smile on her face, her bouffant hairdo and cat's eyes glasses, standing with a hand on each of their shoulders. *God, I was such a skinny kid, like Quinn is now,* Shelby thought. *What happened to me? I look like a stack of cement blocks now.*

She continued to flip the pages, giggling at times, gaffawing at others. There was India sitting on her pink and white kid's bike, one hand on her hip, the other grasping the handle bar, and Shelby perched on a red tricycle, a brown arm stretching out to steady her. Later, another photo, India sitting on her brand new blue Schwinn, the bike she got for a birthday, and Shelby sitting on the seat of the pink and white bike India handed down. Shelby noticed the edge of a full skirt with a brown leg sticking out.

Must have been Gwen.

Shelby turned the page.

Another photo of India grinning, probably around fifteen years old, standing like a champ with her arms raised, holding a fish in the air, dressed in red shorts, a white shirt, her hair struggling to escape its rubber band, the background rocky. They were on a boat in the middle of some lake somewhere, Shelby was sure.

Shelby took a long drink of her chocolate milk and imagined the past come to life.

What Shelby remembered about that particular fishing trip was that she threw her line out as hard as she could, complete with bait and hook, and her father started screaming behind her. Somehow, she managed to throw the hook back into his ear lobe, and since she didn't know it, she had continued to throw the line out.

Oh my God, what a mess that was, Shelby thought, hot shame creeping up her neck. *I'm sorry I hurt you, Daddy.* She turned the page, and the next page and the next one. So many photos of their past, all done, all over with. Shelby clutching a kitten in winter, the fur-trimmed hood of her coat sliding off her head, blond wisps of hair sticking out. India looking up in surprise when Shelby snapped her picture while she was doing homework at the kitchen table before the house was renovated. Another one, Shelby, in a turquoise prom dress, all big hair and taffeta, smiling as she stood in front of a white car.

Shelby snapped the album shut and sat straight up. Her cell phone was vibrating.

CHAPTER FOUR

India

"India, what the hell?" Nick, the program director, shut the door to her office behind him and stood, hands on hips, his jacket flaying out behind him.

"Working, Nick, you know how it is." She was faltering fast but she didn't want Nick to know it. Not professional.

"Well, sure, but India, you're in no condition to work."

"I'm a professional, Nick. I work."

"Not now, not today. I'm putting you on leave."

"No, I want to work. I want to be here." India found herself standing in front of Nick, wanting to challenge but not strong enough to do it.

"Forget it. Go home. I know you're from someplace in Missouri, some little backwater town, go home. I'm giving you leave. Go home, India."

Nick turned to leave.

"Home? What are you talking about?"

Nick stood, his hand on the doorknob.

"India, you're a walking nightmare. Look at you, you are emaciated. You look like hell! What I am telling you is that you are in no condition to report the news for this station, and as your boss and a friend, I am sending you home. Your leave officially begins now, at this moment. So, pack up what you need to and go. Go. I'll send security up to escort you out."

"But, no, no."

Nick opened the door and then closed it. "Don't defy me, India. This time, I know what's best."

***

"Nick wants to talk to you," Amy, Nick's assistant, said as she walked into India's apartment. India watched Amy take an up-and-down look at her seeing dirty hair, no make-up, wrinkled T-shirt, pajama pants. The image of a derelict living under a bridge. India knew she had lines under her eyes, and she knew Amy noticed.

Amy stopped in the middle of the foyer in her black tights, black-and-white checked coat and perfect red hair, holding her purse in front of her. India watched the purse swing back and forth.

"He says you're not responding to his emails, or texts, or phone calls."

"What does he want from me? He made me take leave; what else does he want?"

"I don't know. Call him. Call him, India. Just do it."

India pulled her cell phone from the coffee table, opened her phone contacts and selected Nick.

"You're my witness," she whispered at Amy. "I'm calling him but I don't like it."

"Nick Seymour."

"Hey Nick, it's India. You've been calling?"

"India. Just wanted to check and make sure you're

following through. You need a break. Greg's illness and death was a terrible thing for all of us, but mostly for you. You're heading home, right? Back to Missouri?"

"Look, Nick, I don't know what I'm doing right now. Just putting one foot in front of the other. Why are you so interested in me going back to Missouri, anyway? Why is that so important to you?"

"Because I know what you need, and I'm telling you: go home. You have a sister, right? Back in Missouri?"

"Are you forcing me out, Nick?"

This time, it seemed Nick paused. "Of course not. India, what a ludicrous thing to say. I only want what's best for you, you know that, so, go, get well and come back when you're ready."

"That's not the way this works, Nick. That's not the way the news works, and it's not the way my contract works, and it's just not the way I work."

"Well, I'm telling you, India, as your boss and your friend, don't argue. Just take the time off. In fact, I'll suspend you if you don't."

"Sure. Okay. Thanks."

"Anytime."

India clicked off.

"Am I being forced out, Amy? Tell me the truth. Am I gone?"

Amy's cheeks seemed to redden but other than that, she held complete composure, sitting on the couch beside India, her legs crossed, arms on thighs.

"Of course not," Amy said. "Listen, I have to go. I have a dinner date, if you can imagine that, so I better get going."

"Wait. Amy!"

Amy was already up and moving for the door.

"You're not being forced out, India. Think of it more, like, you've been given an opportunity, although you might not see it now. It'll come to you, whatever it is. And I'm sorry about Greg."

After the click-click of Amy's heels leaving the apartment, India sat for a long time on the couch, staring out the long windows with the city dusk settling outside. The grays and blues of the daylight surrendered to amber, yellow and bright white. Black sky stretched on and on.

I never thought this would happen to me. I've been forced out of the network, no matter what they say. Greg. I wish you were here. God, how I wish you were here. Nothing makes any sense without you.

Coming back to the apartment was hard after Greg passed. He was in every corner, striding through every door. The photos over the fireplace, photos of India and Greg on vacation in France, photos on the beach, Greg walking with his pants rolled up. His hair was long, and he held his sandals in his hand. His stuff lay on the bathroom counter. The razor, his deodorant, the last of his dirty clothes in the hamper. The day Greg died, India slumped to the bathroom floor, pulling the garments out of the hamper, one at a time, gathering the last of Greg's scent to her. *You're here but you're not*, she sobbed.

He was all over the kitchen too. Greg's Keurig sat on the counter, now unused since India didn't care anything for a Keurig, and his special knives in the knife drawer. His coffee cup was in the dishwasher, along with that damn soup cup, the one with the Campbell's kid on it. Greg held that thing since childhood. His prized frying pan, the one that was supposedly "green," and his spices and the rooster lamp he bought once in New England on vacation…and so much more.

India looked around the apartment, tears building, her eyes filling.

Go home, she thought, remembering her conversation with Nick. *Easier said than done. And I'm not sure Missouri is home, but I can't stay here either.*

India plucked her phone from the coffee table and wondered if her sister, back in Missouri, would be around. How would Shelby feel about hearing from her? India was well aware of Shelby's claims of India's superiority, the gap between them, the confusing intermittent communication about Shelby's life, and sketchy information about her niece, Quinn, some of it troubling.

India sat back on the sofa, staring out the windows, watching the miniature cars bustling, the lights blinking off and on, mostly on.

This could be a terrible mistake, going back there. What am I doing, acquiescing to Nick's recommendation? I could stay right here and wait it out. Everything's bound to blow over sooner or later, right?

India stretched her legs out, reaching the coffee table, and then curled back up on the couch, staring out the windows.

Leaving here would be like leaving Greg all over again. But maybe it's time to go back, just for a while, as long as it takes me to get back on the network. Mistake or no, maybe it's time. Time to go home.

India dialed Shelby's number and waited.

CHAPTER FIVE

Quinn

Quinn's bedroom door opened without warning.

She glanced up from her tablet to see Shelby's shadow, looming large in the hall. She was lying on her bed, stomach side down, messing around on Facebook.

"Knock, please," Quinn said, going back to her tablet.

"Um, look, baby, I have to tell you something."

Shelby Graham perched on the edge of the bed, depressing it a bit as her weight settled in. The dull hue of Quinn's Mickey Mouse lamp turned Shelby's skin yellow. The bulb blinked a bit.

"What?"

Quinn rolled over, holding her stomach. What now. What freaking thing now.

"India's coming back."

"So?"

"And she's moving in here for a while."

Quinn sat up, knocking the tablet to the floor.

"Mom, no. I don't like her. She thinks she's better than us. You don't like her either."

She watched Shelby turn the ring that loser, Phillip, gave her a year ago before all the trouble. Quinn couldn't stand Phillip; thank God he was gone. But Shelby still wore that cheap Cracker Jack ring. Quinn couldn't understand why her mother even had that ring anymore. *She should have burned it.*

Her aunt, India, was coming back to town.

"I don't want her here."

"Quinn, she's family, she's my sister. We'll handle it. Was I supposed to say no?"

Quinn stood up.

"Uh, yeah."

Quinn watched Shelby's face turn downward.

"Why is she coming back here? Her life is in New York, or Bagdad or Somalia or some other where."

"Well, she's had a little bit of bad luck, like her boyfriend dying of cancer and all, and she's taking a leave from the network."

"But why here?"

"She grew up here, Quinn. I mean, technically, this is her house too. Er, rather, this is her house. Period."

"No. Mom, seriously?"

Shelby sat silent, a toad squatting on Quinn's bed.

Quinn waved her hand in dismissal.

"Forget it, Mom."

The urge to run hit. Fight or flight, and Quinn favored flight. Quinn ran out her bedroom door, down the stairs while Shelby called for her to come back, all the way down to the main hallway and out the front door, down the walkway to the sidewalk.

Once on the sidewalk, Quinn looked left down Madelaine Street and right for oncoming traffic, and then crossed the street and began running north, on Tenth Street. Her instinct to go turned off. Now she just wanted to run. She felt better when she let go, bursting against the air, pummeling the sidewalk with her tennis shoes inextricably pinned to her pumping knees.

Her mother's voice followed her down the street. "Quinn! Quinn Antonia Demarist! Come back here right now!"

No way. No way would she share a house with that snob, India. India, the big reporter woman, been all over the world and back, been on TV, India who didn't remember her family so far as Quinn was concerned.

The real problem was, Quinn knew as she bicycled her legs up and down, was the impending change in the status quo, and Quinn didn't like change. She didn't like feeling as if she was standing on shifting sands, arms akimbo, legs trembling and spreading to accommodate the moving ground beneath them. India's arrival reminded Quinn of all the telephone conversations she overheard as a child of her grandmother, Shelby and India's mother, talking to India on the phone, begging for help and advice on What To Do About Quinn. Quinn remembered conversations between her mother and her grandmother about Quinn's hair, or rather the color of it at any particular time ("too gimmicky,"), her jeans ("too tight," her grandmother would argue), her makeup ("What are you doing, Shelby, painting her up like a doll?" To which Shelby would argue back, "None of your business, she looks beautiful. I'll do what I want with my daughter.") There was also the Phillip situation, which Quinn hated thinking about, and the marks on her arms, which she sometimes thought of as battle scars, and other times thought of as junk.

As far back as Quinn could remember, or at least after her grandmother died, it was Shelby and Quinn, and Gwen, even though Gwen didn't live with them in the big house on Madelaine Street.

No, another adult in the house, especially one she

hardly knew, was toppling her.

India. What did she look like anyway? The anchor Quinn saw on TV looked a little like her, with brown hair and an angled face, but the eyes and ears were different. Quinn's eyes were brown, her complexion was dark, and her ears resembled a taxi cab riding with the doors open. India's eyes were blue, and her ears weren't prominent. But still, sometimes, when Quinn and Shelby, and sometimes Gwen too, watched India on TV or saw photos of her, Shelby would point out something about India's pose, her stance, her eye movement, and she'd say, "Quinn, you do that too. You're so much like her."

Quinn hated being compared to her aunt. She barely knew India. She had so few memories of her, and didn't really know if she liked India or not. All she had to draw from was what her mother said to her about India, and in that case, Shelby found every reason in the world to say India thought more of herself than she should; that India left their town and family to be a big star and didn't care about them; that India thought she was better than them. Did Quinn like her aunt?

I don't want her coming here, Quinn thought as she ran, fear gripping her stomach. *She'll change everything.*

"Hey now, slow down, lady."

A voice came out of nowhere, propelling Quinn to stop and face Gwen Baker. "You're gonna make me trip and fall all over you."

Quinn came to an abrupt halt in front of the family friend.

"Oh, hey, Gwen."

"Where you running to, girl? And why you runnin' when you can stroll, hunh? You young folks, always in a hurry to get somewhere, but you ain't goin' anywhere."

In spite of her internal turmoil, Quinn grinned and realized she ran straight to Gwen's block, to her bungalow, in fact. How did that happen?

"You want to come in?" Gwen said. "You look like you all out. Come on, I got Coca-Cola, and I know you like that."

The brick porch with the taupe door opened an invitation. Quinn stood, contemplated going forward into this wonderful reality, and then decided she would.

"Come on, child," Gwen said. "Tell me what it's all about."

The screen door rattled as Gwen shut it behind Quinn.

Gwen and Quinn ended up sitting at Gwen's Formica table in her kitchen. Quinn gazed around at the red apple clock hanging above the sink.

"You all got power on over there?" Gwen asked. It wouldn't be the first time the power company shut off the electricity on account of Shelby forgetting to pay the bill, once for three months. And then where did the money come from to catch up the bill and get the power back on? Gwen often wondered what Shelby was up to. Shelby didn't have money. Sometimes, Gwen wondered if Phillip was giving Shelby money every once in a while, even though they were supposedly broken up and living separate lives. Gwen would not have been surprised to find out Shelby was seeing Phillip on the sly. Nope, Shelby went head over heels for that guy, and he proved to be a total fraud, and an even worse issue. Gwen remembered the day Shelby demanded he leave, Gwen standing on the porch, listening to the conversation just inside the front door.

Shelby stood her ground one time, and then I figure, she crumbled because she really believed Phillip loved her. She would have suffered with his foolishness til her dying day if the girl hadn't gotten pregnant.

Gwen sighed in spite of herself.

"Yeah, we got power," Quinn said. "The electric's

on. It's not that."

"The flag team? I know you was havin' some problems with that."

Quinn sat back in her chair. "I quit the flag team."

"But you loved being on the flag team, and I saw you, I came to games, and I watched you. You were really good. Why would you let somebody bring you down like that?"

"Things. She didn't like me. Our instructor. She didn't like me, and she said something I didn't care for. So I quit."

"That's a shame," Gwen said. "You can't go through life quitting everything because someone says a word to you."

"Yes, I can."

Gwen drew back.

"Well, you ain't gonna work very well at life then. What is it then, Quinn? What's got you all upset?"

Gwen shifted in her chair, watching the girl across the table.

A long minute passed. Gwen slurped on her bottle.

"My aunt India is coming back," Quinn said, setting her Coke bottle on the table. "I can't stand it."

"Oh, India. Well, I remember her as a girl." Quinn saw Gwen's face light up upon the suggestion of India. "You don't like her?"

Quinn stared into the speckled table top before answering. She had nothing to borrow from as far as India was concerned, when India was a girl or whatever. Quinn wasn't even alive then.

Quinn burrowed her hands in the pocket of her jacket.

"I can't stand her. She thinks she's above us. She's a snob. I don't want her here. She's gonna change everything."

"Change what? Everything's a pretty big word,

Quinn." Gwen belched. "Excuse me."

"She's gonna change my mom, she's gonna change me, she doesn't fit in here. My mom says she thinks we're trash. I hate her!"

"But you don't know her, right? You don't know whether or not you like her. You're going with someone else's opinion, I think. What do you think, Quinn?"

"I don't know what I think. But I know my mom is gonna let her come and move in with us whether I like it or not."

"When will she be here?"

"Tomorrow morning, I guess."

"Why do you think she's coming?"

"I don't know, and I don't care."

Quinn stood up, but was instantly conscious of Gwen's hooded stare.

"Maybe, Quinn, just maybe, your aunt needs support right now. Maybe she's not as strong as she portrays, or what you think, and maybe she's not as highbrow as you imagine. Maybe she's a real person. Think about that."

Quinn sat back down on the edge of the chair.

"Uh, no. She's a jerk."

"I doubt she's a jerk. The India I remember wasn't a jerk. Quinn, you only know what you've been told. People hold prejudices; everyone does."

Quinn stood.

"I gotta go."

"Okay. I'll drive you."

"No, I'll run. Thanks."

"Well, in that case, I'll call your mother and let her know you're on your way, right?" And with those words, Quinn found herself out the door on the sidewalk. Running back home. Nothing was changed in Quinn's favor, as far as she was concerned. India was still coming, *tomorrow*, and Quinn didn't quite know how she would deal with that.

CHAPTER SIX

Shelby

Shelby Graham perched on a stool at the nurses' station, monitoring her Droid for any message from India, or Quinn, for that matter.

Outside the windows, the deepening dusk enveloped the mauve and blue lobby with its colloquial Colonial couches and armchairs, then the hallway, and as the dark fell over all, Shelby relaxed, in for a quiet night with the residents of Oaks River House Nursing Home.

"Oh, guess what," Shelby said to Sarah, the other nurse on. "Guess what the fuck what."

"What," Sarah said, looking up and down the chart of duties for the night.

"My sister. You know, the one on TV? She's moving back here."

"What the what, girlfriend? Your sister? India's coming back here? What for?" Sarah's chart banged on the nurses' station, her elbow landing on top of it.

"Don't ask me. I guess her boyfriend died of cancer or something and she's supposedly taking a leave. Something like that, I guess." Shelby stood up and then sat back down. "You wanna take rounds?"

"I can," Sarah responded, eyes wide. "And I can relate to the boyfriend's passing, so tragic, but Shelby, I just gotta ask, do you want her back here?"

Shelby tucked her hair behind her ears. "I don't know. She's the oldest, the golden child, the one prone to glory, you know? Thing is, I live in her house, which was our house when we were kids, but our mother left it to her when she died and India's let me and then Quinn live under what would be her roof. If she lived here, that is. I don't know. I think India sees me as a charity project, a no-good mess. I'm not looking forward to her being here, I'll just say that."

"Tell her to get a hotel or something. Don't let her in your house," Sarah said.

"Sarah, you miss the point," Shelby said, stretching the stethoscope around her neck. "It is her house."

Shelby turned back to the charts and notes on the desk. "Time for you, girlfriend, to go on rounds. Don't worry about me, really. Just don't. It'll work out, or it won't."

Thirty minutes went by, Shelby making the appropriate entries into the log, calling doctors about patients, all the duties she executed beautifully, night after night, after night.

"Shelby," Sarah came running. "You gotta come. It's John, and he's asking for you."

"He wants to show me his toast collection again?" Shelby stood, wrapping her stethoscope around her neck, chasing after Sarah, who was already running back to John's room.

"No, I think he's dying," Sarah gasped.
Code, code, code.

Shelby entered John's room to find the 92-year old sitting on the side of his bed, dressed in a smoking jacket, looking quite dapper for a man of his age, and not in any danger of dying at all.

"What is it, John?" Shelby approached the old man.

"Oh, thank God you're here," John gasped, reaching for her hand. "I prayed you would come."

"What's wrong, John? What are you all worked up over?"

Dried spittle lined the old man's lips, his eyes a blue rheumy glaze, but he stared up at her with such intent Shelby thought she might fall to her knees. In an instant, John reached out and grabbed her hand with both of his.

"It's this – I'm in love with you, and I want to marry you," John said. "No, no, I know I'm older than you, but I love you with all my heart, and I want to make your life easier. I'm quite wealthy you know, and my stepdaughter takes care of everything for me financially. You would never want for a thing, and I would ask your father for your hand, but I don't know him at all, and I want to ravish you the proper way," and he winked. "I've always been quite good at ravishing."

"Awww, that's so sweet, John," Shelby said. *Why couldn't other men appreciate her the way this one would? So old fashioned and…nice…and proper.*

"Now, I have a ring," John said, letting go of her hand, digging in his jacket pocket. "I wouldn't come to you without a ring. It's right here."

The silver glitter of aluminum foil appeared in his clenched hand. When he unfurled his fingers, a band made of wrapped up foil popped out.

"It's beautiful, John," Shelby said. "I'm so honored."

She pushed the ring onto her middle finger, since it was too big for her ring finger. She pressed her stethoscope against his chest.

"Can you breathe for me? Just in and out, that's right."

"I don't have much time," John whispered easing back onto his bed. "I just know you would be a happy, fulfilled woman with me."

Shelby grinned at Sarah and helped the old man pull his feet up. She took his slippers off and tucked him into bed.

"Now, John, I'd be so happy to be your wife," Shelby said. "I'm sure you'll make a wonderful husband, and we'll spend many years together."

"Oh, I will, I promise you, I will," John whispered, grasping her hand. He took a deep shuddering breath and closed his eyes. "I'm a lucky son of a gun," he said, and fell asleep.

Shortly after 10 p.m., Shelby looked up from her desk to see Sarah running toward her.

"What's the matter, babe?"

Shelby noted Sarah's pale face, how she was sweating, how she could hardly breathe.

Sarah stopped at the nurses' station, grasping her stomach.

"Oh my God, Shelby. I'm so sorry. Shelby, it's John. Call the doctor."

Code! Code! Code!

Shelby's heart dropped.

Damn, the first honorable man I've met since my father, and this one goes and dies on me.

CHAPTER SEVEN

Gwen

Gwen Baker saw the green-grey fog, the smoky issue, even before she saw Quinn, enveloped in her aura, running toward Gwen's house.

Oh boy, here we go, Gwen thought, and so she walked to the corner because Quinn was coming that way, and when she saw Quinn, Gwen saw the green-gray aura surrounding her.

Jealously. Fear. Indecision.

Quinn was running, hair flowing behind her ears, eyes wide open. Gwen stepped in front of her, because no one else was going to rescue this girl, and Gwen knew Quinn needed rescuing.

Colors, auras, whatever you want to call it, Gwen saw them. Shelby was dark pink, like a spring rose, the color of unconditional acceptance. Normally, Quinn's aura was sea foam green, the color of expectation.

She didn't know why she saw these things, she just did, and over the years, Gwen came to accept the strange halos surrounding people she knew and cared for.

The green-gray aura surrounding Quinn was troubling. But perhaps temporary, until she and India settled in together and got used to one another.

Gwen's mind's eye scrolled back to Phillip's last day in the Graham house; Shelby screaming, Phillip penitent at first, and then as Shelby accusations continued, Phillip's shouting to match Shelby's shouting. And finally, Phillip exiting with his stuff, ramming his form into his new Ford pickup, squealing out of the driveway and leaving Shelby sobbing inside the house. At the time, Gwen didn't know quite what to do. Should she comfort Shelby in her time of need or remind her she was better off with Phillip gone?

Gwen jumped when her cell phone rang. Shelby called and said Quinn was home safe. It was a condition Gwen held with Shelby, to always call and let her know Quinn's status.

Too much confusion. Gwen watched her dark brown hands washing up the last of her dinner dishes. She glanced up to see her reflection in the kitchen window. Big eyes, close-cropped black hair, chocolate-colored woman. How strange to see her own brown hooded eyes bulging in the thick glass.

Too much fear. The girl hasn't had much of a chance. Sad to blame Shelby, but she should have done better. Should have kept those men away from Quinn. Should have protected her from such dark things. But Shelby's got her problems too. Nobody's got a bigger heart, but probably nobody's as short-sighted either. That combination's got poor Shelby in trouble more times than once. Oh, Shelby, always wanting some man's love. Never getting the real thing.

Shutting off lights from the kitchen to her bedroom, Gwen pondered the Quinn question as she often did. *What are Quinn's options in life? She hates school. She hates getting up in the morning. Routine? She bad at that. How's she gonna get a job, how's she gonna live when Shelby and me are dead and gone? Is she gonna have to marry some no-account man probably because she's pregnant, and suffer his wrath the rest of her life? Or just be somebody's baby mama and collect welfare and have more babies by more baby daddies, what? The girl don't understand how valuable an education is; she don't understand what work means. Shelby, she don't help it none. She so indulgent and lazy. She ain't shaping that girl right. Funny though, how much Quinn runs. If she applied that kind of energy to school, she could do anything.*

Gwen undressed in the dark and pulled her nightgown on. Easing into bed, the thought came to her.

India will be here soon, and she just might be the answer to all of this.

CHAPTER EIGHT

Shelby

Shelby roamed The Bee Bouquet, looking the cluttered shelves up and down. This week's paycheck was cashed and resting in her wallet. Her cell phone bill was due in a few days, and as usual, Quinn went over the limit, and Shelby had to pay an extra $34.85. Tony's child support check was already spent, covering the light bill. Shelby voted not to think about any of that.

What would India like as a welcome home gift? What speaks India in this place?

She picked up a small statue of bone china, glimmering white, a lady dressed in Grecian flowing garb, carrying a basket of flowers on her head, one arm flung back, the other hanging tenuously to the basket.

Nope.

A pair of bookends caught her eye and she picked them up, examining them from top to bottom, clicking the bookends together. No, too flowery, too cloying. She set the bookends back down.

Finally. The pendant lay on a sheet of delicate lace. It was old, rustic gold steampunk style, with a large clock face in the center, antique-looking face and an image of the Eiffel Tower behind the black hands. Turning it over, Shelby saw a small opening for a battery. The thing could actually be made to keep time. Delightful!

Shelby flipped over the tag and stopped for a second.

Fifty bucks. But it's really pretty, and I know she'll love it, and once she gets over being mad at me for leaving her stranded, she'll be happy about it. I mean, she's got money.

Sold. Shelby grabbed her package off the counter and almost made it out the door.

"Hey."

Shelby turned and almost ran into Phillip.

"What are you doing here?"

"Saw your car out front. I'm on my way to my brother's place for a barbeque. Thought I'd stop in and see what you're doing, that's all."

Okay, so he's coming way too close. Shelby could smell his breath and what could she do. It's Phillip.

"Baby, I miss you," he said, running his eyes up and down her.

Shelby was awkwardly aware her T-shirt was wrinkled and her jeans were tight enough to make her wince if she moved just right.

"I don't miss you," Shelby lied. The grey roots of his stubble were appealing.

"Like hell you don't," Phillip said, leaning in close. Shelby quivered. "You miss me. I can smell it."

"I have to pick up my sister in St. Louis."

Phillip pulled back.

"India? You're picking up India?"

"Uh yeah," Shelby said, easing away.

"Why you picking her up?"

Shelby shook her head, feeling lost, out of control. "I promised I would. She's coming in for a while, that's all."

"And you have to drive all that way and pick her up?" Phillip was back in her space, hot breath stinging Shelby's upper lip.

"I told her I would."

"That bitch can find her own ride," Phillip said, leaning in again, pressing his lips on hers, forcing her mouth open.

How did it happen? Shelby would never know.

An hour or so later, and a few texts from her sister later, Shelby sat at the end of Phillip's bed, pulling her jeans back on. Phillip stood at the sliding glass doors in his robe, smoking a cigarette, smoky tendrils circling above his head.

"You know what," he began. "You said all that stuff about how I molested your daughter, you made me the asshole in that whole thing, but I'll tell you this right now, right here. Your daughter lies."

Phillip turned, dramatically, his robe furling around his bare legs. "She can say what she wants, but I'll tell you this. She strutted her stuff in front of me, daring me to take a bite, and you know how hard that is for a man? But I never did. Not one time. Quinn lied to break us up. She hates me."

"Why would she do that? You don't know what you're talking about." Shelby grabbed her sweater and pulled it over her head. "Besides, you grabbed her."

"Shelby, stop being blind. I'd be living right back where I was, with you, if it weren't for that snot of a daughter of yours."

"Oh yeah?" Shelby wanted to slap the arrogance off his face. "Need I remind you about how you brought an eighteen-year-old girl to my house, *my house*, and fucked her in my daughter's bed? Huh? How am I supposed to feel about that?"

Phillip stubbed his cigarette out in an ashtray on the dresser. "Well, at least it wasn't your, I mean, *our* bed."

"You're an ass."

"Well, Shelby, I'll tell you something. You took that innocent little daughter of yours and made her up to look like she was ten years older than she was. You dressed her up like a Hugh Hefner bunny and let her have a Facebook account when she was nine years old, posting all those pictures. It was you, parading her around in front of middle-aged men cruising the internet. You know you did that, or you allowed that. It was you that messed her up."

Shelby turned away.

"My daughter is beautiful. She's perfect. I was just taking pictures. She wants to be a model."

"Look at me, Shelby." Phillip took her chin in his hands, forcing Shelby to look him in the eye, causing her to tremble, tears forming at the corners of her eyes. "I may be a no-account fucker, but one thing I ain't, Shelby. I ain't no child molester, although she gave me reason to want to. Quinn's got problems. Real ones, and you know it."

"Stop it, stop it," Shelby started. "She's my daughter, why are you talking this way?"

Phillip dropped his hand and walked back to the sliding glass door, pulling another cigarette out of the package on the dresser. As he lit, he stood staring out the glass doors. "Shelby, the elephant's in the room. All you got to do is look at her arms, right?"

Shelby fled, same as Quinn would, to the living room, the front door, out to her car and slammed the driver's door shut. The impact gave her a headache.

Her arms, right?

All she wanted to be was beautiful, and I helped her

be that. I was so proud of her. She looked so good in those dresses and heels. Shelby jammed the car in reverse and screeched out of Phillip's driveway, the rear end of the car swinging crazily. Righting herself on the highway, she careened toward town. *Asshat. All Quinn wanted was to be beautiful, and she looked damn good in those dresses and her makeup. I did that, her makeup, and it was perfect. She wanted to be beautiful. She wanted to be a model. I never got that. I never got beautiful because once I hit my teenage years, I was always too fat! So what if she was a kid? She was my baby girl to dress and make up any way I wanted. I ain't gonna apologize for that. She was everything I wanted to be and never was.*

Shelby slammed through the four-way stop sign before the square. An indignant blare caught her attention briefly, but she drove on.

Everything I ever wanted to be and never was.

Shelby turned into her driveway and pulled the car to a stop.

Did Phillip ever touch her? I saw what I saw. Did it ever go further? She told me he did, but she hated him. She wanted us broken up. She could have made up that whole story.

Shelby sat with both hands on the wheel for several minutes, staring straight ahead.

India's gonna kill me. I bet she doesn't show up. No, she will. She'll come here and make me feel small.

"Mom?" Quinn's voice brought Shelby out of her thoughts, suddenly alert to the katydids and town traffic.

"Yeah, baby. I'm home. I just got here. Sorry I'm a little late."

Quinn opened the car door.

"You're more than a little late, Mom."

Shelby burst into tears, shaking, gripping the steering wheel.

"Mom, come on."

Shelby was vaguely aware of Quinn scolding her, trying to get her out of the car, and finally, she gave in.

"I'm just so tired, Quinn. Just so tired. India's supposed to be here, and I didn't pick her up, and I don't know...she's gonna be so mad at me. She's gonna be so mad," Shelby blubbered while grasping Quinn's hand, allowing herself to be hauled out the car. "I bought her a gift, a homecoming gift, but she's gonna be so mad."

Struggling toward the porch, leaning on Quinn's slight frame.

"Where were you anyway, Mom?"

"Uh, nowhere really. I just lost track of time. I ran out of money, and I couldn't go to St. Louis, and I just messed up. I just messed up."

Shelby slumped into the wicker loveseat on the porch. She saw Quinn's eyes flash, and she tried to focus on the porch railing. Weariness washed over Shelby like a warm wash rag. She didn't want Quinn to know she went to Phillip. Shelby didn't want anyone to know that. How could she willingly go to him, really, after what she thought he did to her daughter? What kind of mother would do such a thing, knowing her daughter accused the man her mother loved of inappropriate behavior? Shelby turned to her daughter, tears in her eyes.

"Uh huh. Liar, liar, pants on fire, Mom."

Out of the corner of her eye, Shelby watched Quinn turn to the front door and pass through it, leaving Shelby alone, on the porch under a yellow light.

I'll sit here and wait, Shelby thought. *If India's coming, she'll be here soon. I'll sit here and wait.*

CHAPTER NINE

India

Seriously? India checked the time on her phone, 1:55 p.m. And then checked her messages to Shelby. All of the messages confirmed she would need a ride at 12:30 p.m. and Shelby confirmed she would be there.

India texted her. "Are you on your way?"

The text back was baffling. "Yeah, just left. Been shopping."

"What the hell." India said to no one in particular.

India stared around. Airports in general are not pretty but this one, in St. Louis, Missouri, seemed uber-dreary, unclean and depressing. The plastic chairs, the stench of human. All India wanted was to go to a warm bed and quiet, clean surroundings.

"So, are you coming?" India texted back.

No response.

Fifty-five minutes later, India texted again. "Are you on your way? Been waiting here all afternoon for you."

Ten minutes later, a text came back.

"Sorry, can't make it. I don't have gas money."

"You're kidding me, right? I'm stranded here."

"Don't know what to tell you. You're the big reporter with the swank life. Sorry."

India clicked the phone off without replying.

You've got to be kidding me. Unbelievable.

India looked left and right. People were teeming about, prospective passengers chatting together, the operation, a well-oiled machine, everything clicking neatly in place.

Except for her.

Welcome home, India.

"Rental car, you want rental car?" the Indian attendant shoved a form over the counter for her to fill out. And then another form and another one. She turned over her credit card and then her driver's license.

"What's all this for?" India asked. Her neck hurt.

"Rental car." The attendant punched her information into a computer, dark brows furrowed, intent on his computer screen.

"Okay, rental car. What car can I get?"

"You like Volkswagon?"

"Sure, I don't care. Just so it drives."

"I have very nice car for you. I take good care. We'll have the car brought around for you."

"Right, thank you," India said, imagining a brand new gleaming Volkswagen, maybe a red one, pulling up to the door.

India winced and loaded her luggage into the trunk of the rental, a 2008 black Jetta station wagon with Arizona plates. She settled in for the long drive home.

Some things never change.

All eagerness to see her sister faded, India tried to remember the last time Shelby came through on anything. She couldn't.

It's not like I couldn't go somewhere else, bag on them like they bagged on me. It's not like I have to go there. I'm not sure I should. But I can't go back to New York either.

India kept driving and thinking, both hands on the steering wheel, her eyes hidden behind heavy shades.

What about Quinn? Will she be happy to see me?

India drove on, lost in thought. Quinn wouldn't mind seeing her, maybe. But India's current irritation and bewilderment with her sister was seething. No gas money? Shelby promised to pick her up, wouldn't that mean she'd make sure she at least had gas money? If she didn't have money, she could have asked India. Why wasn't Shelby straight with her in the first place? If she didn't intend to come, and she didn't have gas money, why didn't she just say so?

The radio in the Jetta quit. India didn't notice.

She pondered the long time strain between her and her sister.

India was the structured one, the oldest daughter, the daughter who pushed always to the next level, always striving to make their parents proud. By contrast, Shelby was the free spirit, never giving a thought about anyone but herself, who didn't care if their parents found pot in her underwear drawer, the one who searched for love and hoped for fairy tale endings.

Sisters. Blood. Why were they so different, she and Shelby? *You're the big reporter with the swank life.*

Where did that come from? Why does she keep bringing that up? She had choices too, and she made them.

True, India and Shelby hadn't been close sisters as children, but they respected one another's space. India was so serious, studious, curious about the world outside their hometown, impatient to see it for herself. Shelby was the other side of the coin, the flim flam, adopter of stray pets, the one so in love with her life, she would most likely never leave their hometown, who didn't give two nickels for what was going on outside of Oak Ridge, Missouri. They were different as children and seldom got along, but there were times of laughter, joking, confiding, great anger at the betrayal of confidences, guarding each other's backs, borrowing one another's clothes, spying on each other on a date, all the things sisters did for and with one another. They didn't long for each other as some sisters did. They weren't best friends. Did that mean they didn't love each other?

But still...*where did we go so terribly wrong? Why are we so uncomfortable with each other?* India thought back to their parents' deaths. Shelby was fourteen to India's eighteen when their father died. Shelby, a child with blond curls and geranium red nail polish, more bluster than brawn. India stood quietly beside the casket on a hot day in August, silent tears seeping into an all but invisible handkerchief. The sisters' suffering was different with their father's death. Shelby grieved loud, as if she wanted everyone to know she was grieving. India stood silent, still, holding her mother's shoulders as the box holding the man they loved was lowered into the ground, shovels of dirt landing on top of the cement box.

Why do you want everyone to look at you, at YOU alone? India wondered at the time. *We all lost him, first of all, Mom. Why are you putting yourself in her place?*

So perplexing and so aggravating. India's brow furrowed.

When their mother passed, a mere four years ago, Shelby again grieved loud, but this time pulled Quinn into the funeral itinerary, having the girl stand in front of the casket for most of the ceremony as some sort of symbol to how much their mother loved Quinn and only Quinn.

At the time, India protested quietly, "This isn't good for Quinn," to which Shelby's reply was, "Oh, so you think she didn't have a bond with Mom?"

There was no fighting it. India decided not to struggle. The pain of their mother's death was insurmountable. And to stab the wound even further, Shelby said, "Stop waving that 'I am the oldest' flag around. You do it all the time."

India didn't know when she ever held such a flag to the wind, but she also knew Shelby was floundering in unknown waters, trying to preserve a hold on her life, crying out to the universe, protesting the change their mother's death brought. India wanted to say, *but I am the oldest and I can't change that*, but in the end, she said nothing, and allowed Shelby to live in their childhood home and claim the birthright India was born to.

Oak Ridge, population 4,800, lay tucked between a series of Ozarks hills. Residents were proud to boast the town was incorporated in 1883, after the Civil War, and settlers chose the area because of the many pure water springs and the abundance of farm land. The settling of the town pivoted outward from the city square with no planning involved. Many of the streets ended with no reason or curved to incorporate a different street. The town square remained, flanked by three-story brick buildings, including the post office, a bank, a Mexican restaurant, Henderson Foods, and the local newspaper office. There were no stop lights on the square, only two stop signs. In the summer, the local farmers brought their vegetables and herbs to sell. In the winter, the gazebo in the center of the square was adorned with lights and a Christmas tree in the middle. It was the kind of town that might be put on a postcard, if only it was better taken care of.

The house India and Shelby's parents owned on

Madelaine Street, where India and Shelby grew up, the house Shelby now lived in, was left to India in their will, but India never wanted it. She didn't argue when Shelby and Quinn moved in, out of a trailer court on the sadder part of town, where Shelby married and divorced Quinn's father, Tony Demarist, and eventually where that Phillip guy, the one India was pretty sure molested Quinn while her mother pretended not to see, moved in and then out.

The house was big, surrounded with old oaks, fragrant mock orange bushes and stately rhododendrons, with a welcoming front porch, large windows, gingerbread trim, a fire place, massive pocket doors, and chiseled glass doorknobs. Built in 1898, the house was one of a row of majestic homes declaring a more gracious bygone era that would later be left to decay and eventually torn down. Newer bungalows came in the 1940s, and later, some ranch-style homes sprouted up alongside. Only a couple of the original homes remained, and one of them was now a law office, but the Graham house stood in its time-honored way. India and Shelby's parents gave the house a pale yellow Hardy siding, window boxes trailing with vinca and petunias, some French doors, an herb garden, and a chef's kitchen with a great gas stove and an island in the middle. It was a comfortable home. Nice, quality digs.

The second floor room in the turret was India's room. It was a romantic space, the long windows looking out to the back yard on one side, curving and turning to the neighbors on another side, and then turning again to look down at Madelaine Street. India grew up with lavender walls, wood floors, the metal bedframe painted a pistachio hue, an ivory quilt embroidered with wisteria vines, and the lamps India's mother made for her a long time ago when her mother was into ceramics. The lamps were a matching pair, identical Dutch girls in blue dresses with white aprons and hats, wearing wooden shoes, and a white shade over each bulb. Nothing in the room matched, but it was the most beautiful room India could have ever imagined a girl could grow up in, and India grew up in that room, surrounded by those cherished artifacts.

Pulling off the interstate at the second exit to Oak Ridge, India drove slowly, deliberately into town, checking off the road signs to where her sister would be, where India's old life existed only in her memory.

Her old life, and her present life. India felt no connection.

She only felt sadness.

The pangs of Greg's death still came, stabbing her in the gut, forcing India to remember she was the victim of a tragedy. As she drove along, India wondered whether she would want to share her loss with her sister, this life-changing event, and she realized she didn't want to.

What I've been through is too personal for anyone else's consumption. And in the end, Shelby is only concerned about making me the bad guy, the sister who left the family for the big city life, the one who got away. I got away alright. And now, I'm back.

A new stop light had been put up since she was last there.

But I wish we could share. I wish we could act like equals.

The streets looked largely the same, except older and in more disrepair. The homes India remembered seemed dusty somehow, as if they'd been abandoned by time to rot and fall in on themselves. At the corner bar, India smiled at the newly painted exterior, and then the Dollar Store, and the red-brick high school with its multi-paned windows and double front metal doors.

A new wing had been added onto the old brick high

school. India's graduating class was fifty-six people.

She turned left on the street she knew and drove slowly past the park, where softball games were probably still held during the summer months, past the tennis courts, and then a right turn, to her block. It seemed, to her, she passed by Gwen Baker's house on the way home, the brick bungalow with the wide front porch, but she wasn't sure. The trees lining the block seemed enormous.

All so familiar, but different too.

Easing down the familiar street, India paused. How strange to have grown up here, on this block, in this huge home, the Victorian with the wrap-around porch, the gingerbread trim, and the mature trees, all the bushes and plants, and to still recognize it from so many years away. The house seemed a little more worn, the trees seemed bigger, it seemed a little foreign, and yet... not.

India pulled into the driveway. Someone was sitting on the porch steps. In the deepening dusk, India realized Shelby was sitting there. Waiting.

Why is she sitting there? You leave me stranded and you sit and wait?

India's throat tightened. The figure on the steps straightened to a standing position and began running down the steps to India's car.

Stepping out of the car, India found herself embraced in a mammoth-size hug.

"You made it. You made it," Shelby sobbed onto her neck. "Quinn! Come out here. Your aunt came home."

Came home?

"Well, I'm here, but no thanks to you," India said, extricating herself from Shelby's overwhelming embrace. "Why didn't you tell me you weren't coming?"

"I got tied up, that's all. But you're here now, right?"

Before India could answer, Shelby turned and yelled, "Quinn!"

India looked up. A young woman stepped out on the porch, the lights of the house serving as her backdrop. The girl was clearly not the child dressed in pink ballet tutus India remembered, but rather a teenager, astonishing in her too-tight jeans with holes and whiskers, the obvious breasts in a pushup bra, the lacey camisole top clinging to her teenage figure, and the gauges in her ears, Dreamsicle orange hair. And the passive-aggressive slouch of a teenager used to doing whatever she wanted.

India's stomach tightened.

Is this Quinn? Of course it is. I've been gone too long. She looks like a wanna-be thug. Okay, but she's my niece, my blood.

India started up the stairs.

"Quinn. Hey."

"Yeah, sure, hey," the girl said and shrank away from India's embrace, eyes downward and away.

Shelby tittered in the background.

"Uh, Mom, I'm out of here," Quinn said, looking past India's shoulder. "Me and Ivy are gonna hang out for a while."

Quinn loped to the end of the driveway.

"Okay, baby, have fun," Shelby called.

India saw the car, a pale metallic colored sedan that opened up to allow Quinn entrance. Quinn folded into the back seat and pulled the door shut.

"You're kidding me, right?" India watched the red taillights disappear from view. "Shelby, who are these kids? Who is driving that car? Where are they going?"

"Quinn's friends," Shelby said. "You just got here, now don't start."

"Do you know her friends? Their parents, all that?"

"It's okay, India. It's okay. Nothing ever happens

here."

"So, you don't know them? Any of them, the kids, the parents?"

"It's okay. It's just a bunch of kids, friends."

"Oh well, okay, I guess you just let her go, just like that?"

India stared down the driveway, where Quinn last was. No way this would happen in the city. No way would a child of any age just walk down the driveway and vanish.

Shelby already turned away. Quinn was out of sight, out of mind, and Shelby was heading back into the house. India stared after her for a second and then followed.

I'm not in Kansas anymore, India thought. *Or rather, I'm back in Kansas via Missouri but the good witch left for Florida a long time ago.*

Back in the kitchen, Shelby seemed bubbly, giddy.

What's up with this?

"I got you something," Shelby said.

"Why?" India asked.

"You could act a little grateful," Shelby said.

"I don't even know what you're talking about. You didn't have to," India said, settling on one of the chairs at the island.

"No, I did, and I hope you love it. It's sort of a 'welcome home, glad you're here' kind of thing, and when I saw it today, I just had to buy it. I mean, it's so you, and I think you're gonna love it. I mean, I really do."

India stared as Shelby went on and on but could only think, *she saw it today? When she was supposed to pick me up?* The sound of Shelby's voice was drowned out by India's thoughts. *Okay, hello, India, what did you expect anyway? She went shopping instead of coming to the airport like she promised.*

"And here it is," Shelby said, and India was vaguely aware of a package being shoved across the island toward her. "So, welcome home."

"So, you leave me stranded two and a half hours away, but you get me a gift."

"What, it isn't up to your standards, huh?"

"Shelby, I haven't opened it yet but I'm sure it's very nice. Come on, lighten up, please?"

"I just wanted you to like it."

"And I'm sure I will. So, let's open this bad boy up, okay?"

India tore the packaging open and found the pendant. Pulling it out, to the light, she could only say, "Oh my."

Under the lights, dangling from India's fingers, the pendant shone like fine antique bronze and glass and the most delicate tea-colored tapestry.

'It's beautiful. Thank you so much," India said, reaching across the island to her sister.

"I knew it was you. I just knew it was you."

"It's beautiful. And I do love it. Thank you." India laid the pendant out on the island. "But listen, I have to ask you, why did you leave me at the airport when we agreed you would pick me up? I mean, it was St. Louis. Not like I could just walk the rest of the way."

India's stomach dropped when Shelby stepped back, tears appearing in the corners of her eyes.

"I got this for you," Shelby groaned.

Something else is wrong. Something.

"Okay. I wanted to get you something, like, because, to welcome you home. And I still thought I could make it to the airport in time but the truth of it is, I spent all my gas money on this gift and then I, um, I ran into an old friend, and then, um, I just lost track of time, that's all."

"So, those bite marks on your neck, they happened

today?"

"I messed up. I mean, you know, that's what I do. I mess up."

"Uh, well, you're not twelve anymore, and I'm not sure I buy all this. What is the deal, Shelby?"

And then the lights went out.

CHAPTER TEN

Quinn

"I hate gym class," Quinn whispered to her best friend, Ivy, as they sat on the steps leading up to the second tier of the gymnasium.

"I know, me too," Ivy whispered back.

"Too sweaty."

"Gross." Ivy collapsed against Quinn's shoulder giggling. "Hey, can we go to your house for a while, hang out?"

"I don't know. My aunt's here from New York. It's a whole weird deal, she's here and my mom said she could stay here, and I don't like her, but she's, like, up in my face all the time."

"What do you mean, she's up in your face?" Ivy pulled a Ding Dong package open and offered Quinn one of the cakes.

"She's just, like, where are you going, who are you with, do you know the parents, all that kind of crap…did you do your homework, did you eat lunch? I mean, she's just over the top. And it's like she wants me to like her, but I don't. I wish she'd never come here. She's a pain in the ass."

Quinn took a bite of the cake and swallowed loud.

"She's like this big time reporter and stuff," Ivy said, shoving the last of her Ding Dong in her mouth. "My mom thinks she's awesome. She watches her all the time on the news."

"Yeah, like, who cares? She's on some kind of leave, supposedly because her boyfriend died. She just pisses me off."

Quinn wiped the last of her Ding Dong from her lips.

Ivy shifted on the stairs. "Why would that piss you off? I mean, like, she's on leave because of a death? Sounds kind of romantic to me. I mean, you find true love and then your true love dies? Sort of like a movie."

Quinn rolled her eyes.

"Believe me, romantic, it's not."

"Hey," an unknown voice interrupted their conversation. Quinn turned and saw a boy she saw around school. He dropped down casually beside her as if he was invited.

"Hey," Quinn said, hanging her hands between her knees.

The boy looked past her at Ivy. "Ivy, right?"

"Yeah," Ivy said, staring straight ahead.

"We're just having a little girl time," Quinn said, "So..."

"Yeah, I get it. My name's Adrian, by the way."

"Okay. Hi, Adrian. You're the new kid, right?" Quinn looked straight at him. She noticed his hazel eyes and, suddenly feeling self-conscious, mentally checked her clothes wishing her favorite blue top wasn't in the laundry, and that she put on better jeans that morning.

"I've been here since the beginning of the school

year."

"Well, yeah," Quinn said. "I *know* that. You're new from last year."

"I moved here over the summer right before school started," Adrian said, stretching out his legs.

"From where?" Quinn asked.

"Joplin."

"Joplin," Quinn repeated. "How did you get here?"

"My dad. My dad moved us here."

Quinn decided not to ask any more questions.

He seems sort of skinny, but he's cute, Quinn thought. His tennis shoes weren't new, in fact, they looked pretty scuffed up. She didn't want to look him straight in the eye.

He might be cool, I don't know.

Quinn stared at her shoes, dirty pink high tops against the grey concrete of the steps. Ivy got up and walked away, disappearing into the crush of students. For some reason, Quinn wasn't sorry to see her go.

"Hey, Quinn, can I walk you home?"

CHAPTER ELEVEN

India

All in all, returning to Oak Ridge, Missouri, wasn't as welcoming and pretty as India might have imagined, not on any level. Not that warm and fuzzy expectations ever occurred to her in the first place, but being abandoned at the airport irritated her and saying anything about Shelby's broken promise didn't work out well. Quinn's weak, withdrawn response to her arrival pricked India deeply.

But it was more than those things. As India walked through her childhood house, the specter named reality showed up in its best clothing. For one thing, there was no food in the refrigerator, no real food anyway. And the house was dirty. Not messy and lived in, but dirty. It gave off a scent of abandonment, of people taking their shelter for granted, except for a faint rancid memory of a fast food party here and there.

India pushed her finger through the dust on the lamp next to the couch, and left a meandering trail behind. Stringy cobwebs dangled from the ceiling fans. Dirty dishes lined the kitchen counter and stacked up in the sink. Dust bunnies skittered to the corners as India walked through the house.

Finding the bloated corpse of a mouse in the cabinet under the sink startled India even more. Slamming the door shut, she leaned against the counter and looked around breathing heavily.

Seriously, they're living this way? Unbelievable. Our parents would never tolerate this if they were here. Guess what. I won't tolerate it either.

India searched the kitchen and laundry rooms for cleaning products but what she found was a congealed bottle of liquid dish soap, a half-used can of Comet and an unopened gallon of bleach. India grabbed the bleach, filled a spray bottle she found in the laundry room with that and water, and went to work in the kitchen first. She would rather have slept for a while after the flight and drive back, but she couldn't stand seeing and smelling the house the way it was.

Once the house was clean, India felt like cooking. It seemed the only way to restore the beautiful house to its former glory.

The ingredients for a great quiche:

10 eggs, mixed with a half cup of half-and-half.

Four or five strips of bacon, browned and crumbled.

Chopped onion.

Pie crust, either store-bought or homemade (India would opt for the store-bought, roll-it-out variety).

Gruyere cheese, maybe some parmesan too.

Mushrooms.

Kosher salt, pepper and cayenne pepper.

Of course, Shelby's refrigerator yielded none of these things.

"Crap," India said, bent over staring into the cold

interior.

What has Quinn been eating all these years? There are no vegetables around here, not even much meat. Not much of anything.

Riffling through the miscellaneous, nondescript items in Shelby's refrigerator, India sighed. Store run.

India grabbed the keys to the rotten rental and drove to the nearest market, making the most of little time, and returned.

Throwing her grocery store bags on the counter, India went to work.

Bacon and onion sizzled in a skillet, its gorgeous aroma filling the kitchen. Throw in the mushrooms.

Ten eggs, cracked into a bowl, *wisk, wisk, wisk*, stir in some half-and-half. Salt, pepper, cayenne pepper. Stir the cheese in. Preheat oven.

The lights flickered.

It's an old house, right? India hoped the power would hold. When the power went out the other night, Shelby ran downstairs, jiggled a breaker in the circuit box and everything came back on. India wasn't sure which breaker it was, or whether she'd know what to do in the same circumstance, and so she hoped and prayed the power would hold.

Store-bought pie crust lined the pan. Pour in the egg mixture. *Woosh*, Let the bacon and onions cool a bit, then stir in.

India flexed her back and shoulders just a bit, wondering if Shelby or Quinn would have any interest in a quiche. Quinn, in particular, seemed to have been raised on chicken nuggets and not a whole lot else.

Sigh.

India shoved the quiche into the oven.

Salad: torn romaine, iceberg, carrots, radishes, red onions, feta cheese, roasted pecans, blueberries. Salad dressing.

India glanced into Shelby's refrigerator again. A bottle of ranch dressing sat in the door, dredges of brownish goop sliding down the label. Nope.

Okay, so we make salad dressing. Except we have no olive oil, no lemons, no garlic. India sighed and grabbed her purse. Luckily, she had about an hour before the quiche would come out, and the store wasn't far.

Back home with her purchases, again, unpacking, grabbing a bowl from the cabinet. Whisking Dijon mustard, olive oil, chopped garlic and lemon juice together in a bowl. Salt, pepper, some more of that cayenne pepper she found in the refrigerator. Two store runs and she still didn't have dinner made. *Good lord, you're a mess, India. And, you're trying to impress a kid who's made up her mind she doesn't like you.*

Speaking of, where was Quinn? She should have been home from school by now. India ran to the bay window in the dining room, and looked out.

She doesn't like me, and she'd be mortified if she thought I was worrying about her. India ran through the hall and stepped out on the front porch. *Quinn, where are you?*

"Shelby, Quinn's not here," India said into her phone.

"Uh, yeah, she went with Adrian after school. She'll be home soon. He walks her home sometimes."

"Who's Adrian? When is soon? She's not here yet. I'm worried." India glanced at the clock again. 4:10 p.m.

"It's only four o'clock, India."

"I didn't know she was going somewhere."

"Adrian's a boy she met at school and he's going to walk her home. Are you yelling at me? Seriously? Like *you* ever had kids!"

India pulled the phone away from her ear for a second and stepped out on the porch. "I wasn't yelling. School is out at 3:05, and she's not here. We're five blocks from the school. I just thought she would be here by now."

"I know what you're saying. Don't you tell me my daughter is immoral. I've seen plenty of girls like her, and she isn't one of them. She might turn out to be more moral than most."

"You're not making any sense. I didn't call Quinn immoral, but I don't know where she is, she's late, okay? This is about dinner. Listen, I made a quiche. I thought we could all have dinner together, and she's not here, that's all."

"*FanCEE*. Well, I'm at work 'til seven."

"Fine," India said with a sigh.

"Okay, well, I have to go. I've got rounds to make."

"Sure. See you at seven."

India stepped back into the house. A dark house.

"What?" she flipped the outdoor light switch. Nothing.

The smell of half-baked quiche filled the dark house.

"Crap!"

She dialed Shelby back.

"The power's out…"

"So, go flip the switch."

"Switch?"

"The switch in the basement. Remember, the other night, like we did before? Come on, India, you grew up here too."

"Right," India raced downstairs to the fuse box and turned her phone to shine light on the box. "Main switch, right?"

"Right." Shelby sounded bored.

India flipped it and flipped it back. Nothing.

"Nothing."

"Do it again."

"Still nothing."

"Huh."

"Well, now what?" India ran back up the stairs. "I guess I'll call someone, right?"

"You big city girl. Pull your pants up, would you?"

"What? I mean, we had maintenance people in the city, but I know enough to call an electrician, for God's sake!"

"I'm sure you do," Shelby said.

"Why are you so condescending to me anyway? Oh never mind."

India disconnected.

Phone book, there has to be one around here, right? No wait, search on phone. Search for electrician in this town and hope to God somebody can come out right away before the house burns down. The house won't burn down, right? Get ahold of yourself, India. You're not helpless. City-fied maybe, but not helpless.

But, what if the house does burn down? Could it? Probably not, but anyway.

Scads of electrical contractors appeared on her phone. India scrolled down the list and put her finger on one. Funar Electric.

I have no idea who you are, but at this point, I don't care. Just come, please.

India dialed the number, hoping for the best.

Fifteen minutes later, he was standing on the porch. India opened the door, and her stomach flipped.

There you are, her soul said, clear as if she said it out loud.

Red heat creeping up her neck put India in a mild state of panic. She only hoped he didn't see.

India felt a flicker of recognition in his brown eyes, a lift of the eyebrow, something knee-jerk and real, and although they never met before, India felt connected to this man, as connected as they would be had they known one another for a hundred years.

She stepped back, holding the door open.

He didn't hear that, right? Shit.

"Thank you for coming so fast, Mr. Funar. It's pretty dark in here. And I had the oven going when everything blew," she said as he entered the hallway, her eyes on his dark blue shirt. Fact was, she was afraid to look him in the eye, but finally, her gaze traveled from his shirt up to his neck and onto his face where the same brown eyes peered down at her.

"It's no trouble," Paul Funar said. He was still giving her that queer look, sort of confused, sort of on guard, maybe? India felt crazily uncomfortable, and she didn't know why.

"Um, well, okay, I'll show you to the basement, where the fuse box is," she said a little too loud. "If you'll follow me…"

India led Paul Funar down the stairs to the basement, his flashlight leading the way. India gestured to the fuse box and stood aside.

She watched him open the door and inspect the box. After a few minutes, he asked to see the attic.

"Right," India said, leading him back up the stairs and to the second staircase, wondering if her butt looked big, trembling all the way.

"Yeah, so here it is," she said at the top of the attic stairs.

Paul Funar's flashlight moved left and right, up and down, tracking the floorboards, traveling up each wall to the ceiling, and across, over and over again.

"Okay, I've seen enough of this," he said and gestured toward the stairs.

Startled, India followed. Down the attic stairs, down the second floor stairs, and she started to ask what he found.

"Hey, it's dark in here," Quinn said. "What's going on?"

India jumped.

"Hey, I've been waiting for you. I tried to make us dinner, but it turns out, I put the lights out. My bad," India said.

Quinn rolled her eyes. "You're so uncool, you know that?"

Paul seemed to be grinning, which was even more humiliating.

"Um, you can fix this, right?" India turned to Paul.

"Well, I can fix it, but it's going to take probably the next eight or ten hours of your life."

India found herself staring at the ceiling. No reason, just staring, maybe mostly so she didn't have to look at him.

"It's gotta be fixed," she said, finally, after reviewing each and every beam mounted in the living room ceiling. "No choice. So, what are you going to charge me?"

Paul moved forward. India didn't move, her eyes following Paul Funar's every movement. His sheer presence brought a certain kind of comfort and a sense of history. India breathed it in, all sage and eucalyptus.

But wait.

"The quiche," she said finally. "It's probably ruined."

India rushed to the kitchen and opened the oven door to find the quiche actually was doing quite nicely as the oven hadn't cooled entirely yet.

"So, what's going on now?" Shelby entered. "What about the quiche?"

"It's mostly baked, but it's gotta be finished or it'll ruin."

"Half-baked quiche? I'm gonna call Gwen and tell her to preheat her oven," Shelby said. "She can finish it. Half -baked quiche, ha ha. That's a riot."

"Mostly baked," India responded.

"You guys are weird," Quinn interjected.

"Half baked," Shelby said again, dialing Gwen.

"No, mostly baked," India insisted. "Tell her mostly baked."

"Ladies," Paul said from the shadows.

Three pair of eyes turned on him.

"I can fix this," he said, "but I've got to give you an estimate and you've got to do some paperwork with me, okay?"

"Okay," India heard herself say. "Sure."

In the background, India heard Shelby and Quinn twitter identically.

India looked into Paul's eyes and felt herself melt into another person, a person who suffered grief, but at the same time, a person who felt sunshine and pretty flowers around him, a feeling of stability, someone whose life wasn't left on shifting sands, someone not left waiting to fall into the abyss.

You're here, India thought, *and I can barely believe it.*

"Let's start with your name," Paul said, pulling a notepad out.

Shelby jerked her head at India.

"We need to talk," she said, moving toward the hall.

"What, now?"

"Yes, now," Shelby jerked her head toward the door again.

"Excuse us," India said. *Embarrassing.*

To the hallway, whispers of light filtering in from the dining room.

"What do we need to talk about?" India dug her hands in her pockets.

"You should see how you're looking at him," Shelby whispered.

"What? How am I... I am not looking at him,"

India said.

Shelby pursed her lips.

"Mhmm."

"I mean, yeah, I'm looking at him but I'm not *looking* at him. What's wrong with you? We've got business to do here. Right?"

"I'm gonna say I told you so one day, but you're looking at that man like you think he's the Michelangelo."

India rubbed her forehead. "That's a nutty thing to say. What if he's already married, huh? Did you think of that?"

She's not backing down, India thought. *Okay, I looked at him, but this is all crazy. He could be a married man with ten kids.*

A ripple of fear shot through India as she saw Shelby square her feet.

"Trust me. That man, that one in there, he's gonna be your husband one day. And when that day comes, I'm gonna remind you of this moment right here."

India stiffened, glancing back into the dark chasm of the kitchen.

"I hope to God he didn't hear that," she whispered. "What do you know about me, anyway? All you've done since I came here is insult me, and I'm tired of that, and you're acting crazy."

"What, me, crazy? That's been known for years but, I'll tell you again, you're gonna marry him."

"Quit it," India hissed. "You're embarrassing."

"Okay, I've got an estimate for you," Paul said, appearing in the doorway.

"Let's go out to the porch. We can see better out there," India said, glaring at Shelby.

"Good thinking; that's where I wrote this up, actually." Was there a glimmer of a smile around his eyes? *If he heard what Shelby said...* Dropping through the floor was not an option but India wanted to desperately.

India led, Paul and Shelby followed. Quinn disappeared somewhere into the depths of the house and within moments, YouTube music videos started playing.

"Gwen's here," Shelby announced once they stepped out on the porch. Sure enough, Gwen was pulling into the driveway in her white Chevy Impala, parking behind India's rental wreck.

"Okay," Paul began. "Once again, let's start with your name."

CHAPTER TWELVE

Gwen

The scene on the Graham porch was a little unnerving. All those auras, bumping and mixing together, crowning under the roof and bouncing back again in a gang fight of who's who. Gwen moved the car into park and took another look before shutting the ignition off.

A white service van was parked on the curb. Not surprising, since Shelby told her on the phone the power was out and an electrician was onsite.

But what's going on here? These girls interrupted my "House Hunters International," for what? And the episode was in Paris too. I've never been to Paris. Would have liked to have seen that one.

Shelby looked the same as usual, except her aura was pulsating just a bit more than normal.

India. *India.*

India's aura was jumpy, nervous, white-tinged with an electric yellow casting sparks into the middle, breaking up and moving to the rim again and again.

I've never known India to be out of control.

The colors jumped again, smacking into one another.

Gwen's eyes moved to the man standing beside India, holding a notepad, tucking a pen back in his shirt pocket. It was obvious the two were having a conversation when Gwen pulled up.

My. Gwen turned the ignition off watching India's confusion.

She saw India startle and pull herself away from the man to acknowledge Gwen.

His aura, I'm not sure. Yet. But it seems to be blue, which could be a good thing. Loyalty.

Gwen got out of the car.

"Hi y'all, I hear you've got a quiche that needs baked."

"Well, I'll get started," the man in the blue shirt said, stepping off the porch right next to Gwen, walking to his service van.

Gwen stared after him. In a minute, his aura came clear.

Gwen shuddered, turning back to the girls on the porch.

"Well, hurry up, I ain't got all day now," she heard herself say. "Bring that quiche and let's go."

CHAPTER THIRTEEN

Shelby

Shelby paced the floors of Oak Manor House, inconsolable.

John was gone, never coming back, and ever since he died, she felt out of whack, off kilter, as if there was a whole world going on out there without her. She was on the outside looking in, nose pressed against the glass. Loneliness swept over her like a tidal wave crashing to the shore, knocking her over in its wake.

Good thing Sarah was working tonight. At least there would be a friend to talk to.

He was such a good man, and whether or not he meant any word he said to me, he was still a good man. He served his country in World War II, he was kind and smart and really kind of sexy. He was a man I would have loved for a thousand years, if only he'd come to me in my time.

John's family, such as it was, one cloddish daughter and her bespectacled soft-spoken husband, came to collect the body and make arrangements for burial. And then the room John lived in, the bed he slept in, was cleansed of the person before, leaving no marks, and another resident came and occupied the space that once was John's space.

Shelby paused in front of Room 212 and prayed a little prayer.

There would be no more toast collection, no more exclamations of love, no noble man standing in a ruby red smoking coat, declaring his undying love, and asking for her hand with glittering eyes.

The dinner trays were passed out, the nighttime medications distributed.

Sarah was occupying Shelby's chair when Shelby came back from rounds.

"I was waiting for you," Sarah said, getting up, moving to the next chair.

Shelby sat down with a plop.

"It's been pretty quiet around here. I'm really tired tonight, Sarah. But I'm glad you're on with me tonight."

Shelby folded into her customary chair. Sarah settled into a seat next to her.

"How's it going these days for you? You said your sister was coming, right? How's that going?"

Shelby pushed her glasses up her nose.

"Where are the snacks?" shouted Ava Brashears from the common room. She was a white-headed resident confined to a wheelchair, a former high school teacher who ended up taking early retirement when she was found on the city square wearing her nightgown too many times, having no idea where she was or how she got there. "I came here for the snacks, and there's no snacks."

Shelby watched an aide rush to Ava's side, speaking to her quietly. "I want peanuts," Ava was saying. "If you don't have peanuts, I want a bowl of cherry chip ice cream. My show is about to start. I want my snack."

Shelby turned back to Sarah. "Uh, pretty much what I expected and dreaded too. She's a big city girl, and she thinks every time Quinn walks out of the house, something's going to happen to her, like she might disappear. She's, like, some kind of Nazi police, if you know what I mean."

Sarah laughed.

"'Property Brothers' gonna start in five minutes. Where's my snack?" Ava Brashears twisted in her wheelchair. "I gotta have a snack if I'm gonna watch those two hotties. They make me crazy, I tell ya. Those boys are cute."

Shelby scratched her forehead. She knew the aide was well able to take care of Ava Brashears, but nonetheless, listening to the exchange was frustrating.

Mr. Lloyd approached the desk from the shadows and asked for a box of Kleenex. It was the second box he requested that evening. Shelby handed him the box on the desk.

Shelby turned back to Sarah. "And she cooks and cleans like a freak show, which I don't do any of that, so more power to her. But, on the other hand, she paid for the electricity work that had to be done on our house. Or her house, whatever. The house we live in."

Shelby sighed.

"Every time I open my mouth, I say something wrong," Shelby said. "And I don't even mean to, it just comes out. Fight or flight, I guess."

"One big happy family," Sarah laughed.

"Yeah, one big ole happy family," Shelby said, stacking files. A rubbery squeak next to the desk turned Shelby's head.

"It's 'Property Brothers' night," Ava Brashears called. "The Martians have stolen the show and the snacks. Who's responsible, dammit?" Madame Brashears rolled off in her wheelchair.

Shelby sighed again.

"Yup. One big old happy family."

CHAPTER FOURTEEN

Quinn

She'll never stop talking. Why doesn't she stop talking?

"And what is your name?" India was saying.

Quinn groaned and looked around the gymnasium. The football game was finally over, and she stayed and waited for Adrian to shower and get back in street clothes before they went out for ice cream or whatever. Just something to get her out of the house.

Parents and children were reuniting with friendly hollers about the game, friends were hooking up, throwing bags and purses over their shoulders as they exited into the darkness, laughing and shoving one another. Ivy waved as she passed by with her parents.

"Adrian."

"Oh, I love that name. Adrian. Strong, masculine, poetic." India stuck her hand out. "I've heard about you. I'm India, by the way. India Graham. Quinn's aunt."

"India Graham, the news correspondent?"

I'm gonna throw up. Yes, India Graham, the

reporter. The wanderer of the world, that India Graham. On the international news, like, all the freaking time, in every freaking country you can think of and some you can't. That's her, my aunt, and I can tell you are about in love with her.

Quinn shoved her hands in her jacket pockets and squirmed inwardly.

"I follow you on Twitter. I do! Seriously. You are my idol."

"Thank you, Adrian. That's so kind."

Quinn watched as India re-wrapped the scarf around her neck. *Maybe it'll choke her.*

"Do you have aspirations of being a reporter?"

"I'm studying journalism, yes."

"Wonderful. I'm so happy to hear it." Quinn was forced to endure two or three more minutes of India's gushing about the news business as she fished around in the depths of her purse. Finally, she pulled something out, tossing her hair out of her eyes, and extended it to Adrian. "Here's my card. Call me anytime."

Call me anytime, really? Gross.

"Well, Quinn, are you ready to go?"

India appeared to be begging. Quinn shrugged, hands in pockets, looking at Adrian.

Save me! I'd rather stick a needle in my eye than go with her.

"Uh, if you don't mind, I'd like to take Quinn for ice cream, and then I'll bring her back."

Thank God.

"Really, auntie, I want to go for ice cream." Quinn did her best to appear compliant.

Quinn looked from Adrian to India, and back. Adrian looked so cute. And she'd give anything not to have to go anywhere else with her celebrity aunt.

"Sure. Okay," India said. "But have her back home in one hour. One hour, okay?"

"No problem."

"Great to meet you, Adrian. I hope we see each other again. Quinn, remember, one hour." And with a toodle-oo of a hand, India was gone.

"Let's get out of here," Quinn said, taking Adrian's hand, practically dashing for the door.

CHAPTER FIFTEEN

Quinn

Autumn leaves swirled at Quinn and Adrian's feet as they walked home from school, backpacks filled with homework assignments.

Quinn looked sideways at Adrian, at his dark curls falling over his face as they walked downhill to Quinn's home, and said, "What was your mom's name?"

"Uh, Marilee, why?"

"Just wondered. Is she dead?"

"Um, no, not as far as I know. She's alive. She lives in the boot heel," Adrian shoved the bangs out of his eyes. "She has a different husband and a couple of kids. I live with my dad now."

"Okay. You don't have to talk about it."

"I might, but only to you. I feel comfortable talking with you."

Quinn shifted her backpack. "Why do you like me? I mean, nobody else does, really."

"That's not true. I think you make that up, really."

"No, they make fun of me. Like, all the time."

Adrian seemed to be staring at the sky. "What do they make fun of you over?"

"Like, my hair, for one thing."

"I think your hair is beautiful, but that's me. It's just hair. I can see how those kids might think it's weird or whatever. They're in a box, you know? They're scared of not being accepted so they all stay the same, like vanilla. So, what else?"

Quinn kicked a rock. "I don't know, not much else, I guess."

"So, you have it pretty easy. It could be a lot worse, you know. I mean, it's not like you're a cripple or deformed or something like that. I don't know what you listen to those schmucks for anyway. They're all up their own asses."

Quinn giggled. "Here's my house."

"Nice house."

"It belongs to my aunt. We just live here."

"The aunt I met the other night?"

"Yeah," Quinn said, her heart sinking.

"She's cool," Adrian said. "My dad and me live outside of city limits, like just outside city limits. Over that way," Adrian pointed to the right.

"Is it far from here?" Quinn wasn't crazy about the idea of Adrian walking a long distance, but on the other hand, since she didn't drive yet, and nobody was home who might drive him, there was nothing she could do.

"Nah, not really. Probably a couple miles but if I jog it, it doesn't take that long."

"Oh. I run too," Quinn said.

"Really?" Adrian said, his hair falling over one eye.

"Well, not always. Just when I get stressed."

They stopped and turned to one another. Quinn pulled her backpack to her front and wrapped her arms around it. "I like being with you," Quinn said. "You're like a real person."

"Well, yeah, I mean, I think I'm real. Here, pinch me," Adrian said, pulling her hand to his forearm.

Quinn laughed again, squeezing the flesh just under the long-sleeved T-shirt.

Adrian winced. "See? I am a real person. Right? Okay, stop pinching now, ow!"

"You want to come in? We could do our homework together."

"I better get home," Adrian said. "My dad will be looking for me. But, I'll take a rain check."

"Sure. See ya," Quinn waved, walking backwards up the driveway. "Next time."

Adrian waved. "Next time. For sure."

"For sure."

Quinn watched him jog away from the house, disappearing finally down the street. When she couldn't see him anymore, she let herself in, closing the front door behind her, smiling in the afternoon dusk.

CHAPTER SIXTEEN

Adrian

"Hey! Boy!"

Adrian cringed, sitting at the kitchen table, pouring over his school books. A big test in American History II was happening tomorrow, a third of his grade all semester, and no way was he going to fail.

Please God, don't let him come for me and start a bunch of crap. Just let him fall asleep.

His father loomed from the shadows of his bedroom, careening down the hall, drunk as usual. The wall lamps lent an eerie orange glow and shadows falling behind the man.

"Boy!" Adrian felt the nudge of his father's thick fingers on his shoulder. The stench of whiskey and beer streamed from his father's mouth.

Adrian winced.

"Hey, Dad," he said, watching his father weave back and forth in a drunken mess.

"Boy, there's $200 missing from my room, you take

it? Hunh? You take my money? Hunh?"

"No, Dad, I didn't take your money. I don't even know when you have money. I didn't take it. Are you sure you didn't just misplace it?"

"Shit potatoes, boy, are you being smart? Because I think you're being smart, you're disrespectful, and that I gotta punish."

Adrian watched his father advance clumsily, his belly poking out from underneath his T-shirt, knowing the man could fall any minute. Adrian prayed he would.

"You no-good son of a whore, you piece of shit, you whore's child. I don't know if you're even mine."

"Dad! Dad, listen," Adrian started. "I am your son. You know I am your son. We've talked about this before." The litany went on same as so many times before. "Dad! I'm studying. I have school work. I want to pass, Dad. I want to pass with the highest grade in the class. Dad, do you hear me? I want to pass with the highest grade in the class!"

"Why? Why you want to pass with the highest grade? What's so important about that, boy?" Adrian watched his father sway and turn and sway again, his eyes squinted.

"Because I have to. I have to get the highest grade in the class so I can get scholarships and go to college and – never mind." Adrian went back to his books, and his notes.

"What? You mean, you don't think living in a trailer is good enough for you, boy? Not good enough for your stellar brain? Yeah, right, you get the highest grade in the class. You get those scholarships, you go to college, oh yeah, and we'll see where you end up, you piece of shit."

His father shoved a piece of chew from a Copenhagen tin into his mouth, and stumbled to his recliner and then collapsed in front of the TV. The chair heaved back, the footrest snapping up with a tinny sound.

"The highest grade," his father muttered. "You just take that highest grade and shove it straight up your ass 'cause that's all the good it's gonna do ya."

Adrian rose, taking care not to make a sound, standing before his father, watching his dad's chest heaving up and down, his jaw slack, heavy breaths coming through his mouth. His father raised one arm and then dropped it heavily onto the armrest.

Adrian bent over his father. "I want to do better than you! Okay? I don't want to be bound up with bitterness and resentment, and I don't want to live my life soused in alcohol, and I want to be smart and good and have a good life, and I don't care if you don't! I want it. I do! And I can't have that if I'm not educated, and I can't get educated unless I'm first in the class! And there's a girl. She's like me, she has her ups and downs, and she's had bad breaks, and I like her a lot and she likes me too. I want to be with her, and I have to be viable before I can even do that. Okay?" Adrian shouted again, "Okay?" before he realized his father's face turned toward the arm of the chair. The snoring began, and there was no more left to say.

Shit.

He dragged the blanket from his father's bed to the living room and spread it out over his father lying in the armchair.

I can't end up like that. I won't. I just won't.

Adrian stepped back to the kitchen table in the trailer house, jaw clenched, raising the LED light over his books, and continued studying. He gave one last glance to his father's heaving chest, and swallowed hard.

I won't bend. I'm going to make it. I'm smart. I work hard, and I want better than this, and I'm going to get it. Whatever it takes.

CHAPTER SEVENTEEN

Quinn

Quinn pulled her sweatshirt tighter around her and wondered what she was doing at the beach and the bonfire party. Ivy was nowhere in sight. Random figures crossed and recrossed in front of the fire, an orange orbit surrounding their black figures.

Some guy, Clay, an upper classman, brought her a glass of something.

"I've seen you around school," he said, pushing the glass toward her.

"I don't drink," she said.

"You'll drink this," Clay said. "Come on, drink up, little girl. Don't be a porch puppy."

"I don't want it."

"It's good," Clay crooned. "Take one drink, that's all. Come on, you want to have fun, right?"

Clay was cute, with dark hair falling over one eye, muscular, built. Quinn knew he was one of the biggest athletes in school. All the girls wanted him to notice them, and here he was, bringing her a drink, like she was the best thing going on today. *Take that, bitches, take that.*

Quinn brought the glass to her lips and took a swallow. It was good, fruity and hot and something else. Soothing. Another sip.

Clay brought her a new glass. Quinn was beginning to feel warm and languid.

"Come on, baby girl," he said, pulling her hand. "You are so beautiful. Drink up, let's party."

"Uh huh," Quinn said, her swollen tongue filling up her mouth. The bonfire was distant now, only an orange image in the background. "Party," she said and giggled.

There was a car. Somehow, she was in it, floundering in the back seat. No sign of the bonfire in her peripheral. The fire was a distant thought, and now there was only dark.

Clay was pawing her breast, trying to force her down.

I'm going to puke right here, right now.

"No," Quinn struggled. "No, stop." Her limbs felt like Jell-o. She lay splayed out on the back seat as Clay planted messy kisses all over her face and throat. Quinn couldn't breathe. Clay's weight settled onto her, pressing into her crotch.

"Let's have fun," Clay whispered. "You want it. You want me, come on, girl."

Quinn tried to wiggle away from him, the bulge in his pants boring into her thigh. The struggle of arms and legs. It was too much.

"No, let me alone. Let me out of here."

"Who are you, a little frightened virgin?" The smack to her face stung.

"Wait, no, stop."

"Settle down, come on. We're having a party over here, come on."

"No, no!"

Her pants were pulled down, her private parts exposed, chilling her to the bone. If she screamed, would anyone hear?

As Clay tried to force himself inside her, the only thing Quinn could think about was stars, twinkling, shining overhead, beautiful diamonds cascading over a midnight sky.

She stiffened, tightening her legs, her thighs. Maybe he wouldn't get there.

"Come on, come on," Clay muttered.

Quinn shut her eyes, tight, steeling herself against Clay's intrusion. Stars. Great big, sparkling stars. Stars blink, they twinkle. *Twinkle, twinkle, little star.* What was with guys in the first place? Why this? Why? "No," Quinn said again, thrusting under Clay, grabbing for her underwear, trying to pull it back up.

"Uh," Clay grunted.

A gust of cold air hit her legs. The back door was open. Quinn, enveloped in a fog, could only surmise what was happening, but a voice pierced her brain.

Adrian? Oh my God, if it's you, I am so relieved. Please let it be you.

Her eyelids felt swollen, permitting only a small amount of light and vision to come in.

"Get off her, motherfucker!"

Clay instantly came to attention. "Get lost, fuckhead!"

"I said, *get off her you motherfucking son of a bitch!*"

Somehow, Clay rolled off her backward, sliding out the door, twisting and thumping on the way out. Quinn grabbed for her pants, struggling to pull the knotted up mess back on. Rolling, she poked her head up and watched the boys outside.

"You wanna go, motherfucker?" Clay was yelling

as he tucked his shirt back into his pants. "Hey, she asked for it."

Adrian stood straight, fists clenched, his chest hard.

Ivy suddenly appeared on the edge of Quinn's vision.

Scuffle, hard punches, bodies landing in grass, grunts, skin on skin, curse words, panting. Quinn could hear it all as she turned to Ivy.

"Where were you?"

"Come on," Ivy said. "I got you, Quinn. It's okay now, I'm sorry I left you. Can you forgive me? Come on, put your arm around my shoulder, come on. Walk. "

"No," Quinn managed to squeak out from under Ivy's arm. "Where's Adrian? Is he okay?"

"I'm okay," Adrian stepped up behind the girls. "But Clay, he isn't so pretty right now."

Quinn broke from Ivy, throwing her arms around Adrian's neck. Fear and humiliation, coupled with an exhilarating relief, flooded her, and she sobbed into Adrian's shoulder. She felt his arms come around slowly, cautiously.

"Quinn, you have to call your mom. You have to tell her what happened so she can take you to the hospital. You need to see a doctor, seriously," Adrian said.

Quinn jerked back.

"I don't want anybody to know!"

Ivy came around her shoulder, stroking her hair back. "You need to do this, Quinn. You might be really hurt."

"I couldn't be any more *hurt* than I've already been. No way. Not calling my mother. She'll turn it into a circus." Quinn pulled away and gathered her sweatshirt jacket around her. "You two have to promise me. You'll never tell. Never. Promise?"

"Quinn, you have to tell someone, someone you

trust. If not your mom, who?" Adrian was peering intently at her, and Quinn felt scared and naked and vulnerable in so many ways, she couldn't even count.

Gwen? Gwen would be the perfect choice. I love her, she loves me, I've known her all my life. But she'd probably tell Mom no matter that I'd tell her not to. I can't think of anyone I can trust.

Quinn turned away, staring at the lights in the sky. She felt Ivy take hold of her hand, her voice seemed to be coming from a distant place. "You remember Stacy Hill? She's not in school this year. Yeah, her mom and dad transferred her to a different school. You know why? She got raped. And nobody knows who it was, but she said he had arms like Clay. What if?"

Ivy's eyes were dark. "Quinn, don't act like this doesn't matter. Stacy got raped."

Quinn felt warm pressure from Ivy's hands.

"You can tell my mom, if you want."

Quinn shook her head. "There's nobody. If not my mom, nobody."

India.

Quinn shook her head again.

India.

"I don't like my aunt. I don't want her to know, especially."

Liar. Above all, you want India to know.

"Let's get out of here," Adrian said, jolting Quinn from her thoughts.

Adrian's expert guidance, with a swelling eye nonetheless, brought them to his car, and they all piled in.

"Seriously, you guys," Quinn began. "I don't want anybody to know. I don't want to be that girl in school. I don't want a bunch of attention. Let's keep it between us."

Adrian stared straight ahead. "Quinn," he said,

putting the car in drive, pulling away from the party. "If you don't tell, if you don't expose this asshole, he's going to make you a target, and you're never going to be free of it. He'll keep pushing. Trust me, Quinn. You have to tell someone. And besides that, it's possible he's s done this before. He needs to be stopped."

Quinn rolled against the door.

"He didn't... I mean..."

"What?" Adrian snapped, jerking his head around, one hand on the wheel. "He didn't what?"

Quinn watched the black trees speed by, illuminated only by the headlights of Adrian's car. So surreal, ghostly, menacing, but not.

She felt herself falling, a curious buoyance that was neither solid or liquid, but falling just the same into an abyss.

"He didn't... he, he didn't... I'm okay. I'm okay."

Ivy leaned up from the back seat, caressing Quinn's arm. "He didn't get in, is that what you mean?"

"Yeah. That's what I mean." Quinn leaned back in the seat, exhausted.

"But still," Adrian said. "He's gonna make you a target, Quinn. What then? He's gonna say you went all the way, and you liked it, like you wanted it, he'll talk about it all over school. He's gonna think he can do it again and not get caught, you know?"

"I don't know. I just don't know," Quinn said, staring out the window at the darkness, imagining stars, bright, beautiful stars flowing all over her body, and she began to feel alright. "I'll work it out my way."

"Which means you'll bottle it up," Ivy said. "You can't do that, Quinn."

Quinn turned back to the window. "I don't want to talk about it anymore. Not ever again."

CHAPTER EIGHTEEN

Ray

Ray Henderson stood at the last checker station and watched the customers pass through his store, Henderson Foods. Ray inherited the grocery store business from his father, and sadly, Ray, being the last Henderson, an only child with no descendants of his own, stood alone with the business. That fact bothered Ray, because when he died, where would the business be? Who would take it over? Would the legacy his family left to him be left in ruins upon his death? No easy choices. In fact, no choices at all.

Crappy luck. Or fate. Or whatever.

Ray stirred at the checker station. He hated thinking of his own mortality. He hated thinking about how the family business would die once he expired. He often wished he was someone else, not the sole heir of the grocery store fortune, which was quite nice in and of itself. Being raised a rich kid, being dropped into a successful family business wasn't all bad, but it didn't appeal to Ray the way it might to someone more shallow, someone who loved money a bit more than Ray did.

He often wondered what his life would have been had he married young to a lovely wife, a woman he would idolize and ravish, with whom he sired beautiful children who would no doubt resemble his wife, children who could follow in his footsteps and to whom he would leave the grocery store and the family Colonial home on five acres with mature trees, and then one day, who celebrated his old age with a gold watch and a cruise to the Caribbean. Ray visualized the scenario, a lot, and sometimes wished he would have walked that path.

Fact was, he never walked that path. Not even close. The traveling life was sweet, such as the time he flew to Aruba, alone, and spent two beautiful but uneventful weeks strolling on the beach, watching the sunset, dancing with female tourists, sleeping until noon, eating great food, and drinking far too much rum.

Ray regretted that trip for one reason.

He went alone, and he stayed alone.

Ray wanted someone with whom to share his life. Never married, no children in his younger years, when Ray would have been able to throw a football or play foosball or trundle children back and forth from piano lessons and soccer practice, do homework, all the domestic things Ray would have loved to do, had he had the opportunity

Ray sighed, looking up at the clock over the windows. 10:14 a.m. It was gonna be a long day. He was standing with his new checker, Shasta, the girl with the black painted fingernails.

Did I not tell her no fingernail polish? Ray wondered, and then dismissed the thought.

Carmen Stauffer, owner of the local newspaper, *The Herald*, appeared in a cloud of perfume, armed with expensive jewelry around her neck and on her fingers, and a shopping basket laced on one arm.

"Hello, Ray," she smiled invitingly. Ray could see two steaks, a head of lettuce, a cucumber, two baking potatoes, and a bottle of red wine in her basket.

"Carmen," Ray said.

Carmen set the basket down on the conveyor belt and struck a pose, one hand on her hip. Ray could see she was pushing her chest out, straining the fabric. She was smiling, a too-red lipstick full-tooth grimace.

The hair went up on Ray's neck.

"What do you think of my dress, Ray? I bought it in California last spring. I didn't know if it would be in style now, here in the Ozarks, but I got a great deal on it, and the sales lady told me it was to die for on me. What do you think?"

Ray stepped back.

"Uh, it looks quite expensive."

Carmen pursed her lips. "You know, Ray," she began, gesturing to her groceries, "Here I am, with two lovely steaks and all the fixings for a wonderful dinner. I'd grill these tonight if you wanted to stop by. Please tell me you'll come by for dinner. Say around 7?"

Ray felt Shasta's eyes on him. He didn't dare look at her, but he knew her eyes were bugged out.

"Uh, well..." he began and looked around in desperation.

The door opened with a *ding!* Shelby Graham walked in with her daughter, Quinn, and Ray's heartbeat picked up a bit. Watching Shelby and Quinn pull a cart out, whispering between themselves, and giggling together, Ray said, "Carmen, thank you, but I'm sorry. I won't be able to make it."

Shelby and Quinn disappeared into the dairy aisle, and Ray apologized again.

"I have to go. Good day."

"Seriously?" Ray heard Carmen say as he rounded the corner into the dairy aisle and found Shelby pulling a gallon of chocolate milk out of the dairy case as Quinn animatedly told her some sort of story. He was sweating, almost panting, but thankful he managed to extricate himself from conversation with Carmen.

"Ah, Shelby," Ray said. "Are you finding everything you need today?"

CHAPTER NINETEEN

Quinn

Quinn stared down at both her arms, gazing at the not-so-intricate web of white scars marching over her skin. Picking up the razor blade she left earlier at the bathroom sink, she looked at her reflection in the mirror.

I look like a rat, she decided, under the votive lights. *Who thinks I'm pretty?*

Facebook. Her iPad lay on her bed, grinning in the dark like a blue-black talisman of evil. She could see it from where she was at the bathroom sink. The last message she received took hold of her mind.

Ivan. He seemed cute at first and since he said he lived in Australia and he was her age, Quinn didn't fear him.

What do you like to do for fun, Quinn? By the way, I love your photograph, the one in the gauzy white shirt, your hair blowing back in the wind. Gorgeous.

Uh, thanks. My mom took that picture. I am a DJ at a radio station and I love that, but when I'm out of school, in the summer, I like to be her model. She's a photographer.

You're beautiful.

Uh, thanks.

How old did you say you are?

19. I'm 19.

Good. You're an adult. I'm older than you think. I have a fantasy about you.

Quinn went offline, scrambling off the bed, running to the bathroom.

Sick bastard.

Quinn gaped in the mirror. So, here it was. Another cut. The only way she could feel peaceful again.

I just wanted to be pretty, and Mom said it was okay. She wanted me to be her little princess. Yeah, she made up all that shit, but I liked it too. I liked the pretty clothes and the high heels and the photography. I wanted to be a model. I wanted to be somebody. Mom said it was alright. She said the compliments were good, that meant I could be a model.

But I'm not a model, and now I feel like my mom betrayed me somehow. I'm dirty, damaged goods. I shouldn't be alive. I wish I wasn't.

She chose a spot just above her right elbow, on the inside of her arm, matching the blade to her skin.

Quinn stared at her reflection in the mirror

I could end it all, right here, right now. I wouldn't have to feel dirty anymore, just peaceful, as if I was on wings.

The idea appealed to her: being on wings, aloft, away.

It wouldn't be so bad, to be buoyed away by the wind.

The bonfire. Clay. Quinn saw him every day at school, but from a distance. Only one time did she see him face to face, and that was after gym class, as she walked out of the girls' locker room going to her next class. He was at the water fountain in the brick-lined hall, bent away from her, slurping up the stream of water hitting his face.

Quinn hoped to squeeze by without him noticing her but as she slipped around him, he stood up and turned.

Quinn startled at the angry stare, the black eyes.

In an instant, he was leaning over her. Quinn looked up.

"Don't you ever tell," he whispered. "If you tell, and you ruin me, my life, I'll make sure you suffer, and I mean that. Don't ever tell."

Quinn stared back, her heart beating madly.

"So you admit it," she said in a low voice. "You admit what you did to me."

"Shit," Clay said and shoved around her, loping away.

Quinn feared the worst. Clay would spread rumors, or he would cat-call her in the hall, jeer at her, make sure his friends knew, and would spread rumors, and a hundred other awful things. But so far, high school life wavered on the high school sea, a nauseating calm.

But still, Quinn felt an unnerving fear winding up her spine into her belly, up her neck. School became a never-ending obstacle course. She learned Clay's routes and avoided them altogether.

So tired. Quinn stared at the razor blade clutched in her hand.

Another memory, probably the worst of any of it.

Her thirteenth birthday. Shelby insisted they dress up and go out. Shelby chose the heels, the dress, the makeup, and made it a girls' night out, just her and Quinn. Once made up and dressed, Quinn remembered looking at her reflection in the mirror, thinking she looked like the model she dreamed of being. Plush, plump lips, eyelashes stretching across state lines, a pretty little dress, short and low cut, spaghetti straps, tight, short, showing her cleavage and her legs.

"You're stunning," Quinn remembered Shelby saying, her eyes beaming. "My little girl's all grown up. Turn around, let me look at you."

Quinn twirled, giggling.

"Beautiful, just beautiful," Shelby sang. "I wish I could wear a dress like that, baby. That thing is made for you. Turn around, look at your butt."

Quinn looked behind her in the mirror. True, the dress clung to every curve, hill and valley she had.

"Hot, oh so," Shelby said. "Yeah, yeah, that's my girl, smoking hot. You got it goin' on, baby, you got it."

Quinn twirled again.

Phillip appeared in the hallway.

"My god, you," Phillip said.

Giving in to impulses, feeling so good and sexy, Quinn pushed her body against his, and kissed him full on the lips, spreading her mouth to allow his tongue to come in. Quinn sucked at it. Phillip's hand crept to her ass.

Then Shelby's voice screaming in the background. "What are you doing to my baby? Get out, you motherfucker! Get out!"

The shocking truth of what she did hit Quinn full on, running over her like a freight train, spewing her human pieces in every direction.

I didn't mean it. I didn't mean to do that.

Crushing guilt, a suffocating, nauseating feeling that nothing would ever be right again. Never.

Phillip moved out. Shelby alternated between mourning the loss of his companionship and consoling Quinn about the incident for days.

It's my fault. I am to blame.

After the criss-cross lanes of white traffic began

appearing on Quinn's arms, somehow, Shelby got a counselor involved. It was either that or DFS would be calling, Quinn was pretty sure. The counselor, a woman with too much education and too little intelligence, didn't do much except suggest Quinn join a social club with her peers, and get active in a church. "Forget about all this," the counselor said. "Get with kids your own age and do things kids your age do. It'll make a big difference, right?"

Quinn remembered thinking the counselor was a big, blond moron. She walked out of counseling and never went back.

The point was, my mom didn't protect me the way she should have. Why couldn't that dumb bimbo see that?

Reality threw a hard punch, and Quinn didn't know how to process it. Her mother's betrayal followed her day and night, like a constant poke in the back. She wasn't clear on which way to turn, or who to turn to, which was why she started running when things got too hard, too real. Sometimes she talked to Gwen. But she never talked to her mother about the shock she endured, about the price she paid for masking her age with heavy makeup and short, tight dresses. Quinn was better off pretending she didn't even feel it. One thing she did know, she would never be a model. She was never wearing heavy makeup, and she sure as shit wasn't ever going to put on high heels and a cocktail dress for the rest of her life. In fact, she wasn't posing for any photographs ever again.

I don't want to be like her, Quinn thought. *She's a loser. I don't want to be a loser.*

Quinn collapsed on the toilet seat. The razor blade still waited in her hand, her tee shirt sleeve still pushed up, her arm prepared for the silver blade to begin sawing, drawing red oozy blood.

Quinn stared once more at the whitened highway on her arms before a jolt of internal lightning shot down her spine.

I have a friend now, and he's like me. We're alike. And he likes me.

The blade fell to the tile floor, toppling over with a quiet tinkle.

Quinn stood up, pulled her sleeve into place, and walked out of the bathroom, her spine straight, shoulders back.

I am never doing that again. Cutting's over.

CHAPTER TWENTY

Shelby

The Missouri humidity caused Shelby to sweat more than usual, and for that she was edgy and pissed. Besides that, her hair was frizzing up like a Brillo pad and that also put her out of sorts and somewhat unsociable.

My whole life is a big old what-the-hell, anyway, Shelby surmised as she walked into the kitchen. *Like, back when I was nothing but a sperm-meets-the-egg-of-his-dreams, the universe was saying, this fetus here, this is one big ole mistake, but we gonna let her go live anyway, because we gotta have some kind of fuck-up in this world.*

Shelby opened up the cabinet door, looked at the bags of chips on the shelf, and shut the door. The refrigerator, while having a nice bright light, didn't hold anything to enthuse her either.

"You know that guy, that guy who owns the grocery store, Ray? Do you know who he is?" Shelby paced around the kitchen island, willing India to look up from her laptop.

"What? Who?" India was perched on one of the chairs on the island with her laptop in front of her.

"Ray, the owner."

"No, I don't know who that is." India remained intent over her computer. "What are you talking about?"

Shelby's shoulders sagged. *What is she looking at anyway?*

"I think he likes me." Shelby paused for a minute. "No, I think he really likes me, like, he *likes* me, you know?"

"No, I don't know. Say what you mean, Shelby."

"Would you look at me for a minute? I mean, hello, I'm trying to talk to you here."

India looked up, frowning at her.

"What?"

Shelby groaned. She watched India push her glasses up her nose, and resumed pacing.

"Would you stop with that? You're making me nervous."

"I'm trying to tell you something here!"

"Well, what? Spit it out, Shelby."

"I mean, Ray asked me out on a date. That's what I mean. He asked me to go to dinner."

India sat up straight, her hands in her lap.

"That's great, Shelby, what's wrong with that? I mean, why not?"

Shelby stood still. "I don't know if I'm even attracted to him, I mean, he's older than me in the first place. And he's going bald and he's sorta fat, but I mean, look at me too. I'm no Charlize Theron. I mean, I guess, if he's willing to go out with me. I mean, I don't know."

"Well, I don't know either, but what's wrong with going out with him for one date? It's not the rest of your life, Shelby," India said. "And you just might have fun. You might enjoy his company and make a friend, right?"

"Right," Shelby said, thinking of Phillip. *I have to let go of you. You are no good for me, but, you're good with me. And, if I ever find out for sure that you touched my daughter under age, I will kill you. But somehow, I still want you. I must be the craziest woman in the world, and why would anyone like Ray want me anyhow?*

"You know, he's never been married. I mean, is that a red flag, you know? I mean, like, is he some kind of weirdo?" Shelby looked at India, who was back to looking at her computer.

"I don't know, but I kind of doubt it," India said a minute later, or at least it seemed a minute later to Shelby.

"But, how do I know?" Shelby persisted, pulling a soda from the refrigerator.

"Well, you don't, really, until you get to know one another. What's wrong with going out with him one time, really? I mean, haven't you had enough of those losers, those pieces of shit?" India's eyes gleamed behind her glasses.

She means Phillip. How does she know? Did Quinn say something?

"You should not have said that," Shelby said, slamming her hand on the counter. "I didn't go to fucking New York, and I didn't date millionaires and I didn't experience what you did, but you should not have said that!"

India was standing up, holding up her hand. "Wait a minute, Shelby, stop right now," she was saying.

Shelby wanted to go in for the kill, but she stopped, seeing her sister's hand up. Still, her rage took over.

"What's wrong with me?" Shelby shouted. "Why do I even listen to you, you're so hoity-toity, you are so far gone from this world. Everything with you is style and status, why do I listen to you? I've been here while you have not, and I know what's going on here, and you do not, and I wish you would just pack up and go back to your world and leave us alone!"

India stood straight across the island. "Shelby, stop. Take a deep breath. I am not going anywhere right now so get used to it."

Both sisters paused. A dog nearby barked in greeting to its owner, and then was quiet.

"Shelby, listen to me," India continued giving her a dead stare. "We don't need to be arguing here. We can't change the decisions we've made about how we live our lives. That's neither here nor there right now, you know what I mean? Since I've been here, I've picked up on some things."

"There's nothing going on," Shelby said pushing her soda can around.

The kitchen island seemed to contract into a tiny square, leaving Shelby feeling conspicuous and over-sized. The air felt thick.

Sweat beads formed on Shelby's upper lip.

India sat back down, folding her arms on the counter. "I think there's something more important to talk about than us. What's going on with you and your daughter? I've seen her arms."

Shelby tried to stare down her sister but was unable. Suddenly exhausted, she sat down on a bar stool.

"Nothing. Nothing we can't handle."

"It seems to me, she's looking for something she can't find with you."

"We're fine. We're taking care of us."

"Well, it doesn't take a rocket scientist to see she pretty much disdains you. She doesn't seem to respect you."

"She respects me," Shelby said, softly but defensively. "I don't know how you can say that."

India seemed to be considering her words.

"Oh, come on, India. Just say it," Shelby said. "You

know you think you know better than me, as usual."

"What do you mean, nothing we can't handle?"

"Nothing. Just a figure of speech. She respects me. You don't have to worry about that," Shelby said, getting up. "In fact, you don't need to worry about me and my daughter. You're the one she *disdains*, as you put it."

CHAPTER TWENTY ONE

Gwen

B*ang, bang, bang!*

Gwen heard the screen door bang and upon investigation, realized India was standing on the porch, beating Gwen's screen door with all her might.

Lord, she look scared, and her color ain't too good. Oily, frightened looking. India has concerns.

Gwen noted the yoga pants, more expensive than anything she or anyone she knew would wear, but yoga pants nonetheless, and the careless way India's hair was gathered up over her head in some kind of band. Except for the obvious quality of her clothes, India looked like any other soccer mom, or aging writer for that matter, except India was no soccer mom, nor a writer, aging or not. Gwen had to remind herself, India came back from New York, from the newscaster paradise. India was no soccer mom.

"Girl, come in," Gwen said, holding the door wide to allow India entrance. "What's going on?"

India strode in, but stopped in the living room. "I'm sorry. I'm sorry to come here and act like a total ass, Gwen, I mean it, but I need answers to some questions. I know I wasn't here for a lot of the time, and I know Shelby blames me for a lot of stuff, mostly for going away, but, and please tell me the truth... what do you know about Quinn and her problems?"

Gwen's heart sank. She noticed the dark circles under India's eyes, the dark frightened stare. *She must know, she must have guessed. After all, she is not stupid. How can I tell her what I know and not have her go off on Shelby?*

Gwen sagged as she watched India pull her hair behind her ears, a signal India was disturbed, not a casual movement.

"Gwen, I saw her arms. By mistake, this morning when she got out of the shower. She knows I saw. And I told Shelby I saw it, and she said, 'we're handling it, stay out of our business.'"

No other way. No options.

You have to explain. It's her aunt.

Gwen brought two Cokes from her refrigerator, opened them and set one in front of India. She noted they were now sitting in the exact same position as she sat with Quinn, at her kitchen Formica table with the apple clock overhead.

"What do you want to know?" Gwen heard herself say.

India's hands splayed out on the top of the table. "I want to know what Shelby never told me. All these years I've been away, working for the network, I didn't know what was going on here. Sometimes, before she died, my mother would call me and hint about bad things here, bad things with Quinn, but she never fully explained what she was talking about. And if I called and asked Shelby, she overwrote the whole thing, like she was handling everything, Quinn's fine, whatever's going on is not that significant, just a bump in the road. I never got any kind of answer to anything I asked. Never."

Gwen twirled her bottle around on the table. "So, you feel you've been lied to, or the wool's been pulled over your eyes?"

"Yes, I do. I feel like things have been covered up so nobody knows, so no one is accountable, particularly Shelby."

Gwen let out a deep sigh. "India, I'll be the first to tell you Quinn's got problems. And, love Shelby like I do, I'll also be the first to tell you Shelby manufactured Quinn's problems. I told her years ago she was asking for trouble, I told her, she didn't want to listen. She wanted a friend, a little doll she could stow away in her purse, decorate up to suit her, and show off, and you know the both of them thought Quinn should be a model."

"A model?" India asked. "Are you serious?"

Gwen sagged in her chair. *This is more terrible than anything I've ever had to do. But India needs to know, she deserves it. She's afraid for Quinn, just like me.*

"India, if I could do it all over again, I would have taken Quinn out of that situation before it became so toxic to her, I would have, and she would have lived here with me, except for Shelby would never have allowed it. Shelby didn't see the monster she created, and she still doesn't. All that stuff, maybe you heard, about Phillip molesting Quinn? Well, the account I got, directly from Quinn, is that her mother dressed her up like she was 21 years old for her thirteenth birthday. Talked her into feeling like she was 21 and a sex pot, but Quinn was thirteen, and she got carried away in the moment and made the advance on Phillip. India, I honestly believe she didn't mean to do what she did."

"What did she do?"

"She grabbed Phillip and kissed him full on the lips, and then Shelby started screaming at Phillip like he was to blame. But he touched her, yes, inappropriately, on her rear end. Such a bad situation. Just bad all the way around."

It was hard to tell what India was thinking. Gwen watched India take it all in.

"My God," India said finally.

"Quinn cuts herself, has for a while, trying to rid herself of the misery and the guilt, make herself feel clean again. Shelby took her to counseling over that summer, and it went nowhere. But I think, or rather, I perceive, something else has happened to Quinn, something she's not talking about," Gwen said. "I don't know what it is but I do know, she's clinging to that boy, Adrian, the one who walks her home from school, you know him?"

"Met him, he seems nice."

"He's a good kid. Lives with his dad, his mom ran away years ago. That boy is real people. He knows the hard side, but he's gentle. He's good and kind. Quinn needs him, and she likes him. That's all I know."

"He told me he wants to be in the news, be a journalist or a reporter."

Gwen let out a large belch and wiped her lips with the back of her hand.

"India, Quinn wants him around for some reason, and he wants to be around with her, you understand me?"

Their eyes met, solid.

"He's good for her," Gwen said, shoving her empty Coke bottle to the side.

India nodded. "Gwen, how do I help her? There's so much distance between us."

"Oh, I know. Shelby's poisoned the well, but I'll tell you, between you and me, and Shelby will never say this because she don't want to see it herself, but Quinn's watching you. She wants to be more like you than like her mother. I'll tell you that. She just doesn't know where to begin."

India let out a lame laugh. "Well, at least she and I agree on that, don't know where to begin."

"And India," Gwen said, stretching across the table, covering India's white hands with her brown ones. "Shelby don't know what love is. She thinks love is pleasing people, giving them what they want. She wants to win a popularity contest."

"Yeah, I know that."

Gwen nodded. "Sure you do. You two, you were as different as night and day. You always had your own identity, but see, Shelby never did. She was always an extension of someone else, your father, your mother, Tony, Phillip, others, and then Quinn. Quinn's struggling too. Quinn wants to break away from the mold, to be more self-assured, more like you."

"You know, since I've come back, since I've been here, I feel like I'm intruding on everyone's time, particularly Shelby's, and it's real weird. It's like if there's room to insult me, she will. If there's a reason to make me feel small for anything or everything, she takes it. I don't know what she thinks I'm doing by being here, but it really has nothing to do with her at all. And it's not like I'm going to kick her out of the house. As far as I know, I'm here temporarily. I just want to get back to my real job, back to my life, I think, except I don't know any more what my life is."

"You might stay."

"No, no, no." India shifted again. "No, I'm here until I get my feet underneath me, and then I'm going back to my job."

"And if there is no job to go back to?" Gwen watched India's eyes dart back and forth.

"There's a job, I have a place," India said. "And I'll go back, no question."

"Well, sometimes India, sometimes," Gwen said with quiet conviction, "you come to a place for a purpose and until the purpose is realized, you just stay.

"It could just be," she continued slowly, "that you need them just as much as they need you. And they do need you, India."

"I'm about to give up, really. I didn't come here to be unwelcome or challenged or anything. I really wonder why I came in the first place." India put her head in her hands for a moment and then looked up, eyes bright. "Where does Phillip live?"

CHAPTER TWENTY TWO

India

Another week of hiatus from reporting the news of the world rolled around.

India poured a cup of coffee, resisting the urge to grab one of the brownies she made the day before, and opened the local newspaper lying on the counter in front of her.

How long have I been here? School started since I came back, and it's in full swing. Greg died in April, I worked another four or five weeks, sat in New York a week or two, and then came back here. I missed Quinn's birthday in May, I know that. Seems like I've been here forever, sort of, or not much time at all.

India stretched out over the kitchen island and spread the newspaper out under her elbows. *Dee dee dee, hum, hum.* The usual litany of the small town events, nothing too interesting there, hmm..., the obituary section....India straightened. *What fresh crap is this? Bad writing poor grammar, bad sentence structure, totally disinterested disengaging stuff, yuck. Your dead people, you leave as a small stone on the giant glaze of humanity? Gross.*

The early September end of summer sun shone through the windows onto the island. India shoved the paper aside and stood straight, feeling an epiphany roll over her.

Could she get a job? Something to do, somewhere to go each day instead of sitting in her sister's kitchen, because that was really the way India saw their childhood home now. Shelby and Quinn seemed to hold no vision, no goals, just hanging, watching the grass grow and the sun rising up and down. India didn't see the point of hanging.

She cooked and cleaned because she had nothing better to do, and at least doing those things produced something, even if it was only a pan of brownies or a sparkling ceramic toilet.

Talking to Nick the day before wasn't satisfying.

"India, listen, everything here is buzzing along. Don't worry yourself about it at all."

"Nick, am I fired? Because you really should tell me if I am," India said as she paced around the kitchen island.

"Don't you think Amy's doing a great job on the evening news?"

India stiffened. "I don't know, I haven't watched the evening news in quite a while. Nick, be upfront. I've been let go, right?"

Nick's voice came back as if in a tunnel, and India realized she was on speaker phone.

"Who else is there, Nick? Who's listening to this call?"

'There's nothing to worry about, India. You're just being paranoid. We'll talk again – "

"Nick, I may be many things, but paranoid is not

one of them. Just tell me, have I been let go and why?"

"India, it's me," Amy's voice. "Don't worry about a thing. I've got it covered until you return…"

"…Which should not be before the first of the year," Nick said. "India, just chill. After the first, we'll get a game plan. Trust me."

"Well, that's the problem, Nick. I don't know if I can trust you. Why won't you answer my questions? We're under a contract, you know."

"You're being a little crazy, India. You know you haven't been able to handle the desk since Greg passed. We're looking out for you."

The room suddenly seemed too small, Lilliputian sized. It was hard to breathe.

"Right," India said, and disconnected.

When are they going to be straight with me?

India stared down at the newspaper.

Small town news. Obituaries, for the love of God. It's not much, but it's a place to start. I need to do something, even if it's small.

India paused only a second before she entered the newspaper hub, a two-story brick building on the square. She glanced around at the tin ceilings and exposed brick walls.

A receptionist sat in the middle of the front behind a wood-topped counter. Two cubicles were apparent, one on her left and one on her right, but only one was currently occupied. A youngish man lurked over a computer screen, but seemed to pay more attention to his cell phone. India stopped to introduce herself, but she didn't need to after all.

"India Graham? What are you doing here, I mean, really?" Carmen Stauffer, owner of *The Herald*, appeared out of nowhere, striding toward India in her white sheath and pearls, her auburn hair in an eternally paused beehive. She was just a little overweight and just a bit more than she maybe ought to think of herself, smug and self-righteous. Shelby knew the type. This woman would sing the loudest in church every Sunday and shout, "Praise Jesus!" after stabbing her neighbor in the back every Saturday night, shouting "hallelujahs" as she licked the blood off the blade. The fact they went to high school together was a small thing. India remembered Carmen Hobbs, now Carmen Stauffer, as a small-town jerk, the big fish wannabe in the small pond, fake, a cheerleader, a Christian by association, and a willing screw if the football team was bored. So.

We may be adults now, but I bet she's still full of shit. India walked straight to her, and extended her hand, which Carmen looked down at with a look of confusion, finally taking India's hand in a weak squeeze.

I figured as much.

"What are you here for, India?" Carmen asked, in a half giggle. "Surely, you're not looking for a job at our humble newspaper?"

"Actually, I want to talk to you about that," India said. "Is there somewhere we can talk privately?"

Carmen turned her head and then turned back. "Look, we don't have any openings here, India, if that's what you're talking about. And besides, why would you, a big city anchor desk celebrity, want to work at this little newspaper? You know? I mean, I don't know why you're here in the first place, I don't know what you want here."

"Is there any place we can talk besides here in the middle of the newsroom?"

"Sure, follow me," Carmen turned and click-clacked her way back to an office at the back of the building.

"Make yourself at home," she said, gesturing to a chair.

India sat.

"What do you want, India?" Carmen leaned back in her chair. India was conscious of the stare.

"Listen, I read the obituaries often, and they suck, really," India said. "They're bad, just bad writing."

"You gotta be kidding me," Carmen said. "You're here to tell me my obituaries suck? Of all things in my paper, you're talking about the obituaries? Are you serious?"

"Yes, I am serious. It's bad writing." India leaned forward in her chair.

"It's *obituaries*, India, it's not world news."

"Well, it's the same as world news to those left behind, and frankly, the writing is horrendous. And it's boring, and leaves nothing for the loved ones to cherish. It needs to be cleaned up."

"And you want to work for me, is that what you're saying? Because we weren't exactly kissy-kissy in high school. Seriously, why are you here? This is not your place, India. Not since you left and went to bigger things. Another question, did you sign a non-compete agreement with your network?"

India leaned back in her chair. *Damn those hurdles.* "I'm sure I did."

"Well then," Carmen said. "I cannot hire you at all."

"I am sure I signed a non-compete agreement with regard to television networks," India said. "I do not think the agreement included small-town newspapers, but I'll have my lawyer contact you on that."

"Well, India," Carmen said, spreading her hands wide. "I think you misunderstand. Number one, there is no offer. No offer to you. As I told you earlier, we have no openings. And, off the record, do you think we could pay you what you think you deserve?"

"And because you have the hots for Ray Henderson, and Ray has the hots for my sister, you're putting me off. Okay, I get it. Okay, fine."

India rose and turned to leave.

I'll be damned if I leave it like this.

She reached the door and turned around. "You know, Carmen, you're right. We weren't kissy-kissy in school, and quite frankly, I couldn't stand you and your phony ways and how you paraded yourself for no substantive reason whatsoever. And when you married that poor crippled rich guy, I thought, well, there she goes, eating off the money train, just like you always did, every chance you got."

India watched Carmen blanch and saw her eyes water.

"My husband, God rest his soul, is dead. And I loved him and so did my daughter. Your sister is white trash, India, surely you know that," Carmen said, receding in her chair, fingering her necklace.

"Oh, well, you might call my sister white trash, and that's all well and good," India said leaning over Carmen's desk. "But what you really can't stand is that Ray doesn't want you. He wants my sister. Maybe you aren't all you think you are, Carmen. Maybe you're just a rich haughty bitch with nothing real."

"She's been with Phillip."

India reeled back. "What did you say?"

"She keeps going back to Phillip. I thought you knew."

India noted the satisfaction in Carmen's eyes.

"Yeah, and while you're speechless, I'll tell you something else, India." Carmen stood up and leaned across her desk. "Mark my words. I'm gonna have Ray Henderson; I know the way to his heart. Ray's an old-fashioned man. Once he finds out about your sister's trysts with Phillip, he won't have any more to do with her."

The truth came whizzing at India like a thousand

flies at a picnic.

Shelby and Phillip.

She keeps going back to Phillip.

I thought you knew.

She backed away, opened the door, and ran down the hall, searching for a way out.

The blue-shirted bulk just happened to be in the way.

They collided, and India felt his hands on her forearms just as she smelled his cologne.

"Whoa, hey now."

India looked up and found familiar brown eyes staring down at her, and the curve of a mouth ready to smile.

"Oh, sorry. I'm so sorry," she said to Paul Funar.

"No problem," he said, bending down to pick up a toolbox. "Just didn't want you to hurt yourself."

"Sure, thanks. Are you working here?" India tucked a strand of hair behind her ear.

"Hopefully. Putting in a bid anyway. I may be putting in a new electrical system in this place. Built in 1902, I think, probably ready for an upgrade, you know?"

India laughed in spite of feeling humiliated, knowing she'd been played by Carmen. "Yeah, I'm sure it is. Well, I hope you get the job," she said, moving closer to the door. He was too close. He smelled too good. His brown eyes were too damned inviting.

"India, right?" he said.

"Yes."

"I knew it was an unusual name, I remember that."

India stopped, her hand on the door latch. "Have you seen me on TV?"

Surprise registered on his face. "No. I don't watch much TV."

"Not even the news?"

"Especially not the news. Too depressing."

"Okay. Well, nice to see you again. Maybe I'll see you around." India shoved the door open and stepped out onto the sidewalk. She held the door open for just a minute. It seemed a gamble, looking into those eyes again, those arresting brown pools, she could slide into them and never come back out, but that was a gamble she was willing to take.

Paul remained standing in the spot she left him in, so disconcerting. India took a deep breath, and looked into his face.

I don't know what to say. And my knees are shaking.

"I'll be here," Paul said. "Or there, depending. Where ever there's work, that's where I'll be."

India nodded and closed the door, wondering where here or there might be, and how she might figure that out.

CHAPTER TWENTY THREE

India

Darkness was falling outside the kitchen windows. India watched the day turning to night and started to work. And there was work to do.

Here I go again, cooking.

She thought about her earlier conversation at the grocery store with Ray Henderson.

He's a good man, India thought. *Shelby needs to give him a chance. Maybe I'll just give them a little shove.*

"I heard you applied for a job at the paper," Ray said as he helped her load her groceries into her car, something that didn't ordinarily happen at that store, unless one was elderly.

"Oh, it's just a little job, but yeah," India said. "How did you hear that?"

"Carmen made sure I knew," Ray said.

The wind picked up, pitching Ray's hair in a wild position.

"Oh yeah, I keep forgetting how word travels in a small town. For the record, and you probably already know, she didn't hire me. In fact, she refused to even entertain the idea." India pulled her sweater around her.

"You don't want to work for her anyway," Ray said. "That's how I see it."

India paused, crossing her arms in front of her.

"She won't treat you right," he added.

"Hey, what are you doing for dinner tonight, Ray?"

"I suppose I'll have some. Not sure what or where."

India took ahold of his arm. Ray looked down at her hand. "Ray, would you come by our house tonight, around 6:30? I'm cooking, and I promise you, I'm a pretty decent cook, I won't poison you or anything," India grinned, and Ray laughed. "We'll have a little dinner party."

"Six-thirty?"

"Yes, can you make it?"

"I will. I will, and thank you."

India shoved the hatchback door down over the groceries in the back of the rental wreck.

"Great. Six-thirty. You know the way."

As she climbed into the rental, and drove away, India wondered whether she was the good witch, presenting Ray with a great gift, one he would always treasure, or whether she just interfered in the worst way in her sister's love life.

Either way, I don't care. It's time Shelby looked at someone new. Someone decent. And I bet he'd be good to Quinn too. Win-win.

Oh my God, what have I done? This could so backfire.

Well, it was too late for regrets now. Still thinking back to her earlier invitation to Ray, India nodded to the darkness outside and began.

Baked Gnocchi and Italian Sausage
4 oz. baby spinach
    2 tbsp. extra virgin olive oil
    1 cup diced onion
    1 ½ cups chopped peppers in green, yellow,
orange
    ¼ tsp. hot pepper flakes
    1 clove garlic, minced
    1 pound Italian sausages, casings removed
    2 15-oz cans fire-roasted tomatoes
    4 tbsp. tomato paste
    1 pound gnocchi
    ½ cup heavy cream
    1 ½ cups whole milk ricotta cheese
    1 beaten egg
    1 cup fresh Italian leaf parsley, chopped
    1 tsp. kosher salt
    ½ tsp. ground black pepper
    ½ cup fresh basil, chopped
    1 cup parmesan cheese, divided
    2 cups shredded mozzarella cheese

India rolled up her shirt sleeves, then started pulling pots out of the cabinets and ingredients out of the grocery bags on the island. The clatter of the pans and the rustling of the bags began to sooth her.

Bring a pot of salted water to boil, and place a strainer in the water. Add the spinach and boil for one minute, and one minute only. Remove strainer and drain, but leave water on the heat. Squeeze spinach to get the excess water out and place in medium bowl and set aside.

India wiped the sweat from her brow.

Okay.

India plunked a sauté pan on the stove, poured in the oil and threw in the onions, peppers and pepper flakes. After three or four minutes, she added the garlic.

Only 30 seconds or so because garlic burns easily. She shoved the vegetables to the outside edge of the pan and added the cut-up Italian sausage.

Yum, what an aroma.

Now for the tomatoes and tomato paste, which she dumped in and continued to stir. Once the mixture was thickened, she moved the pan to a cold burner.

India threw her towel over her shoulder and turned the oven to 375 degrees.

Okay, the pot with the cooking water. India turned the heat back up and dumped the gnocchi into the water. As soon as the gnocchi began to float, she dumped them into a strainer, allowing the cooking water to go down the drain. She dumped the gnocchi into the vegetable mixture, added the cream, stirred until the gnocchi absorbed the cream and then removed from heat.

Good lord, India thought. *All this for a silly dinner party? I must have been crazy. But oh well...* The stiffness was gone from her shoulders, a peaceful feeling growing in her.

It's okay. Good, even.

India dragged a bowl down from the cupboard, clattering as she went. Spinach, ricotta, egg, parsley, salt, pepper, basil and ¾ cup of parmesan cheese. Stir, stir, stir.

Alright. India grabbed the casserole dish she set aside earlier.

Half the meat sauce went in, all of the ricotta mixture, and then all of the gnocchi, the rest of the sauce, and the remaining parmesan cheese. She tossed the mozzarella cheese on top and shoved the casserole in the oven.

Holy cow. Thirty minutes. What else?

Artisan bread, baked, lying on a wooden platter.

Romaine lettuce, radishes, cucumbers, red onion,

feta cheese, walnuts, all tossed into a pretty bowl.

India pulled a green-and-yellow stitched quilt over the dining room table, lowered candles into three mason jars, set them out on the table and lit each one.

Quinn appeared in the doorway.

"Oh, hey," India said. "I'm glad you're here."

"Yeah, well," Quinn sauntered in further and looked the table up and down. "Do you need any help?"

India smiled.

"Sure. Can you set places for you, your mom, Gwen, me, and Ray? Get those plates out that look like pottery, the ones that say they're from Portugal on the back."

"Yeah." Quinn sauntered back to the cabinets.

Everything will be fine, it'll be nice, India thought, watching Quinn arrange plates and silverware. India went for the glassware and lined everything up.

"Adrian might be here," Quinn said. "I'm gonna set an extra place."

"Fine, that's great," India said, running water into a vase for some orange dahlias picked up earlier at the grocery store. "I hope he comes," she said, plunking the vase onto the table.

"Whatever you're cooking, it smells really good," Quinn said.

India wanted to thank her, but the doorbell rang, and Quinn ran for the door to let Adrian in. Ray rang the doorbell nearly as soon as the door closed behind Adrian.

Shelby came downstairs, dressed in a white top with silver embroidery and white pants. Her hair was newly blond, and she looked radiant. India watched Ray suck in his breath.

Gwen arrived, carrying a chocolate cake on an old-fashioned crystal pedestal with a lid. Quinn ran to hug her.

India smiled in the doorway to the dining room, looking at all of them.

I think this little soiree might be a hit.

But that wasn't quite how it turned out.

The dinner party began well. Everyone complimented the food, the lighting, the music, the flowers. Ray and Shelby sat side by side. Quinn was across the table from Adrian. Gwen sat next to Quinn with India at the head of the table. Wine was poured freely.

Shelby was beginning to sway and laugh for no reason.

Quinn and Adrian were not allowed to drink, but it seemed they were watching the adults carefully.

India felt good.

Gwen was wiping her mouth with her napkin.

Ray was holding Shelby's hand. The two of them seemed to glow into one another.

India was about to go retrieve Gwen's cake when Ray asked about India's career, about dangers and intrigue around the world, and being in the scope of a camera.

"I..." India barely began to answer and then Shelby was pulling her sleeve and wanted to go to the kitchen.

"Be back in a minute, folks," India said with no real conviction, and followed Shelby into the kitchen.

"Why am I'm always beholding to you," Shelby said, just a bit too loud, tears starting to fall.

"Oh my God," India groaned, gripping the edge of the kitchen island, hoping to high heaven no one in the other room could hear Shelby crying and shouting. *Not this, not now.*

Gwen's chocolate cake sat on the island. India began dumping heaping spoons of coffee grounds into the coffee maker.

Too much wine, I guess.

"What's wrong with you? We're eating dinner here, we have guests, what's got you all unhinged? What do you mean?"

Shelby slumped onto one of the island chairs, staring into space. "Don't call me stupid, you big city reporter girl. I'm always in your debt, and I don't know why. I stayed here, year after year after year, when I could have had a life somewhere else. I stayed here and took care of Mom and Dad…"

"I didn't call you stupid; quit saying that," India felt as if she was careening on an out-of-control merry-go-round. "You have that idea in your head, not mine."

Ray stuck his head around the corner.

"Everything in here okay, ladies?"

"Ray, no, it's fine, it's fine. Coffee and dessert in a minute," India heard herself saying.

"Okay, sure," Ray said and disappeared.

Shelby's earlier radiant look was rapidly dissipating. "You think you're so much better than me. You look down your nose at me, at Quinn, at everything about us."

"Shelby, no, I don't. We're just not the same person, that's all. You've picked at this scab for years and there's no reason. Calm down. We have guests, Shelby. Come on."

"And then they, or she, left the house to you anyway, not to me, when I was the one here, taking care of everything while you were traveling the world, forgetting about us, forgetting about your home, India. They left it all to you, and now I'm a beggar on your doorstep. Do you know how that feels?"

"Now, wait just a minute," India "It wasn't easy for me to come back here, believe me, knowing what I know. I know you resent me, you have for years. I know you have some kind of chip on your shoulder, but come on now."

"My friends tell me I'm more assertive since they both died," Shelby said.

"Well, Shelby, I don't know your friends, but I disagree. I don't believe you're more assertive. I think you are more aggressive than you used to be."

"What's the difference? It's the same thing."

India sighed. "No, no it isn't, Shelby, that's what you're not getting. Assertive takes other people into account, respect, you know? Aggressive means no respect, just give me what I want."

"Of course, dumb Shelby, wrong again," Shelby stood up, picking up Gwen's cake. "I'm sick of you, and I'm sick of your crap. I can't kick you out, since this is your house in the first place, but I wish you'd leave. In fact, I wish you'd never come back here! Why did you come back? Because your boyfriend went and died on you?"

Gwen's cake slid out of her hands and hit the floor with a crash. Chocolate cake broke apart in clumsy, crackly globs as glass scattered recklessly across the floor, coated in frosting and cake.

***

The guests were gone, as was Quinn, who left with Adrian as soon as dessert was over, but returned alone while India was cleaning up the mess. No greeting, no conversation, just the sound of boots climbing the stairs and a door shutting with a definite *click*.

Shelby retired to her room, after stumbling up the stairs to her bed. Ray left for home, shaking India's hand, and complimenting the food, thanking India, assuring her not to worry about any of the night's events. Gwen excused herself with few words. She simply said, "I'm goin'," and walked off the porch into the night.

India was left alone with the clean-up and her own

thoughts. Being left to clean up was actually sort of a respite, a quiet time to think and follow mechanical rules. *Shove the uneaten food onto one plate. Rinse all the others. Put the uneaten food down the garbage disposal, and look at the dishes you have to work with. Place them in the dishwasher. Put the glasses in the dishwasher, line them up so they don't jostle against one another and maybe break. The pots are already scrubbed and put away. Pour another glass of wine. Shut the capsule of cleaner in the dishwasher compartment and shut the door, program the dishwasher, sit your ass down and drink your wine.*

Which was exactly what India did, staring at the reflection of the kitchen lights in the windows with the dark just outside. It started out so well, and then one unfortunate moment and it all went to hell.

God, I'm disappointed. I doubt Ray gives her another chance now. Quinn was engaged tonight, a nice change, but she was also happy that Adrian was coming, which is probably the reason for that. And Adrian is a nice boy, a solid one. I like him.

India sipped her glass of wine, staring into the darkness outside.

Gwen didn't say much, not sure why. I hope she wasn't uncomfortable with everything, but that doesn't really sound like her. On the other hand, Ray and Shelby seemed to be doing just fine until…"

Until.

Until Ray started asking me about my career. That's what it all went to shit.

India pulled the bottle from the refrigerator and filled her glass up again.

Shelby didn't even blink an eye when Quinn left with Adrian. Didn't even ask Quinn when she would be back, where they're going. It was almost like, oh well, whatever. India saw her reflection in the dark of the windows waving one hand in a flippant motion.

Maybe I should let go. Not worry about this anymore. Their life, their problem, and God knows they don't want me in the middle of it anyway.

Paul. *Maybe I should have invited him to dinner*, India thought, remembering the brown eyes looking at her under the ball cap. *Then, on the other hand, with the way things turned out...*

Her cell phone vibrated on the island.

India picked it up cautiously, not wanting to keep it ringing but not wanting to answer either. The number was unknown to her.

The thing kept ringing, and as India watched it, somehow, she let it go to voicemail.

Which she listened to immediately.

"India, it's Adrian. And I don't want Quinn to ever know I've talked to you."

CHAPTER TWENTY FOUR

Shelby

7:04 pm, a text came in.

"Hello beautiful"

Shelby stared down at her phone. *Phillip. Now what.*

"Hello yourself."

"Hey, wantd to let u knw im getting married. Yeah, this old man is getting hitched and we're having a kid, and u should knw. We're moving to Texas bc her family is there, woopeedoo, but that's where ill b if u ever want to contact me."

Shelby's stomach hit the floor. She shut her phone off. And three minutes later turned it back on.

Another message from Phillip.

"Hey, baby, didn't mean 2 mix u up with that. Cme on, b nice, lets get 2gether one last time. Ur the best i ever had and i don't want to go into marriage without one last time with u."

Oh really.

Shelby carefully typed out a lengthy reply.

"Congratulations on your marriage and impending fatherhood with your teenage bride, and personally, I hope you get to endure all the hell I did when I was with you, and whatever happens to you from this point forward, well, I can only hope you get what you so richly deserve. Other than that, congrats!"

CHAPTER TWENTY FIVE

Quinn

"Well, here's my place, where me and my dad live," Adrian said, holding Quinn's hand as she stepped up the rough, rocky driveway. Quinn's eyes followed his other hand, pointing upward.

"Okay," she said, looking at the house that looked more like a single-wide trailer disguised with some log-like siding and a small porch jutting out in front. "Okay," she said again.

"It's gross, right," Adrian said.

Quinn looked at him sharply. No matter what the place looked like at first glance, she wasn't going to let Adrian think it was beneath her to be there, or for him to live there. "It's not bad," Quinn said. "I mean, look at all these trees, and you got that stump over there to sit on and think, you know? It's quiet, not like living in town with all the traffic and stuff."

Adrian didn't appear convinced. Quinn shook his arm.

"It's fine. I mean, maybe you don't want to live here always but…"

"Hey, boy!"

The shout broke the pleasant calm of the setting.

Quinn saw a short, fat man, wearing a too-small tee shirt that exposed his girth of stomach and a pair of shorts dropping off his ass, step out on the porch. She felt Adrian tense. Upon seeing her, the man stopped short and smoothed his tee shirt down over his belly.

"Dad," Adrian said. "This is my friend, Quinn. Quinn, this is my dad."

"Hi," Quinn said, stepping forward. The man on the porch seemed confused, and then Quinn realized he was drunk. She watched as he pulled a can of chew out of a pocket, never taking his eyes off her, then pulled out a plug and stuck it in his face.

"It's nice to meet you," Quinn said.

The man weaved a bit, pushing the chew can back into his pocket. "Uh hunh," he said, flicking excess chew off his fingers over the porch railing. He seemed to be panting. "What do you think of this weather?"

"It's nice here," Quinn said. "You have lots of nice trees."

"Lots of nice trees," the man repeated, looking skyward, turning from side to side. "We have lots of nice trees. Did you hear that, son? Lots of nice trees."

Adrian stepped up on the porch, leaving Quinn at the base of the steps.

She could feel his awkwardness, the weirdness of it all, his suffering.

"Dad, do you want a sandwich?"

The man on the porch turned to Adrian.

"What? We have lots of nice trees. She said so."

Adrian stepped closer, taking the man's arm, which the man threw off, seeking in his pockets again for the tobacco. "Dad, can I make you a sandwich?"

"You're just trying to make me get sleepy, aren't you. So I'll go to bed and then you bring your girl in here."

The man turned around, jamming at the screen door for a second or two before opening the door and disappearing inside the trailer, sending back one last message.

"Just like your mother."

Quinn blanched. "I'll wait here," she said as Adrian looked at her, his eyes a watery brown. "Go on, tend to him, and I'll sit right here." She plopped down on the top step of the porch.

Here I thought I had it bad. He's suffered too. Not exactly like me but close to the same thing.

It was nearly dark when Adrian exited the trailer.

"He's asleep," Adrian said, holding a pair of keys.

"What're those to?" Quinn asked.

"His car. It's dark, and I think we'll ride back to your house."

On the ride home, Quinn examined Adrian's profile in the dark.

"I'm sorry," Adrian said. "He's just like that."

"Don't be embarrassed," she said.

"No, he's a drunk," Adrian said, bending over the steering wheel. "He's an alcoholic. He always drank, so far as I can remember anyway, but after my mother left, he started drinking more and more and more, and cursing her and every other woman on the face of the earth. He can't forget, and he can't forgive. So he just wastes away here, thinking about how he's been wronged by women, working at the factory, unhappy, drinking the rest of the time he's awake."

"I get it," Quinn said. "You don't have to pretend with me, I mean, just don't. I kind of like your place, all those trees, and the quiet. It's nice."

"I want to be different," Adrian said, turning the

radio off. "I don't want to be that guy, swimming in his own spit and never amounting to anything at all."

Quinn stared at his profile as they pulled up to her house. "Trust me, Adrian. You're not going to be that guy. You're just not."

"I'm glad to hear you say that," Adrian murmured. "You have no idea."

"Oh, maybe I do," Quinn said and fell silent.

CHAPTER TWENTY SIX

India

The first thing India noticed about Phillip's yard was that it hadn't been mowed in some time. Her eyes ran over the small house, nondescript, picture window in front, dingy white door with half-moon glass, black mold creeping up the siding. Phillip's gleaming pickup truck sat in the driveway, an odd-looking jewel in the otherwise bleak landscape. Next to the house was a junkyard with high fences and "Stay Out" signs. Across the busy county road was a church, and next to the church was a bar.

Nice.

Before she rang the doorbell, the front door opened and Phillip stepped outside.

"What you want?" he asked, bare-chested and barefoot, squinting at her as he dragged on a cigarette.

"You know who I am, I guess," India said, feeling a bit unsteady.

Phillip looked her up and down. "I know who you

are," he said after a long pause and another drag on the cigarette. "But what do you want?"

A shrill voice floated out from somewhere in the house. "Phillip, baby? Is everything okay? Who's she?"

He opened the front door an inch or so and yelled back in, "Everything's okay, sweetheart, don't worry about nothing," then shut the door hard.

"Make this quick, reporter girl. I got things to tend to."

He threw his cigarette down, stomped on it with a bare foot, then pulled another cigarette from a back pocket and lit it. "Let me guess, you want to talk about your little niece and what I did to her and how she's suffering, right? Like you care. Funny thing, reporter lady, you ain't been around here in what, five, ten years? Are you gonna stand here on my front porch, with my pregnant wife inside, and tell me I molested that girl?"

"I just want to ask you a couple of questions, Phillip. I realize this is not the optimum time, and I'm sorry, but my focus is Quinn. She's hurt, and she needs help, and I just want to understand what happened so I can maybe help her. That's all."

India gulped and began again. "I'm not here to place blame; I'm not here to point a finger. I just want to get a perspective, okay."

Phillip blew a smoke rush into her face, making her cough. "I'll tell you this much. I did not molest or otherwise harm that girl. Never did. Shelby always said I did, but I did not."

"But what happened?" India shifted her stance.

"What happened is this," Phillip hissed, "Shelby dressed Quinn up like she was someone else, someone Shelby wanted to be, and then bad things happened. Shelby set her up with a Facebook account when she was underage, and Quinn posed as an older girl so she wouldn't get caught on Facebook as a minor with an unauthorized account. Shelby posted photos of Quinn, nonstop. Some of them were pretty suggestive, and I told her it would be a problem, but she wouldn't listen. So, men contacted Quinn all the time, older men, men like me, but not me, understand," he said, gesturing toward his chest. "I suppose most of them caught on with her conversation because she was a kid and she spoke like a kid, but even with that, there were those that knew she was a kid and liked it."

"And?"

"Quinn's birthday, I forget which one, and again, Shelby dressed her up like she was twenty-two, and she came out of that bedroom, and... my God, I'm so ashamed," Phillip said, sagging a bit, leaning into the porch rail. He took a deep breath and continued defensively. "She came out of there, and she was all dressed up in this micro-mini dress, cleavage from here to there, legs, everything showed but her pussy, and she was made up like a model. She came out of that bedroom and grabbed me and kissed me full on the lips. Shelby had her all worked up. She wouldn't have done it otherwise."

India watched the man buckle and shake his head.

"I couldn't believe it happened. But, sure, I kissed her back and touched her, and Shelby started screaming and yelling and blaming me, and she kicked me out. That was our breakup."

"So, that was it?" India put her sunglasses back on.

"That was it. Shelby tried to make it so much more, and I'm sorry for my part in it, but that was it."

The door opened a crack. A plaintive voice again. "Phillip, baby? Are you done yet?"

"In a minute," Phillip roared back.

"Okay, baby, because I just need you right now."

India stared as the door closed.

"She's a little insecure," Phillip said. "We're

packing, moving to Texas. Boxes all over the place. Can't find one damn thing."

"Well, she's what, eighteen?" India asked. "A child."

"Nineteen. I did not molest your niece," Phillip snarled. "I'll swear on that 'til I die. Shelby made a big deal of what happened, but I did not have sex with her daughter."

"But you touched her."

"I did not force myself on her. Remember, she kissed me."

"Doesn't matter. She's a kid. You are an adult."

"I didn't fuck her!"

India stood back. "Well, I'm not sure I'm satisfied with your explanation but, I suppose it's time to take Quinn to the doctor and find out whether she's been violated or not."

India pulled her sunglasses back down and turned to leave.

"You're not her mother. You don't have the right."

Halfway to her car, she turned back.

Phillip was still standing on the porch, lighting up yet another cigarette.

"Hey," India called, "When was the last time you were intimate with my sister?"

Phillip scrambled down the driveway.

"Can you not shut up? My wife is in there."

India rolled her eyes.

"Somehow, I doubt that makes a difference. What's the answer to the question, stud?"

"I don't know, a while. I guess the day she was supposed to pick you up at the airport. That's all I'm giving you. Now, get out. Leave right now."

"Sure," India said, getting in her car. "I'm gone."

CHAPTER TWENTY SEVEN

Adrian

"If I asked you, would you ever be mine? If I asked in you, in another place and time? Would you stand there, just stand and stare? Or would you tell me, you would always be there? If I asked you...if I asked you..."

Adrian's fingers caressed the guitar gently, with a surety of a seasoned musician, as he perched on an old tree stump in the yard, red and gold leaves swirling about his feet.

The air was crisp now, a hint of winter coming on. Adrian loved autumn with its rich colors and fog in the mornings, the impending quiet rest of winter.

It was hard not to think about Quinn, and pleasant to think about her. Adrian continued plucking the strings of the old guitar, trying to make the song just right when the trailer house door slammed open, banging the side of the house.

"Hey!"

Adrian turned to see his father stumbling down the

porch steps, ambling toward his spot on the tree stump.

"What you doin'," his father said. "Pining away for some girl, maybe that little girl that was here the other day? Playing that guitar like some love-struck fairy? Hunh?"

Adrian's father pulled a cigarette out of his pocket, lighting it with a blue Bic lighter. Adrian watched him inhale and throw the smoke back out his nose and mouth. For a moment, his father's face was lost in a white fog. "Come on, Dad," Adrian said, laying the guitar on his lap. "Let's go back in. I'll get a pizza out of the freezer. Okay?"

"I don't want no pizza. You thump her yet?" His father asked, swaying back and forth.

"What?"

"You thump her yet? Like, you gotta let the woman know who's the boss. You gotta make her know you gonna thump her, and you'll thump her hard, don't you know that?"

His father stumbled a step, breathing through his mouth, then righted himself, the cigarette dangling off his lips.

"What are you talking about, like I should beat her up?"

Adrian's father grabbed his crotch. "You know what I'm talking about, boy. You back her up against the wall, pull her hair a little, make her understand you mean business, get her back side, and you thump her," he said, moving his crotch back and forth. "I can't believe any son of mine don't know that. Ain't you any kind of a man?"

"Dad, it's not like that. She's not like that. And we're not like that."

'The hell she ain't. They all are." Adrian's father turned back to the trailer and began stumbling toward it. "They all are, boy. They all gotta be taught a lesson.

They gotta know who's boss. They all gotta know who is the boss."

Adrian watched his father mount the porch steps heavily, breathing through his mouth, fumbling with the screen door and finally, disappearing inside, the half-smoked cigarette wedged between his fingers.

"I don't need no pizza," his father called back.

He'll be asleep in a little while. It'll be quiet soon.

Adrian pulled his guitar back up and resumed working on the song. It had to be a good song if it was going to be for her. It had to say what he wanted to say.

The sun went down in an orange haze, the cicadas began singing, and Adrian kept plucking away on the guitar, seeing Quinn's face as he worked his ballad.

Someday he would sing it to her.

Chapter Twenty Eight

Shelby

The date with Ray happened over a week ago, and Shelby remained entirely disenchanted. *I only went out on this stupid date, after turning him down twice, because India told me to give this guy a chance, and I tell you what, he bored the hell out of me. Nice guy, well intentioned. I just think not.*

In the first place, Ray came to her door with flowers. No reason for the flowers. In fact, why? Shelby took the flowers, put them in water and then listened to Ray ask her out for a date for the third time. She decided to go.

Maybe, if he gets a taste of my life up front, he'll be grossed out and won't ask me again.

Shelby thought she had the odds on her side when she agreed to go out on a date with Ray Henderson.

But a little issue arose, a little complication, a ripple. Shelby supposed it could also work in her favor, maybe.

The current issue was Quinn's father, Tony Demarist. Tony emailed Quinn, asking her to go out to dinner with him, some father-and-daughter time, and Quinn appeared to be amenable to it. In fact, she seemed downright excited. Maybe a bit too excited in Shelby's book.

"He's my *dad*," Quinn argued when Shelby objected to their burgeoning relationship. After all, Tony moved forty miles away, left Shelby and Quinn after the divorce, and also unforgiveable to Shelby, he remarried.

"Why do you want this?" Shelby shouted at Quinn. "Why?"

To which Quinn only responded, "Well, he and me had so little time together, and if he wants to get to know me, that's okay and fine with me."

"But he's an asshole," Shelby countered.

"And Phillip isn't?" Quinn said.

Well, that was bad enough.

Just as bad but on a different level, Shelby and Ray's date.

A dark ring of embarrassment over the dinner party fiasco surrounded Shelby, and took root in her belly.

Should I apologize? Should I bring it up? Here I am, riding along in Ray's car like nothing happened. Nice of him not to bring it up, though.

Ray drove her sixty miles to Springfield, to a steakhouse called Level 421. As the big luxury car's headlights bore into the dark, Shelby wondered, had she gone too far from her home?

After being seated in the posh cool restaurant, Shelby studied the extensive menus, full of all sorts of food with more unfamiliar names than she could even fathom. "Order anything you want," Ray said. "Anything. I eat here any time I can. The food's excellent."

"Right," Shelby said, going back to the menu,

squirming in her leather seat underneath the glare of a single pendant light.

"No really, I want to treat you," Ray insisted again, pushing his glasses up his nose. "Anything."

Shelby scoured the menu, wondering if anything she ordered would be even edible or familiar or odd. She didn't like fish, cancel that out, she didn't really care for complicated food dishes, that was her sister's arena, but nonetheless, she was determined to be a good sport.

In the end, Shelby ordered a steak, medium well, with grilled mushrooms and a baked potato. Ray ordered oysters on the half shell, onion rings, and a tuna steak.

"You gotta try this," he said, shoving a mucous-ridden oyster on the shell at her. Shelby shuddered.

"Have you ever had oysters before?"

"No, and I never want to," Shelby said, pulling back.

"Just try it, here, let's put some hot sauce on it," Ray was saying, pulling a bottle out of nowhere, dousing the unfortunate disgusting thing.

"No, I don't think..."

Shelby's steak arrived, a reprieve. She jammed butter and sour cream into the crevice the steaming potato and smiled. *What to do? Why am I on this date?*

"Shelby, I've wanted to take you out for a long time, but I think you know that," Ray said, slowly carving his tuna steak.

Shelby paused, her mouth full of potato and accoutrements. "I'm surprised you would," Shelby said, gulping her food down. Ray didn't seem to notice. "I mean, in spite of..."

"I know, I've never married, I don't have any children, no reason to even think I could have any kids out there," Ray continued. "I'm a single man, I'm forty-eight years old, and I took care of my mother for years before she passed. I inherited my place in life, really."

"Okay," she said, swallowing hard. So, maybe he wasn't going to bring up the dinner party disaster?

"Don't get me wrong, I'm grateful for my family's legacy," he said, waving his knife. "I've traveled the globe, been to the West Indies, all over Europe, Africa, road-tripped across America, so many other places, and I've always gone alone. Having a partner to go with me on my travels is something I've longed for."

"Okay. My sister travels. Or did."

Ray sat back in the booth and laid his silverware down. Shelby was faintly conscious of the odor of tuna, but more than that, the onion rings. She pulled her iced tea to her mouth and gulped.

"Do you like to travel, Shelby?"

"Uh, well, I… I just haven't, so I don't know."

An awkward silence.

"I'm screwing this whole thing up," Ray said.

Shelby rubbed her fingers on the napkin in her lap.

"No, no… well, yes."

"I was afraid of that. I just wanted to impress you," Ray said.

Shelby wanted to reach across the table, and take his hand, but she found she couldn't. She wanted to do the right thing. "Ray, I'm flattered that you wanted to bring me there, but honestly, I'd rather go bowling and eat a hamburger. I don't need all this, all this… fluff. If it's all the same to you, can we go home?"

"Sure," Ray said. He looked relieved.

They drove back in silence, listening to the radio.

Ray walked to her the door.

He didn't try to kiss her. He didn't press up against her. Not like Phillip would have done. Shelby wondered if that was weird or if Ray was maybe gay, or maybe he just didn't know how to hook up.

"Shelby, thank you for going out with me."

"Sure, Ray. Thank you."

Shelby watched the back of his jacket as he walked back to his car.

So much for that.

But, Ray, the eternal gentleman, sent flowers to the house the next day, a beautiful pink rose display with a generous *thank you* on the card.

Shelby set the flowers on the kitchen island in an old pitcher, believing there was no reason to hope, although she wanted to. She wanted to hope so much.

She decided she would shop elsewhere than Henderson Foods.

And for two or three days, Shelby kept to her decision.

Okay, no. I'm going in.

Since the date, Shelby found herself in Ray's grocery store four times, and each time she entered, she looked over at the cash registers to see if Ray was standing guard, or if he was greeting customers, or if he could be seen at all, and none of those four times was Ray visible. He wasn't around when she came in, he didn't greet her in the aisle, and he wasn't standing by the cash registers when she checked out. It was almost as if Ray didn't exist at all.

What gives?

Ray just wasn't around, and she didn't understand why not.

When the tenth day dawned with no Ray sightings, Shelby was, as her mother would say, "crotchety," or as her sister would say, "bitchy."

Shelby snapped at her co-workers, whined at the staff, and ran Quinn to her room with a "leave me alone for one second, will you?"

Why am I acting this way?

Shelby couldn't take it any longer.

Where is Ray?

The weekend prior, Tony called and said he wanted

to take Quinn and Shelby out for dinner.

"Why?" Shelby snapped. "Like, when was the last time you saw Quinn anyway?"

Tony's voice, rich as dark chocolate, came across the phone. "I saw her a week ago, you know this. I took her for the evening when you went out with that guy from the grocery store."

"So? How do you even know about that?"

"Shelby, quit it. Quinn is my daughter, too. She told me. She's our daughter, and I just want to spend some time with her, and I want the three of us to go out."

"Whatever," Shelby said, biting a fingernail.

"That's real grown up, Shelby," Tony said. "Just cooperate for once, okay?"

"Okay, sure, or whatever," Shelby said and hung up.

They went out, the three of them, to a nice dinner place in West Plains. Shelby drank wine. Tony laughed, joked, and talked to Quinn about her grades and her friends. The lighting was great. Tony was as handsome as ever, swarthy and masculine, dark Italian, olive skin, brown eyes. Shelby kept staring and wondered, *how did I let this guy get away?*

Quinn seemed to be having a great time.

Shelby looked back and forth at the two of them. Quinn shared Tony's brown eyes, but the resemblance stopped there.

She looks just like India when she turns her head a certain way. Other than that, I don't see a resemblance to Tony or me. Figures. My own daughter looks like my sister.

Shelby snapped to attention. The two of them were talking about Adrian. She missed a whole conversation.

"He's really great, Dad," Quinn was saying. "I like him a lot."

Tony's eyes met Shelby's across the table and she

could tell he was wondering, *hello, what? This boy she likes him a lot? When do I get to meet him?*

Shelby raised her hands, palms spread in a helpless gesture.

I need some water.

Her tongue felt like a cotton ball. From Texas. Where, according to rumor, everything is bigger.

Tony turned back to Quinn, and they kept talking in a language Shelby couldn't understand. She asked the waitress for water. Her head was swimming.

Tony drove them home, told Quinn he would be in touch, to call him any time, and he wanted to meet this boy Quinn liked so much. Shelby climbed out of the car and stumbled to the porch, grasping the railing like a life raft.

Quinn kissed her father good-bye, skipped up the steps, and mocked Shelby as she struggled to the front door.

That was a weekend ago.

Tony was hot, no doubt about that. Shelby remembered how his jeans fit just so, how muscular and manly he looked that night they went out. She remembered how he and her fit together so well.

It was all so confusing. Alarm bells sounded in her head. *Don't get involved. Don't get involved.*

What if, Shelby couldn't help but wonder. *What if Tony and me and Quinn could be a regular family again? What if we got a place, a nice house, and me and Quinn moved in with Tony?*

But the musings about a possible future with Tony fell flat. It didn't work before, and there was no reason to think it would work now.

We're divorced for a reason. We couldn't make it work, not even for Quinn's sake. Besides, he got married again. No room for me.

They didn't really matter, the fantasies of a new,

wonderful life with Tony and Quinn. It was all fantasy, after all, and Shelby knew there was no going back or making a new future there. And she couldn't get Ray out of her mind.

Why? He isn't my type. He's overweight, grey, and not real tall. And he wears glasses.

She slept fitfully, tossing, turning, never getting comfortable in her bed, no real rest. But at least she didn't have to work tomorrow.

Late afternoon, Shelby found herself wandering the grocery store and finally chose a gallon of chocolate milk and a box of glazed donuts.

I feel like crap, and I bet I look like it too.

She stood at the checkout counter, the sweating gallon of milk hugged close to her chest, with the glazed donuts in the other hand. The checkout girl stared at her. Her nametag said Ashley.

"Oh yeah," Shelby said, setting the items on the conveyor belt, not noticing the sweat stain from the milk on her right breast. "Hey," she said as casually as she could, her heart was beating in her throat. "I haven't seen Ray around in a while. Is he okay?"

The girl barely looked up. "Um, yeah. He's on vacation, I guess."

"Vacation, okay. Well, at least he's not sick or something." Shelby hoped Ashley might volunteer more information, but Ashley only pushed her items to the bagging area.

"Um, that's gonna be $5.17," Ashley said, leaning on the cash register.

"So, he's on vacation," Shelby tried again. She hoped her tone sounded completely casual. "I hope he's having a good time."

She pulled money out of her pocket and extended it. "Did he go alone?"

"God, I don't know," Ashley said. "I think he's

back tomorrow. Do you want me to tell him you asked about him?"

Shelby grabbed her change and the items. "No, no, no, don't be doing that. No need. I'll catch up with him later."

Somehow her heart felt lighter, relieved.

He's not dead, and he didn't move away. That's a good thing.

CHAPTER TWENTY NINE

Quinn

Quinn learned of the fire at school.

Since she didn't watch the news, and Shelby didn't watch it either, Quinn was oblivious to what was going on in the world around her. And so as she showered, dressed, put on her makeup getting ready for school, she had no idea of what transpired while she slept.

Quinn went to school, looking forward to walking with Adrian. When he didn't appear at their usual meeting place, she blew it off. He could be sick. He might have something going on keeping him from school. She didn't think a whole lot of his absence.

He hadn't texted her, though.

He would have texted her if he was sick, or whatever.

Before homeroom, Ivy appeared out of nowhere in the hall and grabbed Quinn's arm.

"Did you hear?"

"Hear what?" Quinn said, stopping in her tracks.

Ivy threw her bag over her shoulder and whispered, "Adrian's trailer-house. The fire. You didn't hear?" Quinn began to sweat. She felt her face get hot, and her stomach started pumping the bile of fear as it beat up to her throat.

"No, tell me."

Ivy grabbed her and steered her outside, through the same door where Quinn would have met Adrian, except Adrian wasn't there that morning.

Numbness took over now, a shield to the rocking shock her body and mind should be absorbing. Quinn grabbed her stomach.

Fire? Adrian's house?

Quinn's stomach began to fall.

Can't be.

Ivy turned Quinn to face her and spoke slowly.

"Quinn, listen, there was a big fire overnight and Adrian's trailer is gone. Like, totally burned up, gone. There was a body, but they don't know who it is. But Adrian's gone too. Like, disappeared. They can't tell yet whether the fire was an accident or what."

Quinn's legs and arms felt like rubber, and she began to tremble. "Is he dead?"

Ivy shook her head, her dark curls bouncing.

"We just don't' know, Quinn. We just don't know."

Quinn turned her face to the brick wall and began to scream.

A half hour later, Quinn slumped against the wall, sitting on a bench in the counselor's office, fists clenched in the front pocket of her hoodie.

The emptiness was unbearable. *My friend, my good friend, maybe even my boyfriend. Gone.*

She barely looked up when the shadow stopped in front of her and then sat down beside her on the bench. A pair of arms wrapped around her and pulled her into the softness of a woman's chest, and she began to sob.

"India, oh, India," Quinn sobbed.

"I'm so sorry, babe, so sorry," her aunt whispered.

CHAPTER THIRTY

India

A soft ping drew India to her cell phone. A text. A video. It was from Quinn.

India pushed her glasses down over her nose.

It's 12:31 a.m., what the hell.

India opened the video and immediately realized the text wasn't meant for her at all.

Quinn, in a dark, grainy video, grinned at the camera and grabbed a bottle of Jack Daniels from someone off screen, while other teenagers milled around her in random fashion. India peered at the background. The video clearly hadn't been taken at the Madelaine Street home. India saw paneled walls in the background, a plaid sofa, a floor lamp. No, not their home. Where was this happening?

India gasped as she watched Quinn put the bottle to her lips and throw a couple of deep-throated gulps of whiskey down her throat like it was water. Quinn laughed, flipped the bird, and someone off camera handed her a cigarette over her shoulder. India watched Quinn draw heavily on the cigarette and pass it back to whoever handed it to her. India watched her exhale and blow a couple smoke rings, and then the bottle was back. The video ended with Quinn gulping down another couple ounces of Jack Daniels and laughing.

Oh my God. How long has this been going on? Who do I talk to about it? Shelby? Does she know this is going on? I doubt it, and even if she did, she'd make an excuse.

India slumped back on her pillows and watched the video again. Unsurprisingly, there was no sign of Adrian in the video.

I expected as much, India thought, examining every detail. *Quinn's been acting so weird since he's been gone. This explains a lot.*

Gwen. I need to talk to Gwen.

CHAPTER THIRTY ONE

"I think Quinn's in real trouble," India began.

"That would be no surprise, child," Gwen said, as the two swung back and forth on Gwen's porch spring and watched yellow and red leaves drift to the ground.

India's aura wasn't too good, Gwen decided. Indeed, what kind of color would that one be? India's aura wavered, staggered, pulled out and pulled in, but the color seemed to be olive green mostly, mixed with a hideous raspberry shade. Not a pretty aura. In fact, it seemed to be fighting with itself.

"You ain't lookin' too good, girl," Gwen said. "Being back in your hometown don't agree with you?"

"Maybe not," India said. "For a small town, everything seems so complicated here. New York seems simple compared to this."

"So, what's goin' on now," Gwen said. She watched India pull her cell phone out of her jacket pocket, punch in a few buttons and hand it over.

"Look at this."

Gwen took the phone and watched Quinn grinning

crookedly at the camera, brushing her bangs aside, reaching out for the bottle clearly labeled Jack Daniels, tipping it back, accepting a cigarette, inhaling, blowing out smoke, giggling, gulping from the bottle again.

Gwen gasped.

The women looked at each other, so close on the swing they could feel one another's breath.

"Have you told Shelby?" Gwen asked.

"I haven't said a word. I told her about what I saw with the scars, and she acted like I had no reason to be concerned. She'd blow sky high if I said anything" India shifted on the swing. "I don't even know if she's noticed Quinn's been acting strange lately."

"Stranger than usual, you mean? Hold on a second, I reckon we could talk better about this with a Coke. Hang on, I'll bring us some."

Gwen handed India a bottle of Coca Cola. "You were saying," she said as she settled back in the swing. "You know, I haven't seen Quinn in weeks, which isn't usual. What color's her hair now?"

"Oh, come on, Gwen. And it's brown. She's gone back to her regular color for right now."

"Hunh. Well, that would be strange," Gwen said, putting the bottle to her lips. "Pretty, but strange."

"It looks nice. I mean, it does."

"But anyway," Gwen said.

"But anyway, something's going on with her. Before the fire happened, she went out with that boy, Adrian, and Ivy, to some kind of party. I didn't know much about it. Shelby said it was okay for her to go, so she left with them, and then she missed curfew, and when she returned home, she buried herself in her room. She wouldn't talk, she didn't do anything. Things got better, but now, since Adrian's been gone... she's been skipping school, she's been really secretive."

"Did you ask her about it?"

"Yeah, I did, and she looked at me like I was speaking Japanese, turned around and shut herself in her room and locked the door." India said. "But that's not all. I got a voicemail message from Adrian."

"Adrian?" Gwen scrunched her face up in surprise.

"Yeah, yeah, but listen," India began. "He left me a long message, and he told me what happened at that party, the one he and Quinn and Ivy went to. An upperclassman, somebody named Clay, got Quinn separated from Ivy and Adrian. This boy got her drunk and tried to force himself on her."

"What?" Gwen sat up a bit straighter. *No good, no good, no good.*

"Adrian showed up before the deed got done, but he said Quinn made him and Ivy promise they'd never tell. And she refused to tell her mom, or you, or me either."

"Oh my lord, child," Gwen murmured. "This is worse than I expected."

India shifted, tucking her legs underneath her. "And then I got this video out of the blue, but I don't think she meant to send it to me. I mean, why would she?"

"It don't sound right," Gwen said. "I'll say that much."

India shook her head. "Gwen, I think she's oblivious. I really do. I think she meant to send this to someone else and hit me instead."

"You need to show that video to Shelby. And you need to tell her about the other."

"Oh lord, we've done nothing but fight and disagree since I came here," India said. "She won't take this well, especially coming from me. I don't think she'll even believe it."

"All the same, India, Shelby needs to know. If you're right, and I suspect you are, Shelby's got to get herself accountable and deal with her child."

"Mhmmm," India said, pushing her foot back and

forth, rocking the swing. "You know to do the right thing, India."

Gwen watched India's brow furrow.

"Now, let's change the subject for just a minute," Gwen said, setting her Coke bottle aside. "I hear you've been sighted with that electrician, the one who fixed the house."

Gwen watched India jerk to attention.

"What?"

Gwen chuckled at India's wide eyes. "Well, in a small town, everybody knows everything about everybody as it happens in real time."

"Who's saying this?" India asked.

"I don't know, just folks, you know, folks talking."

"Oh, come on, who is it."

'Well, if you must know, India, I heard it at church." Gwen grinned.

"Church? Of course."

"Your old friend, Carmen," Gwen said.

India made a face. "We're not dating. What'd she say anyway? I saw him one time, one time, Gwen, on a day I happened to pick Quinn up from school, because Shelby was working, and Quinn had a dentist appointment right after. He was working next door at some other office and we said hi, and that was it."

"He sure is good looking," Gwen observed.

India appeared as if she might throw up. Her aura color was changing, though. The drab, confusing olive green and hideous raspberry hue was being replaced with a softer, yearning pink.

"I hadn't noticed," India said noncommittedly. "He's nice."

"You hadn't noticed. Oh right. Not much is known about him around here," Gwen said. "He just sort of appeared five or six years ago, alone, and started up a business. And it seems like everybody who's ever hired him, or knows him, thinks he is the greatest thing going today. Better than old Doc Barnes."

"Doc Barnes should have retired a long time before he did, really," India said. "He wasn't a doctor anyway, unless he considered stringing crap together even though your house might burn down with it being a doctor of electricity, whatever that means. I figure he worked on our house, which is why the whole thing had to be redone."

"Shelby thinks you and him are going to get married," Gwen said.

"And Shelby would. I know, she already told me. That's ridiculous. I don't know how unless..."

Gwen grabbed at the chance." Unless what, India?"

India sat quiet, for a long, long minute, until her cell phone, lying between her and Gwen on the swing, began ringing.

CHAPTER THIRTY TWO

India

India looked down at her phone.

Carmen.

"India here," she said from Gwen's porch.

"Hey, India," Carmen's voice came across the line, gravely, like she'd been smoking something. "The fire. The one out there that killed that guy and his son is missing. You know the one?"

"Yeah," India said.

"Listen, there's something fishy about all that. The old man's dead, the son is missing, something isn't right. I know I told you I wouldn't hire you ever, but my bad."

"What do you want, Carmen?"

"India, I'm going against my better judgment here, I won't lie. But here's the deal. I'll hire you on this one assignment. Word is, your niece and this boy, Adrian, were tight, so, what I want you to do, is investigate the fire, get into the history, find out exactly what happened. And bring it back to me for a piece in the paper. Can you do that?"

India turned and stared at Gwen, mouth open.

Investigating something that could ultimately hurt Quinn was an uncomfortable feeling. The idea of investigating a potential crime was intriguing.

"Where is the trailer?" India said.

Carmen recited the address and then added, "But I might be out of town for a week or so, beginning tomorrow. You just work it up and I'll take a look at it when I get back, okay, India?"

A feeling, something clean, evaporated from the air, and something sinister seemed to take its place, and India remembered what she and Gwen spoke of before Carmen's phone call.

But the words were left unsaid between India and Gwen because India felt the urge to leave to follow this new story. If India would have stayed, and if India would have expressed herself to Gwen's "Unless what?" that night, she might have said, "Until I can let myself love again."

CHAPTER THIRTY THREE

India

The trailer where Adrian and his father once resided was no more, simply a blackened charred remainder of metal and black bubbled wood. Somehow, the rickety front porch remained, and as India stood staring at the burned down bits and pieces of Adrian's life, she felt sure Adrian survived and somehow got away.

But I don't know how.

The fire marshal was helpful to her. The chief of police was helpful. The coroner was helpful. The body found inside the home was not Adrian.

But no one could tell India what happened to Adrian, if he'd been on site when the fire was happening, if he was gone before. No one seemed to have seen him at all. Of course, the firemen were busy trying to control the inferno, they may not have noticed a teenager. The fire marshal was monitoring and examining the site. The chief of police was not watching out for a teenage boy.

"Somebody had to have called family services, right?" India asked the fire marshal.

"Dunno," he said, scratching his head. "If someone did, it might have been my deputy."

"But a teenager doesn't just disappear," India insisted.

"You'd be surprised," he said, turning away. "They disappear every day."

Adrian's father perished in the terrible fire, probably too drunk to know he set the fire himself with a cigarette, and most likely died of smoke inhalation before the flames consumed his body.

India sighed, taking several pictures with her phone, writing notes on a pad she brought with her, and then she walked around the property for a few minutes, trying to get a feel for Adrian and what his last moments in that trailer might have been. Or was he there at the time the fire started? It seemed somewhat likely he wasn't there, but yet, where was he and how did he just disappear?

The fire marshal stuck his boot toe into a burned board, shoving his hands in his pockets.

"Bad deal, bad, bad deal," he said.

"Yeah," India said, walking away.

India sat down in the tree stump in the front yard and thought about the scene, the night the fire happened and how it all could have played out.

Could Adrian have started the fire somehow and made it look like an accident? Done his father in? Why would he? India shook her head. *Implausible. Not Adrian. He would never do something like that.* She checked that idea off.

What if Adrian wasn't home when the fire started, what if he came on it after the trailer was engulfed? India thought that was the best scenario. But still, where is he and how did he leave?

India stared around at the tops of the trees, to the

sky. There had to be an answer.

To India's mind, the conundrum, the heart of it all, was what if Adrian was alive but displaced? How would she bring him back to Quinn?

CHAPTER THIRTY FOUR

Quinn

The granite countertop on the kitchen island cooled Quinn's forehead. She doubled over in pain, partially the marching band crusading through her head and partially because she was cramping profusely and felt feverish.

She was skipping school again. But really, she didn't feel good. And she couldn't stand the stares and whispers about Adrian's disappearance and her own breakdown at school upon finding out about the fire.

Quinn pulled her hands through her hair.

Adrian! Where are you? I can't believe you're gone. You can't be gone, I just can't accept it.

The despair was insurmountable. Overwhelming, like a constant kick in the gut.

I miss him. So much. And I don't know where he is or if he's safe or even alive.

Quinn looked around at the comfortable, cozy kitchen and drummed her fingers on the island.

Her brain felt weird, like being stuck inside gigantic

salad tongs, squeezing, squeezing, squeezing.

The night before, Quinn snuck out, as she'd done two or three or four times since Adrian went missing.

It was the only way she could alleviate her pain. Going to the party house, accepting a cigarette, throwing down the Jack Daniels, swaggering around like a big shot, don't care no more, Ivy dropping her off at the corner and then Quinn walking home in the dark, opening the back door so quietly a mouse could have done it, climbing up the stairs, her boots in hand, avoiding the steps that would creak.

Quinn was a pro at sneaking out and in.

No one in the house knew of her absences and reappearances, Quinn was certain. A lot of the time, Shelby wasn't even there because she was working, and India seemed to go to bed around midnight, so all that worked out pretty good for Quinn.

Quinn reveled in the belief that her nocturnal activities were unknown to her mother and aunt.

Those two are clueless. They're just two middle-aged women with nothing going on, rattling around in this old house. And they fight all the time over stupid shit. Well, actually India doesn't pick the fights but, still. They fight over stupid shit. But I knew that's how it was gonna be when India came back here. Gwen thought it would be so grand to have India back. Not me. But maybe she'll leave soon. Mom wishes she'd go. India's bound to be getting bored. I sure would be.

Quinn twirled her cell phone around on the island with one finger, staring into space.

Ping!

Quinn jumped.

She leaned over her phone to see a new text in the queue.

Except, who of all people, would have to walk in at that exact second.

Quinn turned her phone over so no one could see the screen.

"Hey," India said, opening the refrigerator, pulling coffee out, padding around in her yoga pants and fuzzy boots, long plaid shirt on top. "Aren't you late for school?"

"Not going. I don't feel good," Quinn said and laid her head back down on the counter, pulling her phone close. She could hear the rush of the water faucet being turned on, the sound of coffee grounds measured into the paper filter, the *click* of the coffee maker's on button.

Quinn prayed for her aunt to leave the room and stayed down like a wounded animal. Spit formed on the corner of her mouth.

The small can of tomato juice plopped in front of her face startled Quinn. The two aspirin slapped on the counter startled her even more. She slowly raised her face.

India looked formidable.

"Drink this down with these," India said. "And then move your ass off to school. Do you hear me?"

"What's this for?" Quinn asked.

"Listen, Quinn. I'm not stupid and besides that, I was a teenager once too, yeah, news bulletin. This here is a hangover remedy. So, get with it, and get to school."

"I don't have to do anything you say. You're not my mother," Quinn began. "You're a nobody, you're a snobby failure. That's what you are."

"You know, Quinn, you're right about one thing. I'm not your mother, but I'm right here, right now, and I am telling you to choke this down and go get educated so you don't have to end up a loser in a place like this where there aren't any opportunities. And you're not staying here today, lounging around, wallowing in self-pity."

Quinn stood up, regardless of the cramps and the

headache and the fever. She grabbed the aspirin and juice, glaring at her aunt. The relief she felt when India rescued her from school after hearing about the trailer fire was a distant memory. The usual distrust and frustration filled up the void. "Fine," Quinn ran for the door. "But if you think my mom won't say something about this, you're delusional."

Quinn grabbed the doorknob, looked back at her aunt, torn between anger and frustration at something she could not name, and a longing for something concrete, a bond, parameters, something to bring her back in case she wandered too far. And she knew in that moment, she went too far.

India stood by the island, immovable.

Quinn's heart began to crumble.

"Bring it," India said. "It won't be the first time."

Quinn made sure she slammed the door on her way out.

CHAPTER THIRTY FIVE

India

India stared at her phone as the text messages started coming in, one after the other.

The newspaper office was quiet. Few people died that week, so India's work load, if it could even be called a work load, turned out to be light. Carmen was out for the week for whatever reason, and the rest of the staff hummed around, doing this and that, making simple chitter chatter about the upcoming weekend, what was everyone else's plans?

India sat in the reception area near the front windows, since she didn't have an office, curled up in one of the reception area chairs.

Outside, the wind began to pick up. Leaves were flying in every direction, red, gold, brown, the square's grandeur dimming. India could see the gazebo smack in the middle of the square. It seemed defeated. Rain was coming in.

Good lord, India tucked her fist under her neck and

began reading.

The first text began: "What were you doing, yelling at my daughter?"

As soon as that text appeared, another one followed, then another.

"You have no right. She's not your child. You have never had children, you have no idea what it's like. You look down your nose at us, you always have. Those pictures you made such a big deal of with Gwen, they were fake. Just a bunch of kids posing, acting out. It was a joke. Nothing at all was going on like you imagine."

India texted back, "So, let me get this straight. Under your scenario, photos and videos shot in live time are fake, and I'm imagining things. Okay, even if they weren't drinking or smoking, where and when were these pictures taken, Shelby? How is she getting there, how is she getting back home? Do you have any idea?"

India stared outside again, watching the weather turn ugly.

Another text.

"Listen sister, I say this with love, but you don't belong here anymore and I don't know why you came back. Okay, so your boyfriend died, which is sad, and you lost your place on the news. So you're not a big superstar anymore. Life goes on. But you come back here and you immediately start accusing us of whatever. You don't know your niece. Quinn is fine. She is a beautiful, lovely young lady. You want to besmirch her name."

India read and read the text again.

"I'm not sure she's fine, as you call it. I think you bury your head in the sand and act like whatever reality you choose to believe is reality."

"By the way, I know you talked to Phillip. Are you taking his side?"

India uncurled and sat up in the chair.

Enough.

She typed furiously.

"I am tired of you vilifying me. We are sisters, and maybe something's been lost along the way, and maybe how things are now doesn't set well with you, but believe me, you are not the point. Since I've come back and my boyfriend died (and you say it in such a condescending way, as if Greg's life and our relationship meant nothing and I'm making my grief up), and with his death, I lost my place in broadcasting news and it breaks my heart, Greg's death changed my future forever, but in your usual self-absorbed way, you don't see that. Me coming back here is not a reason for a fight, particularly since I've seen Quinn and I see what she's dealing with, and I see more than what I can convey in this text message. You've turned a blind eye so you don't have to deal with it, and be a parent. I don't believe you understand my concern for Quinn. You mistake concern for interference. You pick at the same scab over and over again, for no reason. That's all."

India listened for a text to come back and then quit worrying about it, stuffing her phone in her pocket.

"Well," she said out loud.

Zack, the photographer, was standing outside the office door taking pictures of the square.

India grabbed one of the spare umbrellas from the rack inside the door and eased outside.

"Kinda wet out here, isn't it?" India said.

"I love it," Zack said, wandering down the rain-spattered street, pointing and zooming his camera. "Finally, something besides tee ball games and dried up corn fields to take pictures of."

India followed a step or two and noticed something in the distance. Even with the pelting rain, she could see a small figure huddled up against the window of the jewelry store. She peered into the rain at the pink hoodie and began walking, then running to the person, the loaned umbrella flapping inside out over her head.

"Quinn, what are you doing out here, alone?" India pulled the umbrella over them, jerking it back in place. Quinn's eyes peered out from underneath her hoodie, strands of hair glued to her face. She was shaking, and rain dripped off the bottom of her jeans.

"I ran to the store. I wanted some chocolate milk, and Mom's not home."

"You could have called me," India said. "You're all wet."

"*Yeah*," Quinn said, as if the pelting rain was all India's fault.

"Come on," India said and turned to the street.

A black pickup truck pulled up, the passenger window down. India could see Paul's profile, as he turned to look her way, shouting, "Are you okay? Do you need a ride?"

India looked back at Quinn and decided to accept.

Not only did Paul rescue India and Quinn from the storm, he took them to Henderson Foods, leaving the truck running while he went inside and picked up a gallon of chocolate milk.

He smells like soap, an intoxicating kind of soap. India bit her lip. Sitting beside him in the cab, India felt a queer sensation, an electric current pulsating up and down her leg. She looked over at Quinn, who appeared to be staring straight ahead, glaring at the rain.

"So, how come you're out in this weather?" India asked Paul, staring at his hands on the wheel, looking away, stifling a gulp.

"Supposed to be my bowling night," Paul said, giving her a sideways glance. "I don't think it's happening tonight, though. I figure there'll be a lot of no shows."

"You're in a league?"

"Yeah. It's the next to last week for the season."

"I haven't been bowling in a long time, since I was a kid," India said and then wished she hadn't. There's nothing like revealing you're a loser in a particular game, after all.

"Well, I'm there every Wednesday night, 6:30 for the next two weeks. If you want, come out. I could help you."

"That's nice, maybe I'll take you up on that," India said and then wanted to slap her own face.

They didn't say much more, and when Paul dropped her and Quinn off at her car behind the newspaper office, India felt as if the ride couldn't end fast enough, except she wanted it to go on indefinitely.

"Thank you," she said, climbing out of the truck. "We didn't mean to put you out."

His eyes were dark. "No problem," he said. "You didn't put me out."

India watched the big truck back up and pull out of the lot in her rearview mirror, struggling with her keys, finally dropping them on the floorboard.

"You're lame," Quinn said.

"Hunh?" India grunted as she fished the floorboard for her keys, righted herself and pushed the key into the ignition. "Yeah? You got some chocolate milk out of the deal, right?"

"Right. But you're still lame. He was so flirting with you, how did you miss that?"

"He wasn't flirting," India said.

"Right," Quinn said. India watched her roll her eyes.

"I'm just old."

Quinn giggled.

"I don't see the signals," India said backing her own car out and driving to the intersection.

"Uh yeah, you do," Quinn said before pouring her

concentration into the bright blue screen of her phone and all its icons.

India turned her right turn signal on at the light. "I don't even know him. Let's don't get all crazy, okay?"

Quinn snorted.

"What? What does that mean? Why are you laughing at me?" India turned right again, onto their street, suddenly feeling as if she was not the adult, the one in control, of this conversation. "And since when you the big expert on romance?"

India pulled into the driveway, shutting the car off.

"You figure it out, okay?" Quinn seemed to be laughing, as she leaped out, running for the house.

India stared after her for a minute, before getting out of the car.

No words. I can't even figure it out.

Shelby was standing at the island, pouring milk over a bowl of cereal, when India walked into the kitchen.

"Go upstairs, Quinn," Shelby said immediately, setting down the milk carton.

Quinn shoved the gallon of chocolate milk in the refrigerator and said, "Why?"

"Just go upstairs," Shelby said.

Quinn shrugged and said, "Whatever," letting the refrigerator door bang shut before exiting the kitchen.

India heard Quinn sing, "That's what you ge-ett when you cross my mo-om," as she mounted the stairs to her room.

"What now, Shelby?" India said.

"Let's make something clear, India," Shelby said. "Quinn's my kid. She's mine, okay? You might think I batted out a thousand times as a parent, and I don't care. I don't care. It's none of your business anyway."

India folded her arms.

Might as well go in.

"Well, let me ask you this, Shelby, since you're so on top of what's going on with your daughter, would it surprise you to know she's been keeping a secret from you?"

India watched as Shelby pulled the cereal bowl close to her face and dug out a spoonful, gulping it in.

"Quinn doesn't keep secrets from me," Shelby said after a hard swallow. "She's just a kid, and kids act out sometimes. She has bad judgment on occasion, that's all. She likes to joke a little too much."

India struggled mentally. To tell, or not to tell, what she knew of the bonfire party and that upperclassman who tried, and tried hard, to violate Quinn. To reveal what Adrian told her in confidence. India knew what the right path was. She should tell Shelby what she knew, but would the telling of it cause more trouble? Would it cause more trouble for Quinn, trouble between India and Shelby? Why hadn't Quinn told her mother about what happened that night?

Because she doesn't trust her, that's why. Quinn feels betrayed. The thought came quick, sharp, stenciled in India's mind.

India felt as if she held a dirty truth, but talking to Shelby about it seemed futile. Granted, Quinn seemed to have escaped the worst that could have happened, but still. It shouldn't have happened in the first place, and what if Quinn really was suffering because of it? What if Quinn held the belief that she was only of value for men to abuse? Where would that lead?

I can't approach this with her, India thought looking at her sister, who was spooning cereal into her mouth. *She really doesn't get it. It's going to have to be a delicate conversation. I'll have to feel her out.*

India took a deep breath.

"So, has she ever talked to you about these parties she goes to with her friends, you know, Ivy, and Adrian, when he was still here? Does she ever talk about that?"

Shelby turned to the sink and started rinsing her bowl out. "I don't ask, and she doesn't tell. It's like, her thing, and I trust her."

India looked away for a minute and came back to see Shelby putting her bowl and spoon in the dishwasher.

"You need get your own life in order, which has nothing whatsoever to do with having a kid, and let me handle my daughter," Shelby said. "I guess things are bigger in New York, or at least, the buildings are bigger, don't know, never been, never want to go, but you seem to put a whole lot of value on bigger. Bigger is better, right?"

India sighed. "Once again, Shelby, you miss the point."

"No, I don't think so. But don't you ever yell at my daughter again."

"I didn't yell."

"Yes, you did. She told me you did," Shelby said.

India watched Shelby head for the stairs as Quinn did minutes before. "I don't care what she told you. Shelby, we are adults, get it? Be a parent, Shelby, just be a parent. Quinn wouldn't have so many problems if you'd done that all along."

Shelby disappeared from sight.

The door upstairs shut.

***

The lights were still on at Gwen's house.

It was still raining but not as hard as before, as India ran up the familiar steps.

"You girls," Gwen said when she answered the door.

India nodded.

"Come on, child, come in," Gwen padded away from the door and sat down at the kitchen Formica table.

"Maybe I should go back to New York," India said, dropping into the opposite chair, spreading her hands out on the table. "Maybe everybody's right and I don't belong here, and all I do is interfere with their sense of security, you know? Maybe I should just give up and go away, right?"

India looked down as Gwen reached out and pulled India's hands to her. "India. Now you listen to me, girl. I got no more patience for your whining. You want to go back to New York, just run away from your family and what's here for you? You do that, you run, okay?"

India felt like pulling her hands back, but Gwen's grip was strong.

"You got a job here, right? Working on the paper, yes?"

"Uh, kinda. It's not really a job. Carmen doesn't really want me working for her at all. I'm a bit player, if you want to know the truth."

"Hmm. Fact of the matter is, girl, you can't run, you can't hide from what's here. You gotta stand up and face it."

"Face what?"

"Why are you here in the first place, girl? If you don't know that, I can't help you. You ain't dumb, India. You know you love that man."

India jerked her hands back. "What? What about Greg? It's not the right time, I'm not ready, Gwen."

"Don't you think Greg would want you to go on, India? Did you not know him that well?"

India sagged in her chair, tears forming in her eyes. The image of Paul was so strong, his stance, his walk, his dark eyes, the way he might, no, *would* command her soul.

India felt wrinkled, out of step, in between worlds.

Her grasp on what used to be was diminishing. But, what could be?

"Are you dating him?"

"No, no."

"Okay, okay." Gwen looked up and down the street. "Not dating, okay."

"He gave Quinn and me a ride tonight, because it was raining so hard," India stammered. "A ride. Listen, I was outside with our camera man watching the storm. Quinn was stuck up on the square because she ran up there to go to the store to get some chocolate milk and she got stuck in the deluge, and…"

Gwen wasn't finished. "It ain't only that man, India, and don't act like I don't know what I'm talking about. You all kinds of hot and bothered about that electrician, I know that. But, you girls, you and Shelby, you need to get to a common place. The two of you need to make things right between the two of you. I don't dump all the fault in your lap, but I don't dump it all in Shelby's lap either."

"Kiss and make up?" India said.

Gwen smiled, yellowish teeth in a brown face.

India felt nothing but love for that face. She began to smile, as she peered into Gwen's brown eyes, even though she felt more like crying.

Gwen leaned across the table.

"You was always my favorite, India. Although you probably didn't know it at the time and don't know it now. Now, don't tell nobody that," Gwen wagged her finger and laughed. "It's true, but girly girl, you need to go home and make up with your sister. That's gonna be a big job, but you can do it."

Later, India sagged on her bed in the turret room, staring out the windows at the full-fledged storm waging war outside, remembering Gwen's words.

It's not that easy, India wanted to say.

Her cell phone rang.

Nick.

India answered with a non-committal "Hello."

"Listen, India, I hope you're doing well, but I, or we, need to talk with you, and we need to talk pretty quick."

India straightened up on the bed. "About what? And who is we?"

"Come on, don't fight with me."

Rain rolled down the window panes in undulating folds.

"Fighting? What's going on, Nick? You know I have another year on my contract. I'm only taking time off because you forced me to, remember?"

Nick's voice came back strained. "I only wanted you to get well, to recover from Greg's death. I was thinking of you. You know this, India."

"Oh great."

"India, we need you to come to New York. We need to talk about your future at the network."

"Hey, Nick, you don't need me in New York, unless I'm going to anchor again, and somehow, I feel that is not in the equation. What if, just say, what if I take the role of a correspondent and work from here? Any interest?" India stood up, staring out the windows into the blackness beyond. Lightening flashed, a white gore into the backyard. The rain picked up again.

"That's something we'd talk about, India. When you come to New York."

I don't necessarily know what I'm doing here, but what would I do there, anymore?

"Nick, I'll let you know."

"Don't wait too long, India. I'm well aware of your contract. But we have to move on, the network has to keep moving, and so do you."

"Right. I'll be in touch."

India hung up the phone and searched for her bathrobe.

CHAPTER THIRTY SIX

Shelby

"Shelby, it's me, can I come in?" Shelby heard India's voice outside her bedroom door.

"It's open," Shelby answered, lying on her bed, hands laced on her stomach. Hardly the time, when she was so confused over Ray's absence, not even knowing quite why Ray was on her mind, that she would want to speak with anyone, especially India.

Shelby watched her bedroom door shove open, and India stepping inside, the glow of the hallway lights behind her. Shelby saw her look around at the lavender striped wallpaper, the lace curtains, the blue and green mosaic of the lamp beside Shelby's iron bed, which was painted pistachio. Same furniture mostly, except for the bed. Shelby's 1960s blond wood bed with its sliding doors in the head board was gone. The lamp was new, too. But mostly everything else was the same.

Shelby felt India lie down on the bed.

"How ya doing?" India said.

"Confused. I haven't seen Ray in two weeks. He's not at the store, he's just not around."

"Right."

Shelby folded her hands over her stomach. "I mean, we went out, and it wasn't really exciting for either one of us. At least I don't think so, but since that date, I can't sort out my feelings. I feel like there should be more, there should be more for him and me, and the thing is, I think I disappointed him and failed him, even though he disappointed me too, and I don't know, I'm rambling now," Shelby's voice caught. "And I messed up your dinner party with my big stupid mouth."

Feeling India staring straight at her, Shelby turned her head to the window.

"I don't know how, believe me, but I believe it's all going to be alright. I believe this, Shelby. Somehow, I don't believe he's bugged out. I just don't, " India said.

"I don't know. Adrian's gone too, and Quinn's beside herself. I'm coming to the realization I'm going to die alone, but I don't want Quinn to be alone forever. I don't want her to end up like me."

Burning tears assembled in Shelby's eyes. India's arms came slowly around her shoulders and with each touch, Shelby felt transported, back to the world where she and her mother smiled at one another, sort of a browned old photo curling at the edges, but comforting nonetheless. "I didn't mean what I said, you know, at the dinner party, and other times, about you leaving. I was just mad," Shelby said. "And I drank too much wine."

"I know," India said.

"And I read your texts, and maybe I'm a piece-of-shit mom, but I realize you care about my daughter and what happens to her."

"Right," India said. "What about the cutting? Is she still hurting herself, Shelby?"

"No, or at least I don't think so," Shelby answered

quietly. "She would have told me if she did."

"She would have told you? I think this is something you need to monitor, not wait for."

Shelby felt her face redden and for a minute wanted to shout back, but instead, decided to continue the bonding process.

"What about you?" Shelby asked.

"Um, not sure, really. I think I may have effectively lost my job. And I have no idea what the future holds. I don't know what's going to happen for me. I have no job to speak of, no future. Nothing but this, staring out the window on a rainy night."

"It'll work out for you, India. You were the golden child, remember?"

"Somehow, I don't feel so golden, and I don't know if I ever was, really," India said.

"We used to do this," Shelby said. "When we were kids, we used to lie here and watch the moon, remember? Don't you remember that? But I suppose you've forgotten everything about us once."

"Come on, quit being a sad sack," India said, pointing out Shelby's window. "Look."

It wasn't raining anymore. A sudden quiet emerged out of the storm, and the full moon was just coming up, bringing its glowing face up over the trees, and the women laid still, same as when they were children, basking in its luminous embrace, gazing out the window.

"We should be better friends," India said. "We should be better to each other."

"Are you in love with that electrician?" Shelby shifted away from the windows, leaning on her elbow. India's face was encased in shadows.

"Uh, can't say because I don't know. I've been really absorbed in losing Greg, losing my foothold at the network, trying to find some reason to stay here, because Gwen tells me I'm supposed to be here."

"And I tell you you're going to marry him. And you will. I'm never wrong about this stuff."

Shelby felt relieved when India started laughing.

"Well, he is cute," India finally said.

"Uh no, he's freaking hot," Shelby countered.

"Well then, of course I'll marry him! I have to! He's freaking hot!"

"Exactly," Shelby said. "And don't even bother to say you're not attracted to him. It's like zing!" Shelby snapped her forefinger and thumb together.

"Oh, I don't know what the future holds," India said. "For me, anyway. What about you and Ray?"

"Well, I guess I have to see him again before I can answer that."

"You will," India said.

"I don't know about that."

"What do you want, Shelby? You know Ray is a good man, and he's interested in you. Why fight it?"

Shelby took a deep breath. The way she saw it, she could either blurt out the truth and maybe fix things, or keep her feelings under wraps and go on, keeping guys like Phillip in her life.

"I don't know," she said. "I guess maybe I don't deserve it."

"Deserve what?"

"The whole package, you know, the whole thing. Love, respect, trust. You had that with Greg, right? Well, I had it with Tony, but only for a little while. It didn't last, and I thought it would. And then there was Phillip, and he took me over but he was no good, either. Not for Quinn especially."

"But you're done with Phillip, right? And guys like Phillip?"

"Yup." Shelby sat up.

"Well then," India said. "If I thought I had a love worth keeping, I'd be all in. Both feet, Shelby. I'd give it all I had."

Shelby watched India push herself off the bed and stand up, gathering her robe around her.

"I'm just saying, you need to make some changes. And that might start with giving Ray Henderson the chance he seems to want. Okay?"

Shelby's throat closed as she watched India turn to the door and walk out, closing it softly behind her.

The moon glowed a champagne yellow through the windows, quietly stroking the floor and wall with its delicate luminescence.

Her sister's words echoed throughout the room, skipping around the wood trim, circling back to Shelby's mind.

If I thought I had a love worth keeping I'd be all in. I'd give it all I had.

Shelby leaned back on the bed, smiling, and instantly fell asleep.

CHAPTER THIRTY SEVEN

India

Autumn was slowly, unhappily, giving away to winter, showing its misery with cold mistiness. The atmosphere was pale, shades of grey and deeper grey. The trees on the square were bare, standing at a bent angle in the wind, eternally suffering images of a former glory.

India tucked her sweater around her as she pushed her key into the lock at the newspaper office, ignoring the construction permit sign taped to the front door.

Work was clearly going on within, except it wasn't newspaper work.

Two blue-shirted men were drilling holes in the ceiling. India looked around.

A ladder was positioned to the side of the brick sidewall, and India could see boots and jeans from the knee on down. The ceiling was cut out. Wiring dangled from the beams, skirting the floor. India could hear the pounding, the sound of boots on beams.

"Hello," India called as she approached the jeaned

knees on the ladder. "Hello?"

India peered up into the rafters of the building.

A pair of brown eyes peered back.

India gasped as the blue-jeaned legs started stepping down, and the legs turned into a torso, and then the torso turned into a neck and a face and dark brown eyes staring straight into her.

"You got the job," India said.

"We're gonna update this old place," Paul said.

"That's great. I'm glad you got it."

India turned back to the reception area to find an open computer.

He was too handsome, too sexy, too comfortable, too freaking frightening.

India wanted to turn around and run back to him, jumping high, circling her legs around his groin, kissing him until neither one could breathe.

"India."

The sound of her name made her turn around.

"I'm gonna be done here in an hour or hour and a half, by the time I go through this building and see, hopefully everything that's wrong and needs to be fixed," Paul said. "Would you meet me for lunch at Riverwalk Café, say in an hour and a half?"

She could only nod before she heard Carmen calling for her.

"India, listen," Carmen started in the minute India walked into her office. "Listen, I just got back from vacation, and here are these workers making all this noise, and I simply cannot concentrate with all this, all this *action*, India, and so I'm leaving. I'm going home, and by the way, aren't you even going to ask me where I was, where I went on vacation, did I have a good time, how well I look, hmmm?"

"It's not my business, I don't believe," India said.

"Well, just so you know, I was in Mexico. And I

was not alone, India." Carmen gave India a meaningful look. "And I had a grand time, simply wonderful, and sensuous, a woman's dream."

"Uh hunh, well, look, Carmen, this is not my business and furthermore, I don't care," India said and turned to leave.

Carmen raced to the door before India could get there.

"You might care, considering." One of Carmen's eyebrows shot up.

"Considering what, Carmen? Stop playing games."

"Well, I was with a man on my Mexican vacation. You might want to ask Ray Henderson where's he's been for the past ten days." Carmen's eyes lit up in contempt and triumph.

"I don't think I'm going to do that," India said. "Now, get out of my way, I have something else to do right now."

"I told you, I told you, I'd have him. I told you," Carmen shouted. India pushed past her and opened Carmen's office door. "You told me alright, you told me. But you weren't in Mexico with Ray Henderson and don't feed me that bullshit because I know better."

"Oh you think you know so much, don't you," Carmen patted her hair.

"Quit dogging my sister, Carmen, and yeah, I do know better. I know where Ray was and I know he wasn't with you, by the way. So take your trash talk and deliver it elsewhere. No buyer here." India pushed the door open and ran to the sidewalk, hoping her bluff worked.

"I can fire you, you know," Carmen shouted as the door closed.

India opened the door back up for one second. "Well, go ahead and fire me, Carmen, but you never formally hired me in the first place."

The door slammed shut, and India stared out onto the square, confused.

Where did Ray go, and why hadn't he communicated with Shelby?

CHAPTER THIRTY EIGHT

Gwen

The dull ache between Gwen's shoulder blades intensified, along with pressure in her chest.

Gwen put her car in reverse and began to back out of her driveway. Errands to run, a cake to deliver to the bake sale for her church, groceries to purchase; no sir, a little pain wasn't going to stop her. Not even a little nausea. She hadn't eaten breakfast that morning. Nothing sounded good.

She yawned.

Gwen drove along for a street or two, vaguely aware something was off. She started to feel as if she might throw up. Sweat lined her upper lip. *Lord, I feel so weird, like I'm numb all over. Especially my hands.*

She swallowed hard and pulled into the drive-in bank, presented the deposit slip she prepared earlier, and pulled away.

My hands, I don't feel my hands. They're totally numb. They're swollen, looks like an ape.

She yawned again, and then decided to pull over onto a side street. The pain between her shoulder blades was more intense now, the pressure was making it hard to breathe. She slapped the car into park and waited. The nausea overcame her.

Lord, Lord, Lord. I'm in a bad way. Gwen noticed a couple of street workers wearing orange uniforms climbing around a light pole before the contents of her stomach spewed onto the steering wheel and windshield, soaking her pants and jacket.

The episode was over in a minute, and her hands quietly returned to normal. The pain in her shoulder blades subsided. Gwen began to feel more alert. *I believe I just had a heart attack?* Gwen stared around in fear.

The city workers were now on the ground, looking upward, gesturing and speaking with one another. No one else came down the street.

If I left this earth right here, right now, no one would notice. Gwen sat for another minute or two before putting the car back in gear to drive home.

I'm okay, I'm alright. It's over now.

***

Gwen sat down in Dr. Achebe's waiting room, and, well, waited.

There were good magazines scattered about; *Better Homes & Gardens, Country Living, Midwest Living.* Gwen grabbed the newest edition of *Better Homes & Gardens* and sat down to wait.

She wouldn't have made an appointment at all except for the fact she told Shelby about what happened to her the day before and Shelby went nine kinds of crazy. And then Shelby told Quinn and India, and it didn't take long before the whole gang was standing in Gwen's kitchen reciting all the reasons why she needed to see her doctor and get an evaluation done.

"It's your *heart*, Gwen," Shelby said. "It's like an at-will employee. It may love its job, shoving blood all through your body, but it can quit at any moment without warning."

I don't smoke, I don't drink, my biggest vice is Coca Cola, and I don't eat a lot of crap food. Gwen wasn't ready to make the leap that there might really be something medically wrong with her. *I like butter a little bit, but who doesn't?*

"Come on, Gwen," India said, taking Gwen's hand. "You need to do this. You need to get yourself checked out, and if it turns out to be nothing, then fine. But you need to know either way."

"You need to know either way," Shelby repeated.

She noticed Quinn standing apart, holding back just a little bit.

Quinn's forlorn face made up Gwen's mind, and she made the appointment.

It didn't take long before her name was called, and she found herself in another limbo room, having to call her information in on the phone on the wall and then she sat down, waiting.

She was weighed.

"You're at 104 pounds, not bad," the nurse said, marking it on her chart.

Everyone in the office seemed efficient, pleasant, but impersonal.

Gwen was ushered into a room and asked to wait.

Wait. Wait. Good lord.

A knock on the door signaled Dr. Achebe's entrance. He was an Asian man, short, dark hair clipped close, dark eyes bugging out of his face.

A pale orange circled his head. *Intellectual, over-educated, collegiate*, Gwen thought, wishing she was at home, drinking Coca Cola, at her familiar Formica table under the kitchen clock.

"What can we do for you today, Ms. Baker?" Dr. Achebe asked, looking at her chart.

Gwen recited her concerns, the issues bringing her to make this appointment.

"Okay, well," Dr. Achebe said. "We'll do an EKG, I'm going to set you up an appointment for that. You're going to have to have an echocardiography exam as well. We'll do that along with the EKG. Now, I would also suggest a complete blood workup. I'm sending you downstairs to the lab."

"Right now?"

"Right now. We need to know what's going on with you."

Well, that's how it's done, Gwen struggled into her jacket and accepted the written recommendation.

"Do you have any questions?"

Gwen blinked.

"Well, with all due respect, doctor, I believe I had a heart attack, and I'm not at all sure why you can't tell me that with what I just told you. You want to do all these tests like I didn't experience what I did."

"I'm scheduling you for...next week for the EKG workup and the echocardio, Tuesday, at 8:00 am, are you available?" Gwen agreed to the appointment, zipping up her jacket. "Who is the doctor?" she asked.

Dr. Achebe peered into the computer screen. "I have you scheduled with Dr. Amos. He's very good."

"That's fine, child, that's fine." Gwen pulled her purse strap up on her shoulder. "You do what you do, doctor, you trust in science, you trust in your education, but what I'm gonna do right now is, I'm going to church. You know why?"

Dr. Achebe sagged in his chair, hands limp in his lap.

"Because I have a trust in Jesus, that's why. You a

religious man?"

Dr. Achebe shook his head.

"That's too bad, child, that's too bad."

"It's not my job," he said.

Gwen opened the door, looking back at the confused, forlorn doctor." No, that's wrong. It is your job. It most certainly is your job." Gwen stopped short in the hall after closing the exam room door behind her. *Did I just say all that? Oh Lord, I am going daffy, I really am. I was so impertinent to that doctor. Oh Lord.*

CHAPTER THIRTY NINE

India

India was unsure whether to meet Paul or not – would he actually appear? Would he blow it off? Should she go, not go, why did she agree to this?

As India entered the café, she felt as if everyone inside was staring at her, as if to say, *he didn't show, you desperate quasi-celebrity.*

Not only was he there, he was waiting at a table, and he was holding something.

God, he is so good looking, India thought as she made her way to the table and sat down.

The brilliant white daisy bouquet stunned her.

"So pretty!" India said, sticking her nose into the bouquet.

"I thought you might like that," Paul said.

"I do, I really do, thank you."

Menus were presented and each made their orders. Paul asked for the French dip, and India asked for the roasted red pepper soup with a side panini of smoked turkey, apple, and cheddar.

Paul leaned forward folding his arms. "I remember you asked me if I watched the news."

"Sure."

"Well, I don't."

"Okay," India said slowly.

"So, I'm assuming you watch the news."

India laughed. "Not really. I broadcast the news. Or at least I used to."

Paul swung his head back and forth, grinning.

"I couldn't figure out why you asked me that."

"Never mind. It's okay," India said as their plates were plunked between them. India picked up her soup spoon and stirred her soup as she watched his expression. *So, you remembered that, did you?*

"Well," Paul finally said. "I imagine if you broadcast the news, or used to, that you were good at it."

A lump formed in India's throat.

"I was."

"I suspect you'd be good at anything you put your mind to. Can't you go back?" Paul dunked his French dip in the au jus, waiting for an answer.

India sighed and looked out the window. Finally, she shook her head.

"I think that ship has passed. And to be quite honest, I'm not even sure I want what I used to want anymore."

"Anything's possible, India," Paul said.

"Oh, I know that. But since I came back here, I've felt a longing for family, roots, ties to the earth. I loved my life in New York, don't get me wrong, you know, it was busy and exciting and something interesting going on all the time. I loved my career, I loved my life, but, I'm starting to think there's more to life than constant movement. You know what I mean?"

India searched Paul's face for any sort of

recognition or agreement. His eyes were dark. They reminded her of the stroke of midnight, staring back. Finally, he said, "I know what you mean."

His gaze was unwavering.

All India wanted to do was kiss him.

It seemed to be a mutual agreement.

Money, tossed on the table, landed between the red and white checkered napkins and the discarded food dishes.

Outside the café, Paul pressed her into the clapboard siding, his hands on her face, thumbs smoothing her skin back. His lips met hers, gently, and then as she responded, more forcefully, until she pushed him into the corner of the building.

His lips were perfect, pleasantly plush and willing. The feel of his hands on her skin made India realize how sad she was, how sad she'd been for months. Paul stroked her neck. India moaned just a bit, and decided to turn the table.

India grabbed him by the shirt and leaned in, kissing him, pulling him into her, feeling the beginning of a bulge in his pants. He responded with a low growl, breathing heavily.

Their eyes met.

Behind the restaurant, the walking trails in the city park meandered along next to cement benches and the fall foliage in oranges, yellows and reds.

"Your place or mine?" Paul whispered hoarsely.

"Not mine," India said, grabbing his hand. "Come on."

They ran, the two of them, hand in hand, to a spot India knew of once. There was a small cave at the back of the park property, and India led Paul into it.

Moisture dripped off the stone roof onto the rock below, making tinkling sounds. The coolness of the cavern gave India a rush.

India threw her arms around Paul and began kissing him again, only to hear guffaws overriding the *ping! ping!* of the water drops.

Unfortunately, five or six teenagers already claimed the cave, playing games and hanging out.

A bigger cold water bucket was probably not ever invented.

"Oh lord," India said. The feel of his hands on her waist, grazing down over her cheeks was too good to have to quit. Why these damn kids right here, right now?

Paul grunted and surveyed his surroundings, looking dazed.

God, I hope he speaks to me again, after this.

Their eyes met again.

What the hell is he thinking? Have I blown it?

"Let's go," Paul said, taking her arm, walking her out of the cave, looking straight ahead.

They reached the beginning of the trail quickly. Paul dropped her arm.

"Paul, I'm sorry," India said.

"Me too," he said. "I've never made out in front of teenagers before."

"So, you're mad?" India's stomach flipped.

He stepped to the side, looked right and left and right again, hands on hips, brow furrowed.

After a long minute, Paul walked up, close to her face. His eyes were so dark, India trembled.

"India, I don't fall easily."

Paul looked away for a second.

India could only wait for the next declaration, if it came.

"I've been through this game before, and if it's only a game to you, well, I am not playing. I gotta tell you that. But damn. Ever since I met you, I've been confused, shaken up, wondering who you are, where you've been, why you came back here."

He walked away for a few steps and came back. The sun was going down behind him, dragging shadows across the trail.

"I didn't tell you this before. You said television, you asked me if I saw you on TV. So, I Googled you and I found you. Right or wrong, I read everything I found on Google, and Wikipedia, yeah, I did, so shoot me. I'm not a stalker by any means, but you started it with that whole did-you-see-me-on-TV thing."

He rolled both hands through his hair.

India stood immobile.

"Paul…"

"Thing is, I can't get you out of my head. I wake up with you, you're with me all day long, just the image of you, and I see you at night, all night. I can't get you out of my head, just can't."

Paul's eyes burned like fire.

India reached out to touch his face.

"Paul, you don't have to. In fact, I don't want you to."

Another kiss, and Paul's phone started ringing. Moaning, he pulled away from her.

"I didn't want to quit that," he said, taking a breath, pushing a button on his phone.

"Paul Funar Electric."

India smiled, remembering he answered her distress call exactly the same way. She absently watched Paul conduct business while staring at the landscape.

God, I better get another chance at this.

After a few minutes, he clicked the phone off.

"Emergency job," he said, pulling her close.

"Like mine?" India asked.

She looked into his eyes.

His eyes glowed into hers, and he smiled.

"Like yours. I have to go but, India, but I want to continue this conversation. More than anything, I want

to continue this. Can I call you tomorrow?"
"Yes," India said. "Yes."

CHAPTER FORTY

Quinn

Quinn read and re-read the series of texts five times under the yellow light of her bedside lamp.

"It's me," the first text began. "I suppose by now you're wondering where I am, what happened, all that shit. You might be worried. You might think I abandoned you, walked away, or whatever, but I haven't."

Quinn curled up on her bed and continued reading.

"About the fire. I wasn't there at first. My dad let me take his car to McDonald's to get food for us both. When I got back, the place was up in flames. I was standing on the front yard with a bag of double quarter pounders with cheese and large fries watching flames shooting into the night and not knowing if my dad was alive or dead. So, the fire marshal and the sheriff came over to me, and got my information, and one of them called the division of family services who called my mother and she came right up and took me away, that very night. No one told me for days that my dad was dead. I've been living with her, not too very far away, but far enough that I can't walk to you. LOL. The thing I want to tell you is, I'm about to turn eighteen, and I've already talked to my mom about this. I'm going to emancipate myself and come back and finish out school with you. I've never stopped thinking about you, I have not forgotten you, and I'm coming back. Just wait, I'll be there."

Tears drying on her cheeks, Quinn texted back. "Why didn't you call me before now? I've been worried sick."

"I left my phone in the trailer, so it's gone. I just got a new one."

"Just come back. Miss you so much. Please come back."

"They asked me if I set the fire, if I killed my dad."
"No."

"It's been hard. My mom only came to get me because she figured she had to. She's got a new husband and kids, a new life. I don't fit in here. I'm in the way. I sleep in the attic, on a futon they bought for me. I'm up here with the Christmas decorations, boxes of unused forgotten shit, and old photograph albums. I found my mom's high school yearbook the other day. She was really pretty back in the day."

Quinn began to sob all over again. "I hate that you're there, with that. Adrian, please come back."

"I will. Pinky swear, promise, whatever. I will."

CHAPTER FORTY ONE

India

India paced through the newspaper office, watching the end of the electrical improvements.

He's here someplace, just gotta find him. He'll finish soon and be gone and what then.

Paul was in the very back of the offices, finishing up something.

"Hey," India said.

He turned, smiling. "Hey yourself."

"Looks like you're about done in here." India stuck her hands in her back pockets.

"Um, yeah, about done," Paul said. He leaned forward and India responded.

"You are the best kisser in the world," India said. "I admire your skill, sir."

"You are someone I want to kiss, over and over and over again," Paul said. "And more."

"More?" India said.

"Umm," Paul responded, in mid-kiss. India noticed

he was pointing upward.

"What?"

"I live up there," Paul said, kissing her neck, her throat.

"Up there, where?".

"My place, it's above the newspaper office. Come with me, I'll show it to you."

"You are so full of surprises," India said.

They dashed outside to the ancient staircase, up to the back door, which led into a foyer of sorts. An ancient chandelier lit the spot in a yellowy haze. Huge deep-silled windows looked out to the square.

"Maybe someday they'll let me put an elevator in," Paul joked. "But I like the old features. Look at this," he said rolling his hands over the ivory veined marble walls. "Italian marble, nobody does this anymore."

"It's beautiful," India said.

Paul stopped at the door to the left, pushed a key into a lock, then stepped aside to allow India inside.

Paul's arms came around her from the back, his lips searing kisses on her shoulders. India turned, pulling him to her, sucking his lips into hers. "Where are you from, Paul Funar?" India asked, as waves of desire began to rise. She felt Paul's hands moving down her back, sending her nerve endings into ecstasy. He groaned quietly in her ear.

"Romania."

India kissed him again, harder, pushing him into a backwards walk, shoving Paul against the wall. "I heard you speaking in another language sometimes when you were working on our house. I thought you were cussing at our house in a different language so we wouldn't know how bad it was!"

Paul kissed her again. "I've seen worse, believe me. But I lived in Chicago when I was a kid. And then we moved to California, and then to Seattle, and now here."

His hands moved along her body in a sure and steady way. Her throat, her shoulder blades, her breasts, down, down, down. India felt herself respond, wanting more, wanting more, more, more.

This man is not rushed, this man has a sure hand.

"Ever been married?" India gasped.

"No,"

Paul was devouring her with kisses, soft and slow and then hard, demanding, wanton kisses. One hand slipped between her skin and her pants. The fire in India's belly intensified. She reached for his jean zipper, feeling the erection underneath.

"India," he whispered. "I want you."

She pulled him onto her, unzipping his jeans with one hand, leaning in for one more deep kiss.

"I'll give you one hour to stop doing that," he whispered in her ear.

"Only one?" India whispered. "Come to me now."

CHAPTER FORTY TWO

Gwen

I sometimes think I hate these girls, Gwen thought, twisting the bed covers in her hands. *So needy, the both of them in different ways.*

India sat on the bed, her rear end holding the covers down, which was bothering Gwen, and, even worse, she didn't seem like she was going to move. A cluster of photographs was lined up in front of her. India's aura was good, a calm blue, nearly lavender, but in spite of that, Gwen snapped.

"What do you want, India? I'm tired, can't you see that?"

India's head shot up. Shock registered in her eyes.

"Never mind," Gwen said. "What have you got for me?"

"Shelby showed me some photos from when we were kids. You're in them, right?"

"What do you know about that," Gwen said.

India picked up the photo of the holiday dinner and

showed it to Gwen, pointing at the shadowy figure behind the table.

"That's you, right?"

"Lord child, where did you find that," Gwen said.

"Shelby found these, all of them. She was looking at old photographs the night I called her and said I needed to come back home."

Gwen dropped the photograph, sweeping it away with her hand. "And so now you show them to me. What's this about, that electrician? If so, you got my blessing on that. You'd be a fool to let that one go."

"Yeah," India said.

"Well? You know what you want, and what you need, what's right for you. Child, if I had your chance again, why, I'd get with it."

Gwen faltered, knowing she stuck her foot into unknown territory.

"Gwen, were you ever in love? Was there someone?"

Gwen straightened and fluffed her pillows, pulled the covers up just so.

Since she was sixteen years old, she always thought it would be hard to reveal the truth, embarrassing, somehow dirty, sad. Few people knew of Gwen's past, and she liked it that way. Most of the ones who knew, who were there then, were dead now, keeping her secret along with their own.

It was time. No need to keep the secret any longer.

"India, your sister should be here to hear this, but she's not, and so I'll tell this once and then never again. Do you agree?"

"Yes, I agree," India said, moving in closer, holding Gwen's hand.

Gwen leaned into the headboard, resting on her pillows."There was a boy, India. A good, fine, white boy. Oh yeah, I see you raising your eyebrows, but it's true. There was a boy. He was nice. He was charming. He worked hard, he came from an average family, not rich, but not poor. They were hardworking people. He was very nice looking. He wanted to have his own business, be a regular working man, a plumber."

Gwen smiled at the recollection. So much time was passed since she allowed herself to think of it. Relief began to pour over her in warm waves, and she couldn't stop now.

"What happened?" India asked.

"What happened?" Gwen responded. "I'll tell you what happened. I was sixteen. Me and my sister and my brother, we all went to the state fair that year. My sister, she was dating a boy, and he came with us, and my brother was dating someone too, but I didn't have anybody. We were there, at the state fair, when I saw this boy getting a strawberry snow cone at a vendor station, and he was all alone, and so was I. Anyway, he turned around, with the tip of that pink snow cone in his mouth, and at that moment, our eyes connected, and he walked right to me. He walked straight to me. Why, India, we walked all over that fair together, we rode the rides, we laughed, we had the best time. And at the end of it, he said he knew the minute he saw me. We were meant to be together."

Gwen straightened the pillows again, and continued. "So, he came around, one time, to my house to meet my family. He had good intentions, India. But oh my, this was not acceptable to my parents, a white boy pursuing their black daughter. But I was crazy for him. Him and me, we met quietly. I'd run to the meadow behind the post office where the hardware store is now, or we'd go to the cave in the park. No one knew at first, but then they found out. Not sure how, but they did, and they sent my brother to deliver a message. Stay away from our daughter, that's what the message said. Or suffer the consequences. But they couldn't stop us. We were in love, and we just kept on."

"And?" India said.

"They drove me away from him, India. My parents made sure I was never gonna have anything to do with a white boy. It was different then, India. You're younger, you don't understand how diversity doesn't make sense to a lot of people."

Gwen stared at India for a long moment, watching tears slide down India's face, before she continued. "My mother and my father sent me away to my grandmother's home, in St. Louis. I can still hear my mother crying as they loaded me into the old car, and we trundled off. My mother protested to my father, but he wouldn't hear of it. So, India, my parents left me standing on the front step of my maternal grandmother's home, my few belongings in my hand, as they drove away forever, and I lived with my grandmother until I graduated high school, and then she died right after my graduation, and I left. I had nowhere to go, no one to go to. I wrote him letters. But I never got one letter back from him. I believe my grandmother kept his letters from me and destroyed them. "

"That's the saddest thing I ever heard," India said.

"I graduated a black high school in St. Louis. I came back here for no reason I can remember, but I did. Maybe I just wanted to be close to the only person who ever took an interest in me. My family, well, let's just say my sisters got married and moved away, my brother died in a car accident, and my parents died eventually too. But I wasn't dumb, and I wasn't lazy. I had to get a job, and work and make money. India, take a look at these photos."

Gwen watched India's face as she searched the photographs, a burst of recollection breaking through. The Thanksgiving dinner. India was tiny, squashed into her high chair in black and white, the dining room clearly visible behind her, her mother sitting to her left behind a roasted turkey on a platter, and behind her, a mere shadow, a young dark girl, dressed as a maid, in white, holding carving knives. Another photo, India wrapped up in winter gear, crying, and the arms holding her were dark. The bicycle. A sweep of a skirt and a black leg sticking out underneath.

Tired. Wish she'd go home. Or somewhere. Lord, if she don't pick up on love this time, she ain't never gonna do it.

Gwen watched her, wondering if she was ready for the next revelation.

"I was a maid in your parents' house. I knew you girls as babies."

"I knew something, but I didn't know what I knew," India said. "It just seemed like you were always a part of our lives, always."

"Your mother, India, was a proper lady, a real woman, ahead of her time. Your mother got me a job, a proper, respectable job, working at the school, in the lunch room. Yes, India, I was a lunch lady. And after that, I wasn't at your house all the time. Your mother helped me get my own apartment. She saw to all the details. But I missed you after I left your house. You were so little then, and Shelby came along, and I was working." Gwen felt herself drift off.

"Gwen," India was shaking her.

"Yeah?" Gwen roused, seeing concern in India's eyes.

"What was your young man's name, the one you loved? Who was he? Do you know what happened to him?"

Gwen straightened again. The thought of his actual name brought a kind cheer to her heart, like a whispered greeting, a familiar hello.

"His name was Charles. Charles Gene Perry. All I know about him is he became a lawyer and married well, but I don't know where he is, or if he is even alive now."

"Do you know where he was born?"

"Charles was born in Chicago. The family moved here when he was a baby."

"Siblings?"

"Oh now you're wearing me out, girl. Charles had a brother, born much younger than him, named Joseph. Joseph was a toddler when he died. He got sick, real sick, and his fever spiked, and he died. That was before I met Charles."

"So, there's nobody else who can vouch for Charles' existence?"

Gwen felt herself slipping away, into a peaceful slumber.

She mumbled, "Nobody else," and let her limbs go limp welcoming the sweetness of sleep.

CHAPTER FORTY THREE

Shelby

I feel like it's been raining for a year, Shelby thought as she flipped the window wipers on full speed.

A plastic shopping bag skittered across the street in front of her car, shoved along by the windy rain. The radio station out of Springfield announced accidents and delays due to the bad weather.

Shelby concentrated on driving through the deluge, although thoughts of India's story about Gwen trundled through her mind. She decided to dwell on that for a while instead of being nervous in the rain.

Gwen had a lover? A white man? She was our MAID? And our mother got her a job?

Shelby shook her head in disbelief.

I never knew, and I know now India didn't either. How did we not know she was a part of our family? How could we not see that? We were pretty little but still. No wonder she was in so many of our family pictures. It all makes sense, I guess. Quinn will flip out.

A crack of thunder and a spikey flash of lightening in front of the car jerked Shelby back to attention.

The town square looked defeated, drab, assaulted by wind and rain. She turned her car into the last parking spot in front of Henderson Foods. Despite the ads nearly covering the windows, Shelby saw movement between the ads, within the store, and her breath caught.

A glimpse of khaki pants and a black polo shirt, a husky arm pointing, a side view of grey curly hair, and then the image disappeared away from the windows.

He's back. Ray's back.

Shelby sat still for a moment and considered turning the key back on and leaving, buying her groceries at the new Wal-Mart Supercenter instead, a place where she wouldn't have to see him at all. Or rather, where he wouldn't have to see her and reject her.

Rain pounded the windshield, currents of crystalline running water, down over the windshield and over the hood. Shelby stared into the deluge.

I don't know what I'm doing here. Don't know if I can even face him. Maybe I should like fish more, maybe I should like travel, but travel always seemed to be a pain in the ass. All that packing and making arrangements and then your luggage gets lost, the hotel isn't what it represented, I don't know...just never enjoyed it. He obviously does. I'd just rather be here without all those complications and arrangements and things having to be just so. And Ray, he likes the damn fish too. Shit, I should have been a better date.

Shelby looked around the square, although much of it was obscured by rain.

He likes Quinn. Every time we come in the store, he addresses her by name. I know he likes her, but does he still like me?

Shelby pushed the key back into the ignition and turned the car on. She backed out slowly and gulped as she drove the car down the side street and turned right, then another right and a left until she arrived at the Wal-Mart Supercenter at the edge of town.

Rain pummeled her all the way into the store, and once she was inside, she couldn't remember what she was going to the store for in the first place. All she could see was the glimpse of Ray in Henderson Foods.

Shelby's thighs swished together as she walked around Wal-Mart, the hood of her jacket felt plastered to her back. The bright lights made her eyes burn, the blue and white motif, the whiz of automated carts passing by annoyed her.

Shelby fled to her car, having bought nothing.

She drove slowly down Main Street, suddenly remembering everything she planned to buy at Henderson Foods when she started out on the junket. Hot dogs, buns, pork 'n beans, chocolate milk, ice cream.

Her sister's voice sounded in her brain. *Put on your big girl panties and face that man.*

Shelby swallowed hard and glanced at her reflection in the rear view mirror.

No. See how I look? I'm wet and straggly. I think I smell too.

No time for chicken shit, Shelby. Face the man.

The same parking spot Shelby parked in earlier was still available in front of Henderson Foods. She took a minute to smooth her hair down and adjust her damp jacket before going in.

Ray stood at the endcap of the canned meat aisle, bent over a bit, adjusting cans of tuna packed in oil, lining each can up so that the label matched perfectly to the can above it.

It was almost as if he saw her out of the back of his head. Shelby's hands were trembling, her legs shook. *I'm sure I'm a fool*, she thought as Ray turned as if on cue to face her. She couldn't breathe. Ray straightened into a standing position. A long, long minute and then another minute passed as Ray's eyes locked on hers.

"Are you hungry?" Ray said.

Shelby began to cry, nodding her head. In an instant, Ray was in front of her, cradling her face with his big, sure hands.

"Come on, Shelby, I will take care of you."

Ray held to his word.

He drove her home, to the home he grew up in.

It was a modern ranch style home, built in the '50s. The structure sat on a woodsy setting, resembling a Frank Lloyd Wright house, meaning more than one level, a lot of stone work, big windows, clear lines.

Shelby was impressed by the stonework on the fire place, the big windows, the deep leather furniture, the feeling of ease of the home. Ray's home held a heart and it showed. Inside Ray's kitchen, Shelby looked around and took in the huge gas range tucked into a brick enclosure, the antiqued cream cabinets, the humungous black marble island. The floor was clay tile, a surface Shelby never liked, but it looked exceptional in Ray's space. There were rugs, tasteful oriental wool rugs, placed strategically throughout the kitchen.

I never would have expected this. After that disastrous first date, I imagined he'd be surrounded with Victorian stuffiness, heavy swags, mauve and teal blue. But this is really, really nice.

Shelby turned her attention back to Ray, standing in front of his stove, slipping her dinner in a pan.

He's cooking me a grilled cheese sandwich, Shelby thought, sitting at the island in Ray's kitchen, watching him go through the motions. *This man is cooking me a grilled cheese sandwich, and it's raining like crazy, and I've been a fool, and he could be doing anything else, but he's cooking me a grilled cheese sandwich. Does it get better than this?*

CHAPTER FORTY FOUR

India

It was raining in New York City when the plane landed.

Once she collected her bags from the terminal, India summoned a cab and asked to be taken to her old apartment.

She dropped her bags to the floor and looked around. The woodwork, the windows, the layout of the rooms, it was all still there. But the feeling was clear. It wasn't her apartment anymore.

Amy's made some changes, she observed as she walked through the space. She subleased the space to Amy when she left. In India's absence, Amy made some dramatic changes.

The kitchen was now painted a vivid blue, the rugs in various rooms were changed out, and India's glassware was missing from the built-in cabinet and replaced with leopard print plates and platters.

Her bedroom, or what used to be her bedroom, was purple and pink, a far cry from the white India preferred.

Hmmm, not the same at all.

India dropped her bags in the second bedroom and dialed Nick.

"Are you here?" Nick's voice came across the line.

"I'm here," India said.

"One hour. I need you here in one hour, okay?"

India sagged. The flight was bruising, and she was tired but nonetheless, she agreed to meet in one hour.

She hoped Nick wouldn't mind that she was coming to the meeting in jeans. Small town lifestyle, plus her weariness, taught her one thing. Be comfortable, no matter what.

When India arrived at the station, the group was assembled with Nick at the lead.

After some hugging and gushing, Nick held his hand up and all conversation ceased.

"India," Nick began, "Amy's been doing a slam-bang helluva job on the news, as the anchor. I know you want that spot back but actually, ratings are good, just a hair above your ratings, right. So, what I am proposing is that you take a spot as a correspondent on one of our crime series. Hunh? You up for it?"

India watched Nick put his hands on his hips, splaying his jacket back.

"You called me to New York for this?"

"Face to face, that's what we like," Nick said. "What do you think, hunh, India? Good opportunity. A lot of exposure."

India stood up. Nick appeared to step backwards.

"You know what, Nick? I don't know that I need a lot of exposure. In fact, don't present a contract today. Don't even think of it. Instead, I am gonna walk out of here and go back to Missouri, and you can sit and spin as far as I am concerned. There's no reason I should give up the anchor desk. Sorry, Amy."

Amy shrunk and straightened.

"And no reason my apartment should look like a cheap strip club, by the way."

Amy blanched.

"India," Nick said, "You're giving up a lot here. Just a warning."

India stood up. "Listen, when you have a contract or a deal that I can live with, you email it to me, okay? And then we'll talk. Don't try to intimidate me, Nick. I'm going home. You can reach me anytime."

Inside the elevator, India pushed the down button. Down to the first floor, down, away from Nick and Amy and the network.

The elevator stopped and India stepped out.

I feel emancipated.

India heard the heels of her shoes click and clack along the marble floor until she reached the enormous front doors, and once out, into the dark, chilly night, she wondered if she should reconsider. Was she too hasty, too angry, too something else? Should she go back and apologize, make nice, be conciliatory?

Too late now.

India hailed a cab, and one pulled over. The cabbie loaded her bags in the trunk without comment, and they sped off.

I'm going home. I was stupid to come back here. The town I once loved, I once thrived in, it's just not my town anymore. I never would have thought it.

Bejeweled show marquis, blinking lights above laundromats, the milling throng, other yellow taxi cabs sped by outside the cab window. India put her finger up to the window and dragged it down, leaving a long smudge.

Paul's image jumped into her mind. Dark eyes, dark slightly curly hair, blue shirt, Levis. India thought of him sitting across the table from her at The Riverwalk, his dark eyes peering into her soul, and afterward, being chased out of the cave by the teenagers.

If he is still there for me once I get back, I'll consider myself a lucky woman.

Her cell phone pinged. Nick.

"Yes?" India said.

"Listen, India, I know you're on your way to the airport, but I want you to listen to me just one minute," Nick said.

"What do you want, Nick?"

"India, I pulled a lot of strings for this, believe me. I went to bat for you and I have an offer."

"What strings?"

"The network wants Amy in the anchor chair."

"She isn't qualified, Nick."

"I'm not saying she is, I'm not saying she isn't," Nick's voice blasted her eardrum as the Chinese places, the drycleaners, the banks, the corner delis sped by. "I'm saying they want her there. I guess they like her red hair. And her boobs."

"So, if you can't be a newswoman, be a Kardashian?"

"I don't know, but India, let me get my offer out, would you please?"

India shifted in the cab seat, seeing LaGuardia come into view.

"Okay, but hurry, I'm almost at the airport."

"The network is forming a new news correspondent show, a quasi-*Dateline* or *48 Hours*. I have asked them to consider you as a correspondent. And they said yes. Two episodes a month, the pay is astronomical, close to what you were making as anchor chair, and quite honestly, India, I think you should go for it. Say yes. If you don't understand by now, I'm your biggest fan, and I argued this and argued this, and finally, they gave in."

"Why do they hate me so much? I'm starting to think it's my age, being a 40-something. They would have never chosen Amy over me otherwise. She has nothing, no experience."

The metallic doors and huge glass windows of LaGuardia appeared.

"She's young, she's attractive, and the viewers like her looks."

"She's not credible. Is this what they want now? Entertainment value?"

India pulled her coat around her as the cab driver opened her door and she stepped out to the sidewalk.

"Okay, Nick, tell you what. Email me the contract. I'll look it over once I'm back in Missouri, and give you an answer in a couple of days. Is that fair?"

Nick's voice came back. "More than fair, India. More than fair."

"Okay, well, you'll hear from me soon then. Bye."

India's flight was late. Two hours late.

India paced the airport, checking her phone for any messages at all from Paul, or Amy, or Shelby, Gwen, or anyone for that matter. Nothing.

She bought a stale sandwich from the vending machine and a bottle of water and settled down in a plastic green chair to wait until her flight was announced. The sandwich was like dust in her mouth, and she threw it in the trashcan. But the water was valuable.

The wind picked up, causing a low moan in the atmosphere.

India stared out the windows to the darkness.

It's like when I came back to Missouri. Nobody waiting for me, nobody in my corner, just wait, wait, wait, for nothing.

India stood up, looking for a bathroom.

I hope I'm not going back to nothing now.

Her flight was finally called, and India lined up to get on board.

It seemed like no time passed when the plane landed in Missouri. India picked up her luggage and walked to the end of the terminal. She would need to call a car service or get a rental car, to get back home. The rent-a-wreck was long gone, returned some time ago.

India walked along, pulling her luggage, checking her messages (none), checking her email (only one, from Nick, attaching the proposed contract), occasionally glancing out the huge glass windows to the darkness. Occasionally, another passenger jubbed up against her going the opposite direction, and India adjusted her bags and her coat again, and then again.

An electric shot went straight through India and she straightened up and looked around.

All her nerve endings stood to spikey attention.

Oh my God.

India looked around, every direction.

And then he stepped out of the shadows.

India's heart beat faster.

There you are.

She began to walk fast, pulling the bags, and once she reached him, she abandoned the bags and spread her arms wide, grasping him to her.

The feel of him in her arms, the smell of him in her nostrils, the knowledge of *him* snapped through her body. India clung to Paul, relishing his hands stroking her hair, the kisses that began to the top of her head and traveled down to her lips.

"I had to come," he whispered. "I couldn't let you go through this alone."

"Thank you, thank you, thank you," she whispered, tears rolling down her face.

There you are.

CHAPTER FORTY FIVE

Shelby

Shelby hooted in exhilaration, sitting in the passenger seat of Ray's big car.

"I never thought I'd be going to the zoo, but here I go!" she said.

Ray smiled across the console at her.

"I'm excited!" Shelby said. "Quinn, aren't you excited?"

Twisting around to see the back seat, Shelby noted Quinn slouching, picking at her sweat jacket.

"Sure," Quinn said.

Come on, be a little bit interested, please. He's taking me, us actually, and it'll be fun.

Shelby turned back around, watching the road peel by as they approached the exit to the road that would take them to the zoo.

"I think you'll like this," Ray said, turning the big car into the parking lot.

"I know I will," Shelby responded. "Thank you for

inviting us."

Ray smiled again, his eyes covered by his sunglasses.

Ray bought the tickets, and the three of them began their zoo adventure. Shelby didn't know if a sky more azure blue or clouds so white and billowy ever existed, like a comfortable pillow. Indian summer persisted and there was no reason not to enjoy the day. A slight breeze came up but it wasn't cold, and as she, Ray and Quinn walked the grounds, she began to feel light, and joyful.

"My favorite animal ever at the zoo would be the big cats, the cheetahs, the panthers, the lions. I love all the big cats," Shelby said, turning to Ray, who had taken her hand. She hadn't noticed that before. "But I really love the lemurs too, their little houses and perches out on the lake. They're just so pretty."

"Well, let's go see the big cats then," Ray said, expertly guiding her through the maze of cages and peacocks, past the small horses, through the giraffe barn.

"How gorgeous," Shelby crowed, noting the orange, white and yellow puzzle pieces that make up the giraffes. "How long are their necks? It's like they go on forever."

A baby giraffe bounded out of the barn, headed straight for its mother, standing outside and away from the barn. The baby immediately latched onto its mother's teat, and Shelby laughed. Quinn laughed too.

"Cute," Quinn said, taking her phone out, snapping a picture.

They walked through the monkey exhibit, a long dull-light building filled with screaming and grunting. A huge black ape threw a phone book at the glass, and Quinn startled.

"Wow," she said, snapping another picture.

"Mom, you're really smiling," Quinn said, holding her phone up to Shelby and Ray.

"That's because I'm having so much fun," Shelby said, turning to Ray. "This is the greatest idea, Ray. But why did you pick the zoo?"

"Let's just say, I had a feeling." Ray said, looking straight at her. "Let's just say I thought you'd have a good time here."

"Oh, that's sweet," Shelby said, taking his hand. "And I am. I'm having a great time here."

Wow, I'm so impressed. No highfalutin restaurant where I'm afraid to cough, this is nice. Fun, interesting. Maybe he'll make me another grilled cheese.

They passed the hippo pool, made the rounds to the elephants, the turkeys, the bald eagles, the turtles, finally, the big cats, reading all the placards placed at each exhibit, absorbing the details of every animal or fowl. They made small talk, observations about that bird's wingspan or that animal's color, the beauty of the day ("Won't be many more days like this," Ray said.)

Shelby observed Quinn snapping photos with her phone but said nothing.

I hope she has a good time. I hope she likes Ray.

A blue-black panther stared down at them for a moment before skittering out of its tree and retreating into its stone lair. Presently, the beast reappeared, seemingly unimpressed with the human visitors, and Quinn snapped away on her phone.

The cheetah they only saw in the distance as it ran the back fence of its habitat.

I love it, I love it. So much fun. I've never had a date like this. Just fun, nice, and he included Quinn.

Ray tapped on the glass at the lion exhibit. The brawny golden male strolled up to the glass, his blue-gray eyes staring at the three of them.

"Oh wow," Quinn said, watching the huge lion head turn, still staring at them.

"That is one mighty beast," Ray said.

"Uh, yeah," Quinn said.

"He's just beautiful," Shelby said, wishing she could touch the velvet coat, run her fingers through the massive brown mane.

The male lost interest in the humans and returned to his females, lounging on the sun-swept stones.

"The otters, we forgot to see the otters," Ray said.

"We have to see the otters," Quinn said.

"I second that," Shelby said, and they set off.

After the otters and the lemurs, the tour ended. Shelby smiled as Ray put his hand around her shoulder, and Quinn took their picture.

"Anyone hungry as me?" Ray asked.

I'm as hungry as you, Shelby thought. *But for now, let's eat.*

After consuming burgers and fries at a local steak-burger shack, Shelby watched Quinn skipping ahead to the front porch, with Ray walking behind.

"Thanks, Ray," Quinn said, turning around.

"You're welcome, Quinn," Shelby heard Ray say.

Quinn crashed through the front door and disappeared from view.

Ray stood in front of her, and in the fading light, his silver hair started to shine, his eye glasses glinted.

Shelby wasn't ready for him to leave.

"Do you want to sit on the swing awhile?" she asked, hoping he would say "yes."

She pointed to the porch swing, a tremulous white in the oncoming darkness.

Ray walked over and sat down, the swing protesting his weight with a small groan.

Shelby settled down beside him, and again the swing groaned, a little deeper this time.

They swung in content silence for a moment or two, Ray's arm resting across the back of the swing.

"Ray," Shelby began. "I had such a fun time today.

This was a perfect, perfect day. Thank you so much."

She saw Ray's eyes light up and a smile.

"Thank you for including my daughter too. And India likes you."

"I was glad to do it, to include Quinn," Ray said as Shelby relaxed, leaning into the arm across the back of the swing. "I like India. I do. Shelby, I know our last, or our first, date was awkward. I was trying too hard, not making any sense, messing everything up, because I was so damn nervous that you wouldn't like me, or like being with me, and I ruined it all. I needed to sort it all out, so I went away for a while. I had this trip planned for a while. I always wanted to see New England in the fall, and I went, and the whole time, you know, here I am, standing in the woods, in a small town, watching the leaves turn color, and I'm distracted, thinking about you and our first date. I wanted to make it all up to you. I thought about what you would like, where you would like to go, and I thought about Quinn too, can't say that I didn't, because she's a big part of you, and well, all I want to say, Shelby, is that I had a great day too, and I hope we'll have more great days together. I wanted a second chance, and I hope I got one today."

Shelby shifted in the swing, which sent another chorus of squeaking upward.

"You're asking me for a second chance? Nobody's ever asked me that before."

Ray put a hand on her shoulder.

"Nobody's ever seen your true worth, in my opinion."

It's true. Nobody's ever seen me because I've been so eager to give it all right away.

"Do you like me, Ray? I mean, *like* me, for who I am and in spite of who I am in some ways."

"I like you for everything you are, Shelby. I always have. Surely you've noticed me rushing around the store to help you out. That's not coincidence."

Shelby giggled a little.

"Ray Henderson, I will give you a second chance, or a third chance, or whatever this is."

Overhead, the porch ceiling gleamed in the quiet porch light. Only a few feet away, off the porch, the trees and bushes were silhouetted by the creamy light of the moon. The soft sound of a dog welcoming its humans and the hum of crickets rang in the air.

Lips welcomed lips, warm, soft, gentle. Drawing back, for just a second and then going in again, deeper, firmer, tongues tangling, and the inevitable soft panting.

"I promise you won't regret it," Ray whispered hoarsely. "I'll never let you regret it."

CHAPTER FORTY SIX

Ray

Ray heard Carmen before he saw her.

"Where's Ray?" he heard her shout. "Where's Ray Henderson?"

Ray stopped stocking avocados and turned around. Carmen was coming full on, red faced, stinking of alcohol, her coat thrown off her shoulder.

"Carmen, you're not right okay now," Ray said immediately. "You seem a little frazzled, just calm down, Carmen, calm down."

Ray put his hands out to stop her, and a purse hit his palms.

"Shelby Graham Demarist, Ray? Really? When you could have me?"

Carmen crept closer. The blue of her eyes was almost a stab in Ray's throat.

"You don't think right, Ray. You and me, we're the same, we think alike." Carmen pointed to her temple. "I got money, you got money, we're business people, Ray, you and me. We could make a helluva team. A helluva team!"

"Carmen, it's time you left the store. Come on, I'll walk you out." Ray took her arm and began to steer her to the front of the store. "I think we should talk outside."

Ray passed the quizzical looks of the checkers and nodded. "Everything's alright, just go back to business. Carmen was just leaving."

"He's kicking me out," Carmen said, pulling her coat back up over both shoulders.

Ray deftly led Carmen to her car parked down the block a few spaces and opened up her driver's door. Carmen let go of his arm and plunked into the driver's seat, one leg in, one leg out, her coat falling away again, leaving her shoulders exposed.

"Carmen, don't come in my store ever again making a scene. Don't do it," Ray said.

"Ray, listen to me. It's just that you and me, we fit like a glove, Ray. We're the same kind of people," Carmen said, leaning forward. "We could go places together, Ray. We could establish an empire. Shelby, she's no good, a no-good slut. She goes back to Phillip every chance she gets."

Ray stepped back from the car.

"Phillip's been gone since I started getting to know her. What she did before she and I started seeing one another doesn't matter to me."

"It should," Carmen said.

"Carmen, listen to me and listen to me good," Ray said. "You and I are not cut from the same cloth. We're not the same kind of people. I'm sorry you've led yourself to believe this, but there is no possibility of any relationship between you and me. I'm sorry. Go home, sober up, and don't think about this anymore."

"Oh, you're such a purist. Do you know how much I hate India Graham?" Carmen said, tucking her leg in the car, shoving the ignition key in.

"No, but go home, Carmen. Just go home, and drive safely," Ray said, shutting her door, patting the window ledge reassuringly, watching Carmen back the big car out of the parking spot slowly and drive away.

Ray sighed and walked back into the store.

CHAPTER FORTY SEVEN

Adrian

Adrian slumped in his seat on the Greyhound bus. It was dark, past 7:00 p.m., because of Daylight Savings Time in early November, and the lights of the Greyhound station receded in the distance as the bus pulled slowly away from its spot in the bus line and advanced to the highway.

It was all worth it, to get back to Quinn, and in the end, his mother didn't object to his leaving. In fact, she seemed relieved, wishing him well, pressing $100 cash in his palm the night he told her he was going back to Oak Ridge one way or the other. Her life was changed, she was remarried, two children, a new life, a big house in the boot heel of Missouri, and she seemed to want that more than having Adrian in her life.

While he lived with his mom, Adrian worked at the local Perkins Restaurant & Bakery. He went to school, went to work, and came home to the room in the attic, feeling as if he was the unwanted guest ("It's the guest room," his mother explained when she brought him there, "the guest room."). Except he didn't feel like a guest or even a wanted person in the household, and he spent his free time planning to return to Oak Ridge.

He saved his earnings from working at the restaurant, nearly all of it. He spent nothing unless he absolutely needed something. The sacrifice was fine with Adrian. He had a bigger goal in mind.

Adrian hadn't been happy or unhappy living with his mother and her family, but rather he felt he was more of an inconvenience to a clicking along life. His quasi-stepfather seemed distant, more like an acquaintance than a family member. Adrian's mother seemed as if she was walking on eggs constantly with Adrian's presence in the house. His step-siblings refused to acknowledge him at all, except for brief greetings and short, necessary conversations. In fact, they seemed to be a bit afraid of him.

Adrian knew it was all about the fire, what kind of person was he, could he have done this, set fire to his own home, killed his father in the doing of it, what kind of person was he anyway? He knew and understood their fears, but was helpless against any of it. He could not defend himself adequately against the prejudices surrounding his arrival at his biological mother's home, or more accurately, his interruption in their perfect, convenient lives. And so he chose to fly under the radar and try to exist without causing any trouble or inconvenience to any of them. He knew once he left, no hole would be left behind to mourn and fill up, no sentimental thoughts or conversation, or even really a remembrance he was ever there with his mother and her family at all.

He also knew there was really nowhere to go once he returned to Quinn. The reality was, he was homeless, basically friendless, and without a family.

Across the aisle, he watched a woman read the Bible, her belly pulsing up and down as she read. There were a few other riders, most of them asleep as the bus pushed forward in the night.

The bathroom was disgusting, Adrian soon found out, and he hoped he could make it to Missouri without peeing or crapping his pants.

Outside the windows, the landscape rolled under darkness.

The woman dropped her Bible into the adjoining chair and began to snore, her chin folding onto her chest.

Adrian crept forward, and picked up the book, opening it to where the woman left off.

Psalms 46. God is our refuge and out strength, a very present help in time of trouble.

Adrian sat down again, holding the book. He didn't read any more of it, but simply re-read the passage and then set the book down as he found it.

CHAPTER FORTY EIGHT

India

Locating Charles Gene Perry proved to be easier than India first thought.

Shoving her glasses up the bridge of her nose, India peered into the receptionist's computer screen at the newspaper office. Everyone was gone for the day, or so she thought, and it was dark outside. A report came back in her email. India opened it, hoping she hit pay dirt.

The clickety-clack of Carmen's heels came up behind her.

"You're fired," Carmen announced.

"Yeah?" India said, swinging the chair around. "Show me the contract where it says you can fire me."

Carmen ran her hand across the top of the desk. India sat forward, watching.

"You think you're so smart, India Graham. You think you're really something, don't you."

India sat back in the chair, waiting for the next chess move.

Carmen's appearance was nearly immaculate. Except for the spinach in her teeth and a spot of a little something trailing down her left boob on an expensive dress. India noticed a little redness in Carmen's eyes, and then realized she smelled booze.

"Well, I don't know. You'll have to tell me what you're getting at, Carmen. But first, show me that contract I signed where it says you can fire me."

Carmen's hand smacked the desk.

"Dammit, India! I told him! He doesn't believe me."

India stood up and leaned over the desk.

"Get over it, Carmen. Just get over it."

Carmen didn't seem to hear.

"And then you, *you*, you sneaking upstairs to that apartment, getting naked with a, a *foreigner*, oh yeah, India, don't think I don't know what's going on upstairs, over my head, and in the daytime too," Carmen shook her head in affirmation.

India sat back down.

"Well, first of all, what I do in my personal life is none of your business. What Ray Henderson does at any time is none of your business. And, again, would you show me that contract I signed where it says you can fire me?"

Carmen stuck her finger out.

"You are an at-will employee. I can fire you if I don't like your socks, and for the record, I don't like your socks."

India stood back up and faced Carmen.

"Well, goody. Let's take a walk to the break room, and we'll fix you some tea, or coffee, or whatever you want. Come on, Carmen."

India gestured toward the door, and Carmen turned, shrugging, and walked on through.

"I hate you, you know," Carmen said.

"I do know that, Carmen," India said, walking her down the hallway.

"So you know I hate you," Carmen said.

"You're getting a little repetitive now," India said. "You already said that."

"But you are fucking him, that dark, delicious electrician, aren't you? Right above my head?"

"Not your business, Carmen."

India deposited Carmen in a chair.

It felt a little like a hopeless comedy to India as she searched out the coffee filters and packs of grounds from the scant cupboard in the breakroom, pushing it all into a carafe, turning on the hot water, pulling a cup out of the cupboard, as Carmen slouched at the small break table by the brick wall, her head in her hands. *Here I am, taking care of my drunken nemesis, and that makes no sense. There ought to be a reality show about this.*

India finally presented a steaming cup of coffee, shoving it in front of Carmen like an offering.

Carmen moaned.

"He doesn't love me," she said. "He doesn't even like me."

"Who, Ray?"

"I have never had a man in my life refuse me. He's the only one who did."

India stood next to the table as Carmen stirred sugar into her cup.

"You know you have to let the man make up his mind, right?" India shifted.

Carmen sipped her coffee and set the cup down, sloshing a bit over the edge. She stared at the spill on the table for a minute before she continued.

"He should have understood how good we'd be together. But he didn't. And he doesn't."

"You don't love Ray, and you know it," India said.

Carmen shrugged. "No, I don't. You're right. But

we would have been a good pair."

India startled as Carmen grabbed her hand.

"You know you're my only friend, right? My only friend in this whole God-forsaken town."

India stared down into Carmen's eyes.

"I don't know anything about that, and besides, how could we be friends with you dogging my sister all the time and firing me every other day?"

Carmen let go of India's hand and sighed.

"You're not fired, India. I hate your guts, and your sister's a slut, but you're not fired. You know what?"

"Oh god," India said. "What now, Carmen?"

Carmen's eyes glistened. "I wish I'd had your life, India. I would have liked to make a difference. And be famous, and do cool stuff, go cool places, like you did, and live to tell it. Listen, nobody cares about me, India. I was the prettiest girl in high school, and the most popular, you remember. I married who I married, and that union brought particular benefits. I have a social standing in this teeny-weeny town. I'm on the school board. I'm on city council. I'm even on the planning committee at my church. I am a somebody in this town, and I am the widow of an important person. But, nobody really likes me. Nobody liked me in high school, not for real. I don't have real friends."

Carmen took another gulp of her coffee and set the cup back down.

"People are around me because of who I am, and I'm who I am because of the man I married. The RV tycoon, the investor, the founder of the Industrial Park, God rest his soul, but none of those people care about me. A lawn service takes care of my yard. They love me, I give them cake and lemonade when they come to work on the lawn. I have a housekeeper, and I give her gift cards and she fawns over me, but she doesn't truly like me? I doubt it. My laundry goes out, and you know what? I pay them double what they charge."

India sat down opposite Carmen.

"Why do you do it?"

"I live in a beautiful house, behind a gate. Nobody gets to come to my home without getting past that gate, you know? I have more money than I could ever dream of having because I married well, but India, I don't have any friends. I buy my friends. I seek consolation from the gardener, and I don't know why."

Carmen face began to dissolve into tears. India stared, fascinated and repulsed at the same time.

"Except, you talk about me... there's nothing to like! You know what? I went to Kansas City for a week, and I laid on an expensive bed in an expensive hotel, and I drank expensive champagne, and I spent most of my time trying to convince myself that I'm not lonely. I know, I know," Carmen continued, shaking her head, "I wanted everybody, especially your sister, to think I was with Ray on vacation, but the truth is, I went to Kansas City alone, because I heard he was going away. I don't even know where he went."

"Pretty shitty behavior, Carmen."

"Of course," Carmen responded. "I seem to be an expert."

Carmen shoved her coffee cup away and stood up, her ample chest rising in a deep breath. Smoothing her hair, she said, "I'm going home now. You're still fired, by the way. But, come in on Monday, on time, do you hear me?"

India stood up.

"I'll be here on Monday." India pointed to the back door.

"I wish I didn't hate you so much," Carmen said as she opened the back door, allowing it to slam as she left.

India quietly cleaned the coffee pot, washed Carmen's cup, and set it all to drain on the side board.

I never liked her in high school, that much is true, India thought, shutting the breakroom light off, walking out to the hall. *She didn't like me either. I wasn't cool enough for her crowd.*

India stared out the window for a minute.

God, I hope she gets home safe, but on the other hand, she's brought so much of her pain on herself. I guess I just hope she gets home safely.

India walked back up to the reception desk. Paul would be home soon, but in the meantime, a report on Charles Gene Perry was waiting for her on the computer in the front area.

The thought of Paul, his dark intent eyes, his hands on her body, his fingers, his lips on hers, made India gasp and giggle a bit.

Okay, hang on. We're still on business time.

India sat down in front of the computer and began to read.

Charles Gene Perry was not far away. And he was alive, although retired and widowed. India read and re-read the information she found. He was a practicing attorney for forty-four years. He married and had one child, a daughter, and his wife passed away seven years ago.

Charles Gene Perry was alive and well, living in Rogers, Arkansas. And that wasn't even the best part. Charles Gene Perry wrote a novel, published under another name, Chester Fields, and the book was available at online retailers.

India scrambled to locate the book.

The short synopsis stunned her. India clicked on the "more information" option, read the long synopsis, then the reviews, and then went into the Kindle edition.

India set back, her hand over her mouth, after reading the excerpt allowed on Amazon.

Oh my God. How powerful is this. Gwen should

know.

Amazon Author Central gave her Charles' biography. India did a quick search on Facebook, and there he was. His information held an email address.

India considered all she would ask this Charles Gene Perry, the idea of sharing Gwen with him.

What would I say to him? He's obviously still alive. Gwen obviously still loves him.

A quick text to Shelby about that she found on Charles and then back to the details.

Shelby texted back. "Gwen will kill us both you know but this is so exciting! Could we bring them back together?"

India thought for a while before responding. "Don't know. But it's worth a try."

The blackness outside the windows and the quiet of the office brought India into a place where she could think, compose, reason things out. Then she composed an email, checked it two or three times for accuracy and punctuation, read it again two or three times.

Once I press send, it's out of my control. And what if he doesn't answer, and if he does answer, what if he doesn't care?

India stared out the big, black windows.

Charles Gene Perry made a life. He's lived it, and none of it included Gwen. What if I'm just interfering in an old man's life?

India's finger hovered over the "send" button for a long minute.

Screw it. This is him, the boy she loved.

India's finger bored down and pressed the button that would not allow her to back out.

I hope I haven't created a firestorm, a bad situation. And I want to read his book.

She didn't even hear when Paul came in, running up the back stairs to his apartment.

A few short computer strokes, and India ordered the book.

Her phone dinged.

"Hello, beautiful, down there. Why are you still working?"

India smiled. Time to come back to reality, but it was a good reality to come back to. She had to tell Paul about this book, about Chester Fields and Charles Gene Perry. It was something she wanted to share with him. She wanted to tell Shelby too, but at the moment, she would tell Paul.

"Hello you. I missed you. Been working; thinking of you all day. Coming up now."

In a minute a message came back.

"Come on."

India went.

CHAPTER FORTY NINE

India

India peered down at her cell phone, pulling the sheets up over her bare shoulder, as the text came in.

Charles Perry's book tumbled to the floor. India read the love story of a white boy and a black girl all the way through in just a few short hours as Paul slept. The poignant story left India in tears, all the more hopeful she could help bring Gwen and Charles' love story back to life.

"I'm on my way back. I'm coming back. Adrian"

India felt a palpitation in her heart as she read the text.

"This will be great for Quinn. It's just great, period. We'll all be so glad to see you," she texted back.

With a slight stir to her left, Paul was beginning to wake up.

"What's up, baby?" she heard him murmur.

India set her phone back on the nightstand and turned over to the man whose brown eyes were now open and looking right at her.

"Nothing but good things," India whispered, smiling. "Nothing but good things."

India swam back underneath the covers to the warm man with welcoming arms.

"Tell me about Romania," India whispered later, lying in the crook of Paul's arm.

Paul brushed his free arm across his head.

"It was bad," he said. There's so much social unrest. Lots of cross-class culture. Poverty. If you're this or you're that, you might have a social problem. People disappear. It's especially prevalent if you claim a faith. Especially if you claim to be a Christian."

"So, what about you?" India asked.

"It was a little different for me," Paul said. "I can't apologize for it. I lived a bit more privileged life. My family escaped persecution of any sort, nobody probed us, checked up on us or managed our lives, which happens over there. But I saw people less fortunate than me suffer, and that hurts. My parents, both of them, died in Romania in a car wreck. Essentially, I was an orphan. I came here with my aunt. I was twelve at the time, and I knew nothing of America. Didn't speak the language. I had no idea what was going to become of me. But, my aunt, who did speak the language and had some connections, made sure I got an education. She married pretty fast after we came here, and her husband was an electrician. So, there's that connection. He taught me."

"Did you have siblings?" India asked.

"No."

India perched on her arm, looking down into the face she so now loved.

"You told me once that you don't fall easily. What does that mean, Paul?"

India watched his features turn from quiet to pensive to a little bit sad.

"When we were still in Romania, just a little while before I came over, there was a girl. We were kids, but I imagined one day I would marry her. Her name was Lydia. We were in school together. And we laughed and talked and ran around each other, all childish romantic things. And then she died."

"She died?"

"She had leukemia. She died after I left for America with my aunt. I didn't know she was dead for months. I never knew she was sick, even. My letters went somewhere, but were never answered. And then my aunt told me one day Lydia had been dead for nine months."

India's stomach dropped into a cold pool. Pulling Paul close, she said, "Oh my God, Paul, that's so sad. I'm sorry."

"It was a long time ago, but Lydia's illness and death, and how she might have suffered and I wasn't there to help her, affected me. Thinking that someone you knew or wanted to know, was suddenly beyond your grasp, and you might not even know anything happened, or there is no possibility for a relationship at all, until it's too late. I was shocked, learning she died. That state of shock stayed with me for a long time. I've dated here and there, but until now, I never found anyone I wanted to be this close to."

"Until now? Me?" India looked into the brown eyes she was now so desperate for.

Paul's hand crept up her arm.

"Until now. Until you."

CHAPTER FIFTY

Shelby

Shelby poured a tall glass of chocolate milk and swallowed heavily, savoring the cool chocolate lactose on her lips. The last hangers-on of leaves from the maples outside lay on the ground. Soon, winter would fall. The rains would begin, the temperature would drop, and the rain would turn to treacherous ice, slapping the roads, the streets, the houses, the power lines. Shelby did not look forward to the winter season in the Ozarks.

However, that was neither here nor there at the moment.

Shelby sighed again.

You know, I would have thought, in another life, I would have done Ray by this time, but so far, we've haven't done it. It's okay with me. I took Tony too fast and wound up pregnant with Quinn, and then Phillip came along, and I did him too, and look how that turned out. So, I'm cool with Ray, but India, look at her.

"You oughta look better, all things considered," she

said, staring at India, who was sitting at the kitchen island, drinking coffee.

"What?" India appeared to having been roused from a long sleep.

"I mean, you haven't been sleeping at home lately is all I'm saying."

Shelby took a long gulp of chocolate milk and stared at her sister.

"So, what's he about anyway?"

"Paul?" India said.

Shelby set her glass down.

"No, Humpty Dumpty, India. You been sneaking out to meet with Humpty Dumpty, right? Of course I mean Paul."

"I've never been accused of being a sneak before."

"Okay, but what's he about?"

"He's great. It's good," India began.

"So, when are you getting married? Because I told you that would happen."

"Can't say the subject's come up."

"Well, Gwen thinks he's handsome," Shelby said.

"Well, he is."

Shelby turned at a quiet noise.

The front door opened with a quiet creek, and a gust of cold air, and shut with a declaration.

Shelby saw Quinn's pink sweatshirt, heard her call out, "Mom?"

Quinn walked in.

She wasn't alone.

Shelby shrieked and rushed forward, grabbing Adrian in a bear hug.

"You're okay, I'm so glad you're okay," she said sobbing, hanging onto Adrian.

"Okay, okay, okay, Mom," Quinn said, disengaging Shelby's arms.

"I'm just happy to see him," Shelby said. *So what?*

I'm so relieved he's okay.

India stepped forward and hugged Adrian. Shelby saw them smile at one another as if they had a secret. *What? She knew all along. She knew he was coming back, and she didn't tell me.*

"Um, he doesn't have a place to stay, Mom," Quinn said. "And he has to register for school."

Shelby and India looked at each other at the same time.

"He agreed," Quinn said. "We talked, didn't we, and we know you won't want to have us under the same roof and all that, but we're good, right?"

"We're good," Adrian affirmed. "My mom emancipated me while I was gone. I can register myself for school. And I'll get a job, and I'll help out around here anyway I can."

"Yeah, and it'll be okay, Mom. You can trust us. I mean, we're not having sex," Quinn said.

Adrian appeared to blush. Shelby saw him shuffle his feet.

"That's right," he said, curls dropping over his eyes. He brushed them away. "We're not having sex."

"But you've thought about sex," India interrupted. "Right?"

Shelby glared at her sister. *Shut up already, would you?*

"Sure," Adrian said. 'But it's her decision, and I'm not forcing that decision on her. She's been through a lot. I'm not going to hurt her."

Quinn stepped forward.

"What do you say? We have plenty of room."

Shelby looked at India, who was looking back at her.

The decision was made.

"Yes," Shelby and India said in unison.

"We wouldn't turn you out, Adrian," India said,

taking a hold of his hands.

Shelby put her arm around Quinn's shoulder.

"Okay, let's give him a room down the hall from mine. And don't worry," Quinn said, escaping Shelby's embrace. "We're not having sex."

Quinn led the group upstairs and down the hall from her room, opening a door at the far end of the hall.

Our parents' room, Shelby thought, looking around. *Okay, it's fitting. It'll be fine.*

"Okay, Adrian," Shelby said. "Drop your stuff in here. This will be your room, okay?"

"Okay," Adrian said softly. "Thank you."

"Keep it clean, pick up after yourself, is all I ask." Shelby moved to the door.

"No problem," Adrian said, dropping his backpack on the bed.

"And we're not having sex," Quinn reiterated.

"You said that already," India said from the doorway, laughing. "We got it."

Shelby pointed at Adrian.

"You touch my daughter, and I'll touch you, got it?"

"Got it," Adrian said, unzipping his backpack.

"Mom!" Quinn exclaimed from the shadows.

"Well?" Shelby said.

"Okay, okay," India said. "Anybody want to make pizza? Or is that lame on Halloween night?"

"It's Halloween?" Quinn said. "I forgot."

"So, what do you say, unless you've got plans, anyway."

Quinn looked at Adrian. Adrian looked at Quinn.

"Pizza," they said together.

"Pizza it is," India said.

If this was any other kid, or kids, I'd never believe they're not having sex, Shelby thought as she traipsed back down the stairs with India. *And maybe I don't really, because they're teenagers.*

"This is okay, right?" Shelby asked over her shoulder to India. "I mean, they're telling the truth, right?"

"Yeah, I believe they are."

"They're teenagers," Shelby said.

"Yeah," India said. "But it's okay. He's solid. He wants the best for Quinn, surely you see that. He's not going to force anything."

Shelby accepted the flour canister India shoved across the kitchen island. A bowl came soon thereafter.

"I don't know how to make pizza," Shelby said.

"That's okay. You can learn," India responded, tossing a packet of yeast.

"Can we help?"

Shelby smiled up at Quinn and Adrian.

This is family. Shelby listened as India gave all of them their marching orders, smiling with a sense of pleasantness not felt in a long time. Shelby was given the task of making the crust. Quinn and Adrian cut up vegetables, and a carton of leftover rotisserie chicken was found in the refrigerator. India grated cheese and whipped up an alfredo sauce.

The sound of laughter filled the kitchen and the house, as the pleasant scent of yeast dough, and cheesy sauce rose up.

Quinn grabbed some of the grated cheese and flipped it at Adrian.

Adrian laughed, punching Quinn playfully in the arm.

Family at last, Shelby thought, punching the dough down, smoothing it onto the oiled pan. *I could do this forever, and if Ray was here, it would be complete. And then Paul for India.*

"You goober," she heard Quinn laugh at Adrian.

"Hey now," India was saying. "Let's keep it clean,

everyone."

More laughter.

Later, Shelby pulled an afghan over Quinn and Adrian as they snoozed in front of the TV, old movie credits running.

This is what it always should have been, Shelby thought, turning the TV off. *I couldn't make it happen but here is Adrian, and here is my sister, and now it's happening. Something I couldn't do, didn't know how to do, and didn't want it in the beginning. But here it is.*

Shelby looked around the time-honored house one more time before turning the last light off.

It's what I've always wanted. The only other person I'd want here is Ray. And maybe, just maybe, there's room for that too.

CHAPTER FIFTY ONE

India

Monday morning rolled around in a slow, certain way. The sun rose slowly in a haze of Ozarks humidity, and then began blazing. The trees on the square were completely bare, spindly limbs stretching to the sky, a lovely shade of blue. The beginning of November brought a blast of Indian summer to the Ozarks.

India was beginning to get used to the small-town sureness, in all its slow glory, and as she arrived early at the newspaper office, per Carmen's command, she felt as if she might actually conquer a mountain that day.

She unlocked the doors, put coffee to brew in the break room, shuffled around, and noticed Carmen's big car pulling up in the parking lot. India poured a cup and waited.

Carmen burst through the back door, into the breakroom.

"Well, India, I see you have done as I commanded, being be here first thing today," Carmen said, tossing her bag into the nearest chair, unrolling the sweater around her shoulders tossing that too.

India noticed Carmen was dressed more casually than usual, in a red gingham button-down shirt tucked into dyed blue jeans, the white sweater, loafers.

"I'm here, as you demanded and or requested," India said. "Although I am not sure why."

"Well, of course. I'm going to tell you something, India," Carmen said, taking India's coffee cup out of her hand and nursing it with sugar and cream. "But, first thing, listen, you tell anybody about our conversation the other night, you're fired."

India sagged against the sink. "You've worn that one out."

"Well," Carmen said. "Whatever. Hey, you know, I had an epiphany the other night, India." She took a slurping gulp of India's coffee and continued.

India pulled a coffee cup out of the cupboard and poured another cup.

"You know," Carmen said, waving a hand, bracelets clattering, "my late husband, God rest his soul, well, he provided for me very well, as well as the traveling citizens of this wonderful land of ours, the RV king of the ever-loving world, and he wasn't stupid, India. He wasn't stupid."

India stared.

"Right," India finally said.

"Well," Carmen set her coffee cup down with a sloppy thud. "Well, I should tell you first because, we're friends and all. This place, the newspaper itself, my mansion, everything I own... it's all up for sale! Yeah! You know what? My husband had to have one of those traveling RVs he sold the hell out of, and the hell of it is, I have one, parked in one of my garages."

"What?" India set her cup on the counter. "What are you telling me, Carmen?"

"Oh, girlfriend," Carmen said, putting a hand on India's shoulder. "You opened my eyes to a whole new world the other night. Life is about experiences, and I'm starved for experiences. So, I'm selling everything. Everything. And I'm taking my RV on the road, and I'm going to give life a chance. That's what I'm gonna do."

India took a deep breath.

"Carmen, have you seriously considered this? Is this a knee-jerk reaction to anything I said?"

Carmen didn't miss a beat. "You might want to tell your boyfriend he better find another place to live due to the transition and all. Unless, of course, you want to buy me out. Buy the newspaper, I mean. Well, except you've got that contract pending with New York, don't you."

Carmen tapped India on the shoulder. "And why wouldn't you want to take it, sign that contract, I mean."

"Maybe I will."

"Oh right," Carmen pursed her lips. "Maybe you will. Except you won't."

"Maybe I've redefined what success means, Carmen," India said.

Carmen snorted. "Or maybe you're just horny for the guy upstairs. Whatever, India. But, if you feel froggy about the newspaper, leap. It's not that great an opportunity, considering where you've been, but it's still your line of work. And you could settle back here, and have a life too. Just saying."

Carmen checked her watch. "I really have to go. I have appointments today. Think about this place, India, just think about it. Toodaloo, I'm off."

India set her cup in the sink when she heard the door close and knew Carmen was on the outside of it.

Buy the newspaper? I thought coming back here was temporary.

India leaned over the back of one of the chairs in the breakroom.

I have no idea how to run a newspaper, and besides that, this isn't the golden egg. More like tarnished brass. I always thought I would go back to New York. But then I came to work here, worked out the kinks with Shelby, met and fell in love with Paul. I made so many complications by staying. If I had just gone back every time my head told me to, I wouldn't have to think about any of this.

The contract with the network was still outstanding, left at home on India's nightstand, something to get to, to consider when the house was quiet, something to examine when she felt in a place where she could do it.

Go back to New York, accept the offer, go back to network news.

India saw all the possibilities of being back in the city she loved, walking the familiar streets, eating and drinking at the familiar haunts, jostling amongst the human population, doing the work she loved with people who understood what the world of news journalism meant.

My people. I could make it work again. I was good. Not just good, I was really good, and I could run circles around anybody, especially Amy, on the network. It's a fantastic opportunity, and I didn't think I'd get that again. I could really get into that, make it something big.

She found herself sitting at the receptionist desk, her chin in the palm of her hand, staring at the brick wall in front of her.

India gazed around, at the huge windows, at the glass double doors, the wood floors, the feeling of history held in every nail, every board, every ancient brick.

She's right, this is no golden egg, but it's steady and it's real, and maybe with more advertisements, and moving more forward, it could be a bit more than what it is now. And yes, there is Paul right upstairs. I don't see

him moving to New York to accommodate me, and I
wouldn't ask him to anyway. It's just not his thing. He
came here to get away from all the noise, to find peace.
It wouldn't be fair of me to even ask.

Maybe it's true, you can't have it all. Could I trade
New York and my work there, for the man who looks at
me with so much love in his eyes I can hardly bear it? It
almost makes me faint to be loved that much, that hard.

India clicked on the receptionist computer, and
continued staring into space as the computer booted up.

She sighed aloud, and opened her email.

One new message.

India's eyes widened.

Charles Eugene Perry had something to say.

India read the email and then re-read it.

Wow. India held her fingers to her mouth.

ceperry@gmail.com wrote:

"Dear India,

I cannot tell you how grateful I am for the email
you sent to me. I am an old man, by this time certainly,
and I have lived a full and happy life. I became a lawyer,
I held a distinguished career. I married and had a
daughter. I've traveled the globe, to many countries and
the entire United States. However, India, one thing, *one*
thing, has plagued me for the past many, many years.
What happened to that girl, the one I loved so many
years ago? You know who I'm speaking of, or you
wouldn't have contacted me in the first place. Yes, I've
had a good life, which I believe you know about since
you searched me out and found me. The truth is, she was
my first love, and she will be my last, but times did not
dictate that we could be together. Oh, perhaps we should
have just been brave, stood up to the whole lot of them,
to conventional society, but in those days, that sort of
thing just wasn't done. The consequences of standing
out were enormous, and never ending. We took our

punishment, being separated forever, by race and class. It was the times, India, it was the times. I can only hope she's had a happy life. And I hope also that you will tell me where she is and how she is. I would like to see her, if she will see me. Please respond."

Oh my God.

India forwarded the email to Shelby.

In a nanosecond Shelby wrote back: "He still loves her. He remembers her. We have to do something. We have to get him here."

"But, Gwen doesn't even know what we've done. It's not fair to her, to blindside her."

"India, tell him to come on. We'll handle it after that."

We'll handle it after that. Okay, fine. We'll handle it after that.

India took a deep breath, clicked the "reply" button and began.

CHAPTER FIFTY TWO

India

My Lord. Thanksgiving's coming up fast, and I haven't planned one stinking thing. I haven't even bought a turkey. Too busy, I guess.

India moved around her kitchen, grabbing a loaf of sourdough bread, the deli ham and provolone cheese from the crisper, lettuce, Dijon mustard, mayonnaise, a banana pepper.

God, I'm hungry.

India smiled at the thought of Paul, the feeling of closeness she felt when she was with him. His dark eyes, which seemed to peer at her one minute and glow the next. India thought of his bare rear end as he rose out of bed and traipsed to the shower, his arms circling her, his lips on her skin.

Whew, India brought herself back to the present.

Where there was no turkey.

No autumn vegetables.

No pretty tablescape.

Well, that can't be.

India texted Shelby.

You want to have Thanksgiving dinner? Like a traditional, sit down turkey and sides dinner?

In a few minutes, a response.

Hell yeah. We haven't had that in years. Great idea. I love it. By the way, you're in charge.

India took a bite of her sandwich and stared up the stairwell. It was a Saturday, and India was sure Quinn would be home, but sleeping.

It's almost noon, for God's sake.

"Quinn!" India shouted. "Wake up, I need you down here."

No response.

"Quinn! Come down to the kitchen, I need to talk to you."

India thought she heard the rustle of movement and a door opening and closing, some quiet but half-hearted compliance.

In a moment, she heard foot treads on the stairs, and Quinn stumbled into the kitchen, hair askew, wearing a wrinkled Blake Shelton tee shirt and plaid bed pants.

"Good to see you, chickadee," India said.

"Whatever," Quinn said.

"Listen, it's almost Thanksgiving."

"So?"

India watched as Quinn piled into one of the stools at the island, shoving her chin into her hand. "So, let's have a family-style traditional Thanksgiving dinner." India took another bite of sandwich.

"We don't do that. We've never done that, well, maybe once, but I think Gwen cooked most of it, and we had ham, and Mom burned the pie she baked." Quinn yawned. "I'm not big into turkey. Or any of that stuff. We usually get take-out."

"Not this year," India said. "Come on, let's do it."

"I don't care," Quinn said, getting up. "Knock yourself out. I'm gonna take a shower and cleanse my brain."

India watched Quinn shuffle back to the staircase.

"Okay," she said merrily. "We'll do it, yes, we will."

Quinn waved a hand behind her and ascended the staircase, legs disappearing out of sight.

"Well, that's enthusiasm for sure," India muttered as she finished the last of her sandwich and swallowed the rest of her bottle of water. "We're gonna do it, we're gonna do it, and it's gonna be good," she said, dancing a few jives moves.

It'll be fine. I'll make a list of what we'll serve and all the stuff we need to get.

India stepped upstairs to her room.

The contract Nick sent was still lying on her bedside table, under the lamp.

I need to take care of this, I really do. One way or the other, I need to make a decision and stop hanging out there.

India sat down on the bed, gathering the contract in her hands.

On the one hand, I could make a lot of money, India thought. *I could go back to TV journalism, no sweat. I'd be back to my old life. Except I have plenty of money. I haven't been a slouch all these years. I could make it without this opportunity. But, what an opportunity this is. God, I love the news. I love the chase, the digging, the sweat, all of it. I loved being the anchor chair, but not as much as being in the field, actually uncovering the next big thing.*

India looked out the window for a moment.

Buy the newspaper, surrender to this small town, with its small-town baggage. Could I do that? I mean, I could financially, but do I want to? Paul is here; my family is here. Is Gwen right, saying I'm here for a reason and I should just face it? It's not like I ever thought she was wrong; I really didn't consider what she said because I was fixated on returning to New York.

There's a sureness, a solidarity, here that isn't present in New York. I mean, every day there's more construction, tearing history down, erecting huge soulless buildings in its place. In New York, change happens instantly. It's frenetic, and it can be exciting, but it's exhausting too. Too much change, too fast. Mentally, emotionally exhausting. Ever-shifting sand. I've been here now long enough to see the difference, and appreciate the difference.

India was vaguely aware of the sound of the shower in Quinn's bathroom shutting off.

I could go back, assimilate fairly easily. But Paul wouldn't be there. I've never been faced with this before. Abandoning the job I love for a man. But if I bought the newspaper, such as it is, I'd be here and I'd still be doing news. Sort of. Would it be enough?

India set the contract back on the night stand.

I could always write a book, I suppose, a memoir about my life and experiences in the field. I could be that retired news journalist, glasses sliding down my nose, recounting my glory days.

This is the hardest decision. I can't make it right now.

India stood up and opened her bedroom door to find Quinn standing outside of it with an open cookbook in her hands. Her hair was wet, matted to her head, and she smelled like soap and shampoo.

"I guess your brain's cleansed?"

"Adrian likes nuts, almonds best," Quinn said with no preamble. "If we're having Thanksgiving for reals, I want to make this."

"Okay, let's see what you've got here," India said,

peering over Quinn's shoulder at the recipe Quinn chose. An Italian Almond Tart.

"Good choice," India said, setting her hands on Quinn's shoulders.

"You might have to help me," Quinn said. "I want it to be perfect. I mean, not like I'm going to be Holly Homemaker or anything, but it's got to be perfect."

"We can do that," India said. "We can absolutely do that."

Quinn looked doubtful, but then she shrugged and closed the book, turning away, marching back down the hall to her room.

India watched her go and wondered whether a corner turned in Quinn's world "for reals."

CHAPTER FIFTY THREE

India

India pulled her coat around her, standing in the waiting area for the Greyhound bus. Every once in a while, the double garage door-like doors would open, thrusting a blast of cold air into the reception area, making her blanch and shiver.

I hope we've done the right thing, India thought. *What if Gwen objects, gets mad, won't cooperate, doesn't care anymore? Good god, Shelby, why did I ever listen to you? Gwen's older, after all, set in her ways. Maybe, what if, she doesn't feel the pull from Charles anymore? Except that she said she always loved him. That's what we got going for us. This could be a total disaster for everyone involved, or it could work beautifully.*

India recognized Charles Gene Perry immediately when he stepped off the bus.

It was in his spectacles, the dignity of an older man who'd succeeded. He was not a tall man, but he commanded respect.

India stepped forward and stuck her hand out.

"Charles Perry?"

The man turned, making eye contact.

Those blue eyes. Just like Gwen described.

"Yes, I am Charles Perry, and you are India?"

"I am," India said, grasping his arm. "And I am so pleased to meet you."

"Well, I have to say, being greeted by such a lovely woman in this place gratifies my heart."

India smiled.

"It's the least I could do, and it's wonderful you are here right now to join us for our Thanksgiving celebration."

CHAPTER FIFTY FOUR

India

Quinn and Adrian were arguing in the family room, working a jig-saw puzzle.

Working in the kitchen, India could hear the bantering and bickering in the other room.

"Hey, I got the last piece for the frame. Woot!"

"Okay, fine, big shot. Take this one."

"That's not the right piece, Quinn. Look, it doesn't match."

"Oh buggers to you, here's the right one. I got it."

India laughed and continued stirring, seasoning, chopping.

Shelby came in, discarding her scrubs for a tee shirt and jeans, and she and India counted prospective heads for dinner. "Okay," Shelby said. "There's me and Ray, Quinn and Adrian, you and Paul... Hey, we get to meet Paul formally this year?"

"Yeah, yeah, of course," India said, shoving the leaf into the table. "And Gwen, and Charles will be here."

"So, eight of us," Shelby said, helping India lock the table leaf in place. "How did Gwen react when you took Charles over there?"

"Oh," India sighed. "She seemed pleased, but a little intimidated. It's been such a long time for them. I was worried about that, quite frankly. So much time's passed, and they've gotten older, lived their own lives independent of each other. I didn't know if they'll have anything in common anymore."

India pulled a tablecloth out of the drawer and began unfolding it.

"So, then what?" Shelby said. "What about him?"

Shelby joined her spreading the table cloth over the dining room table.

"He was gallant, nice, polite. He seemed happy to see her too. I read his book, and it's really good, about a love no one approved of, but the characters in that book ended up together. I don't know," India turned away for a minute. "I don't know if this was such a good idea, Shelby. What if it's a waste of time for them both? What have we done?"

The aroma of roasting meat, sage, thyme, and butter filled the kitchen.

"That smells so good," Shelby said. "I haven't read his book, but I feel like this is kind of romantic. What if we did a good thing, getting them back together, if only for a minute?"

"I'm uncomfortable with the whole idea of interfering. Maybe I'm wrong, but I'm not convinced we should have pushed this thing."

India pulled some sweet potatoes out of a bowl on the counter.

"Here, peel these," she said, shoving them at Shelby.

"But he responded to you, right?" Shelby said. "If he wasn't interested, he wouldn't have come all this way, right?"

India pulled the casserole of stuffing out of the refrigerator. "Yeah, I mean, yeah, he responded to me. I just don't want Gwen, or him for that matter, to be hurt, or disillusioned about their love. That's what I'm most afraid of, making the wonderful memories they have of each other seem artificial, forced."

"We'll see. It's up to them now," Shelby said.

India sighed again, wondering if she and her sister did the right thing by Gwen and Charles.

India supervised Shelby's cooking. Shelby set the peeled sweet potatoes to boil. Once they were cooked through, she drained them in the sink with instructions from India, and poured the hot potatoes into a bowl, mashing them with butter, salt pepper, brown sugar and cinnamon.

Quinn's almond tart set on the counter. India smiled, remembering the intensity with which Quinn approached the project, shoving her hair out of her eyes, reading the instructions over and over again, reciting them over and over, lining up each and every ingredient on the island, where she could inspect, peer at it, evaluate it and measure it out.

The girl meant business, India thought.

The tart looked magnificent.

I'm proud of her, although she'd hate for me to say that.

India started setting the table, her stomach flipping at the thought of introducing Paul to her family.

I can't wait to see him, she thought, setting candles in place.

"Mom, India, it's starting to snow," Quinn yelled from the other room.

India and Shelby rushed to a window to see tiny white flakes drifting over the lawn, not really touching anything, but snow nonetheless.

Paul was walking up the driveway illuminated by failing light, followed by Ray.

The sisters gasped and grabbed each other's arms.

Gwen and Charles entered a few minutes later.

"No fights tonight," India said, leaning in close to Shelby.

"No fights," Shelby agreed.

And the rest, I'll deal with tomorrow.

CHAPTER FIFTY FIVE

Shelby

I really thought this would work out better, Shelby thought. *I thought we were bringing two star-crossed lovers back together. Probably should have listened to India. She wasn't so sure. She didn't think it would all work out like magic, and it didn't. Totally blew up in our faces.*

Crushing disappointment.

Gwen was absent when the sisters took Charles Perry back to the Greyhound Bus Station for his return home. She claimed she didn't feel like going.

The day was blustery, chilly, with low white-grey clouds covering the sun.

Oh, this is so sad, Shelby thought, watching Charles walk to India's SUV, fold himself in, and pour himself out at the bus station, and walk in. He seemed bent somehow, sad, disappointed.

Her eyes met India's.

Gwen should have been here.

"I'm sorry, girls, I know you had high expectations, and I did as well, but it just didn't spark with Gwen and me again." Charles leaned on a cane, looking up at the sisters. "We're too set in our ways. And too much time passed. I'll always remember her fondly, though."

"I'm sorry," India said. "We love you, Charles. Please don't be a stranger."

"Yeah," Shelby said, feeling tears starting to burn her eyes. "You're family now."

Charles laughed weakly and turned his ticket in at the queue. "Thank you, girls. I'll always remember your sweetness too."

Shelby saw the busses pull up in front of the door. Charles's bus number was called.

She watched him get on the first step, then turn and wave, before disappearing into the darkness of the bus.

She didn't realize India was holding her hand until she needed to wipe her nose.

"I thought we were bringing a happy-ever-after," Shelby sobbed. "What went wrong? I thought Gwen would squeal with happiness when she saw him, and they'd pick right up where they left off, and everything would be magical."

"She did squeal at first," India said.

Shelby watched the last of the passengers ascend the steps into Charles' bus.

"But I think the more time they spent together, the more they realized it wasn't right. They've lived separate lives for so long. Their memories were golden and beautiful, but they didn't translate into real life," India was saying. "Believe me, I'm disappointed too."

Charles' bus lurched forward, blasting black greasy air out its tailpipe. It stopped, then lurched forward again, its engine roaring in protest, and stopped again.

Shelby held her breath, turning to India, who was

staring at the bus.

"Maybe?" Shelby said.

India frowned, watching the back of the bus.

Shelby turned back to see the bus right itself, roar into gear and slowly pull away from the station, lining up at the terminal exit to get on the freeway. The light turned green, and the bus turned away and finally disappeared from view.

"He's gone," Shelby said.

"He's gone," India responded.

Shelby leaned on India's arm as they walked back to India's vehicle.

"Gwen should have been here," Shelby said. "She could have done that much, even if she didn't really like him anymore."

"Oh, I think she likes him just fine," India said, buckling her seatbelt, turning the engine on, and backing slowly out of the parking space. "I think she didn't want to have the memory of him leaving. She wanted to remember him being here, not leaving. That's what I think."

"But he could come back," Shelby said.

"I doubt it," India said. "Elderly folks are funny. Set in their ways."

Shelby stared at the dash for a long minute.

"Crazy old people."

India laughed, and Shelby started laughing too.

"You're right, but then, it seems like you always are," Shelby said.

CHAPTER FIFTY SIX

India

India dialed Shelby's number, toying with a cup of tea sitting on her coffee table. Snow was falling in New York, wet cold snow, nothing comforting about it.

So much happened in the last few months, India was nearly dizzy.

India recalled the contract Nick sent to her, seeing it on the nightstand next to her bed on Madelaine Street, reading and re-reading it, how the proposal for the new show revitalized her. Carmen's invitation to purchase the newspaper excited her. Weighing the options, back and forth, over and over, made India physically ill. Pros and cons on both sides. Going back to her love, world news, and in the city she loved was a dream come true. Being her own boss, her own woman, on a local business venture could be her dream come true.

What to do?

And then there was Paul.

I love this man. How can I leave him?

It was hard to sleep, hard to rest, hard to eat, hard to do or be anything. Whatever decision she made could be the wrong one.

The pen was a dead weight in her hand. India finally signed on the line above her name, and scanned the contract to her hard drive. As with the email to Charles Perry, India knew once she pressed "send," the decision was done. She toyed long minutes, shifting the pen between her hands.

India laid her pen aside and pressed "send."

The hardest thing to do was to say it out loud.

"I'm going to take this chance in New York, this new show. I'm going back. I'm sorry."

The shock and disappointment, in Paul's eyes, cut India to her core.

But she didn't unmake her decision.

India insulated herself against Shelby's comments, which were hugely negative. "You're making the worst mistake of your life," Shelby said, over and over again. "Why would you leave him?"

Gwen was equally non-supportive. "India, stop chasing glory. Accept what you have, which is priceless. This family only came alive once you got here."

India gave her a baleful stare, which was only returned with a baleful stare of Gwen's own.

I can't be responsible for you people. Grow up, get your own shit together.

India knew the signed contract was in Nick's inbox.

I can't stop now.

Christmas came and went without much notice. The girls had Gwen come over on Christmas Eve for small gifts and snacks. They put up a tree. India stayed with Paul on Christmas night, but the holiday didn't seem celebratory.

It seemed as if every one of them—India, Shelby, Quinn, Gwen, Paul, Ray and Adrian—formed fences around their feelings. The closer India's departure date came, the less conversation they engaged in, the less they looked at one another.

India flew to New York and dove into working on the new show, moving back into her old apartment where Amy now lived. She settled in and turned her attention to her new life. She began to feel her old hustle come back. She felt her arms and legs move faster, her speech too, and felt the slow, meandering small-town lifestyle ease away.

She tried not to think about whether she was happy or not.

The thing about the show was, it wasn't quite what was represented to India in the meetings, and that turned out to be good and bad. A news magazine show, similar to *60 Minutes*, was discussed in the meetings; however, India signed on to do a cold case murder review show, and the premier season episodes wrapped up quickly.

To Amy's credit, she was good to allow India to move back into the apartment, to the guest room since Amy took over the master, but in the end, India didn't care. They made uneasy neighbors.. Amy never seemed at ease with India, and India just wanted to work and come and go as she had to.

"Hey," Shelby said. "What's up?"

"Not much," India replied. "Just checking in, checking on what's going on at home there."

"Home?" Shelby's voice shot back. "You still think of this as home, since you left again?"

India slumped into the couch.

"It was a hard decision, Shelby. I wanted to stay."

"And you had that man eating out of the palm of your hand," Shelby said. "Gwen and me, we just don't know how you could walk away from him. I never knew Greg, I know that, but Paul was everything you ever wanted, and you threw it away. Like he was nothing."

Shelby's stinging words made India wince.

"Have you seen him?" she asked, and then wished she hadn't.

"Once or twice. I heard he moved out of the apartment and bought a house in the country. That's all I know about him. He seems remote. Sad. You know, we really could use a newspaper around here, but no, you wouldn't do it. You were the best person for the job, and let's get real, you have the money."

India's heart gripped, but not for the sake of the newspaper.

She hadn't heard from Paul in a few weeks. In the beginning, Paul responded to her, but then he went silent. Her texts, emails, phone calls, went unanswered.

I gave up what we had, or beginning to have, I know. I don't blame him.

"So you think this is too small-town for you, I guess," Shelby's voice rolled on and on in India's ears.

I had that chance, the chance to produce my own news, and I blew it.

"You know what, India? You're the most selfish person I've ever known. You remember what you told me about Ray? If I had a love I wanted that bad, to fight for it? You remember that? So, you go back on what you say, and you leave the love you have here, you move back to the big city, to the place that made you famous. Oh, well, I guess being famous is better than being loved, am I right, India? Does the money agree with you?"

India held her hand against her mouth to hold back the sobs.

"Listen, I gotta go. Ray's taking me and Quinn and Gwen out to dinner, so I'm signing off right now. But listen, sister, when you get your act together, you might think you're coming back here to save the day, and you might not know that man moved on in the meantime.

Not that he has, so far as I know, but it could happen. Or you could stay there in your big world and meet somebody else and forget all about that man who made you smile all the time."

India heard the phone disconnect, tears running down her face.

Amy burst into the apartment, heels clicking, shedding her coat as she went. She disappeared into the master bedroom for a few minutes before reappearing.

"A bunch of us are going out, you want to go with us?"

India looked up at Amy.

"Thanks, but no."

"No, come on, you need to get out. Just for a little while."

India stood up, wiping her face with a finger.

"No, I'm not up for it, really."

"Well, okay," Amy said. India noticed Amy's shoulders relax.

"You know what?" India said. "I might go out for a bit, just a little while."

Later on, India stripped off her clothes and got ready for bed, wondering why she went out with Amy and her friends. It wasn't that fun. In fact, it wasn't fun at all, and it wasn't the old crowd, the people India knew before, or the places they knew before. Conversation seemed shallow, the friends were superficial, and the drinks were watered down, with too many big screen televisions blaring in the bars and a forced feeling of entertainment. Nothing unique, nothing special.

The blonde seated at India's right elbow kept leaning in, pushing herself against India's shoulder, laughing too hard at jokes told by a slick-looking guy across the table from her. Everyone was laughing too loud, too hard, posing as if they were having fun. India's head was aching.

The blonde, India couldn't remember her name even though Amy introduced everyone, leaned in harder and said, "Listen, I think it's really cool the way you stood back and let Amy enter the arena and take the news desk."

She emphasized her point by waving her free hand in an arc. The other hand held a glass of wine. "I mean, you just stood back. That was generous of you, and it makes me respect you just a whole lot more, you know what I mean?"

India leaned away. "No, I don't know what you mean, but this isn't the place or time to discuss this."

'What?" the blonde said, bleary-eyed. "Oh, oh, I get it."

"Really, I don't think you do."

India shoved her chair back and excused herself, dashing out the door to the sidewalk of waiting cabs. The first one in line rolled his passenger window down and beckoned. India grabbed the door handle and got in, out of breath. The Pakistani driver sang to himself over the radio all the way back to the apartment. India fumed, slapping her hand bag against the leather seat more than once.

Once at the apartment, India took a long, hot shower, and found her clarity under the rushing water.

New York City changed in her absence.

Or did it?

CHAPTER FIFTY SEVEN

Shelby

Blindfolded, Shelby took Ray's hand, allowing him to lead her to a spot on the park's walking trail near the entrance to the cave. It was snowing–she knew that from before he put the blindfold on–and there was a slight frosty breeze. She didn't feel the cold in anticipation of what might come next. Ray promised he had a surprise.

"Where are you taking me, Ray Henderson?" she asked, walking slowly, carefully, allowing him to steady her from time to time.

"You'll see," was the only response she received.

Somehow, I don't think we'll be having sex out here, or at least I doubt it, Shelby thought.

The fact they hadn't had sex yet was beginning to bother Shelby. It wasn't normal for a guy not to want sex after the first or second date, and she and Ray were a thing now. They dated for weeks, and the most that happened was some seriously heavy petting. Just enough to get them both hot and bothered and then have to step back before taking that final step.

Shelby was anxious to get to that final step.

I'm getting more used to him, more crazy about him, crazy for him, by the minute.

They discussed sex from time to time. Ray wanted to wait for the "right moment." Shelby wondered how they would know when that moment came, since they were feeling each other up all the time, but not taking it any further.

Shelby didn't believe he was playing her along. Ray was too decent for that kind of stuff. Ray was not a player. He was solid. She believed Ray really believed in the "right moment," and so she was willing to wait. Or at least she had been content waiting for a while, but waiting was wearing thin. India was clearly having sex, a lot of it apparently, or had been before she left for New York. Shelby almost felt as if she needed to catch up.

She stumbled a bit in the snow. Ray shored her up.

"We're here," he said. Shelby stopped. She felt his breath on her face as she faced him, and he turned her around by her shoulders to take the blindfold off. When he turned her back around, she gasped.

"When did you have time to do all this?" she gasped, grabbing his arm. "You worked today, right? My God, it's beautiful. It's magic."

Shelby took a few steps forward to the mouth of the cave. The trees on either side were strewn with solar lights, which were just beginning to glow in the dusk. She could see a table with a white tablecloth, candles lit and two chairs pulled out, just inside the cave.

She gazed back at Ray in wonder.

Feathery white snowflakes continued to drift down outside the cave opening.

"Actually, I had some help," Ray said.

"Who? Quinn? Gwen? Who?"

"Well," Ray said. "Your daughter helped out quite a

bit with the ambiance. Gwen, well, Gwen supervised. I'm not much of a cook, so I had some help with that."

He swept his arm over an array of chafing dishes.

Shelby laughed.

She was swept away at the elaborateness of it.

"Come on," Ray said. "Sit down, my lady," guiding her to a chair, pulling it out and pushing it back in.

"It's not even cold in here," Shelby said, unfolding her napkin, laying it her lap. "How crazy, is that."

"Probably all these candles," Ray said, sitting down. "Let's see what we've got to eat," and he lifted the lid on the first dish.

Stuffed portabello mushrooms.

"Delicious," Shelby said. "They melt in my mouth."

Ray smiled. Shelby smiled back.

"God, I wish India was here to know this was happening," Shelby said.

Ray laughed. "Well, she sort of is. She sort of is here."

"Oh?"

Ray lifted the lid on the next course. Steak medallions in a cream sauce, with asparagus.

Shelby leaned forward as he laid a piece of steak and some asparagus on her plate and spooned sauce over it.

"That's gorgonzola, right?" Shelby said.

Ray nodded.

"How is India here?" Shelby asked forking a bite into her mouth.

"She's here because I called her. I told her what I wanted to do, and then we Facetimed, and she walked me through this whole menu. Listen, baby, she's tough. She made me make this sauce three times on Facetime, and then she said, 'well, I can't smell it or taste it but it looks perfect, so do it just like that.' She trained me, sort of."

"So, India knows about this?"

"She does."

The expanse of candle flame burgeoned and fell back and burgeoned again.

Shelby's heart swelled. Reaching across the table, she took Ray's hand.

"Oh Ray, this is the most wonderful thing anyone's ever done for me. And this food, it's delicious. The setting is beautiful. I couldn't be more touched. This is truly, truly special."

She saw Ray's eyes glisten. "Well, it's not over yet, Shelby. Let's have dessert."

"I don't know, I'm so full."

"No, really, try this," Ray insisted, handing her a clean plate with a slice of cheesecake, topped by a cluster of ruby red raspberries and what looked like, at first glance, a glittering tiara, half buried in the raspberries.

Shelby peered into the plate.

Her eyes met Ray's. She felt so full of wonder, she couldn't believe what she was looking at.

"Ray, is that what I think it is?"

"I don't know. Pull it out and let's see."

The cluster of diamonds encased in white gold glimmered in the candlelight.

"It's so beautiful, Ray," Shelby said.

In an instant, Ray was at her side, on one knee. Looking down at him, Shelby felt a whole new beauty, a feeling of completeness, a feeling of rightness, and such a sense of relief.

"Shelby," Ray began. "I want to marry you."

He reached out, taking the ring from her fingers.

"If you'll have me, I want to be your husband. I love you. And we've talked about sex, and you know I wanted to wait 'til the right time, and, I think, this time is the right time. I wanted it to be special, for you and for me. I didn't want our first intimate time together to just be a flyby, eat a bag of chips, go to work and forget about it. I wanted it to be special, memorable for both of us. I wanted it to mean something. So, if you will have me, will you be my bride, and you make love to me, and I make love to you? We live happily together and be a family? And, I want you to know, my proposal includes Quinn."

Ray was looking expectantly at her. Shelby was convinced. No need for debate.

"I will, I will, I will, I will," Shelby said, as Ray pushed the ring on her finger.

"Thank you," Ray said, grunting a bit as he heaved his bulk to a full stance. "Thank you, Shelby. You've made me a happy man tonight. I know this is all a bit old school for you, but I love you, and that is a fact. I will take care of you, always."

Shelby accepted his extended hand. "And I will do the same for you."

Later, on the ride back to Ray's house, Shelby said, "So my sister planned a lot of this out?"

"Yeah, and she told me I better get it right," Ray said. "She's daunting, that one, even on the phone, from a thousand miles away. But good-hearted."

"Don't I know that. Well, you did. You did get it right, Ray Henderson," Shelby said as the big car eased into his driveway. "You got it right all the way."

***

It was hard, rising from Ray's oversized bed, getting out from underneath his oversized comforter, but Shelby pushed out and grabbed Ray's bathrobe, lying on the arm of a chair in the master bedroom. Whipping the robe around her, she looked around for her phone. Ray was gone, having left for work about an hour earlier.

Shelby wanted to lie in bed and remember the night before. She wanted to savor the memory of the kisses, the stroking, the final unrobing, the giving all of her to this man who eagerly gave all of him back to her.

Shelby found her phone tossed aside on the floor and walked into the master bathroom. She sat down hard on the toilet lid.

Okay, this might be bad, but I'm gonna interfere in my sister's love life. India put Ray and me on the right path, and India needs a sharp kick in the butt, and get out of that big ole city and come home. To him. Sooooo, well, this is me, interfering.

Shelby remembered seeing the paid receipt for the electrical work at the Madelaine Street house. India tossed it aside, slid it into a drawer, and forgot about it, Shelby was pretty sure, although Shelby hadn't forgotten it, and she actually pawed through the kitchen drawers until she found the actual receipt, the document with Paul Funar's contact information on it.

I'm not stupid, Shelby thought as she turned the shower heads on, glorying in the spray, feeling powerful and optimistic.

Once showered, shampooed and pretty smelling, Shelby put Funar Electric's information in her phone, and called a taxi to take her back to Madelaine Street.

I'm gonna settle this once and for all. Shelby let herself into the house. *Pisses me off. I told her, I did, and there she is out in that big city acting like she's really somebody, I can't stand to let real love die, and that's what India's gonna do if she doesn't get her ass back here.*

Shelby punched the number.

There's no telling what I'm gonna say once she gets on this line. I might screw this whole damn thing up. But I have to try.

One, two rings. Shelby panicked. *I should hang up.*

"Paul Funar Electric," after the third ring.

Oh shit, now I have to explain.

Shelby's mouth went dry. Her tongue seemed to swell up in her mouth to where she couldn't really breathe or articulate.

"Hi, is this Paul?"

"Yes, this is Paul," the voice returned.

Shelby clamped her eyes shut. *Of course it's him, you goose.*

"Okay, Paul, this is Shelby Graham, India's sister."

She felt a slight gasp, some hesitation. Shelby swallowed hard and ventured on, words gaining speed as they tumbled out of her mouth.

"Well, Paul, at the risk of India shooting me dead, or you thinking I'm a candidate for the psych ward, I wanted to call, and um, tell you, um, well, that India's an idiot for ever leaving here, leaving you in particular because God knows she doesn't really need to work, she just wants to, she always has, it's just the way she is, and I told her she was an idiot in this case. I was on your side, man. I mean, I am on your side, but sometimes, well, India's really dumb. I mean, for someone so smart, she can be, I don't know, obtuse? Is that a word? Anyway, I wish I could say she's just really confused right now to ease your mind, but I really think she's just making a huge mistake, and I can only hope she figures it out before it's too late. She might be a dumb broad but she loves you, that's all I know. That's all I know to say."

Shelby ran out of breath. Her heart was racing. *I sound like a stupid child.* Silence on the other end of the phone. "Paul? Are you there?" *Shit, I really screwed this up.* "Don't give up on her," Shelby cried into the phone. "Don't give up."

"Thank you, Shelby."

The line went dead.

Shelby started to cry. *If I screwed this up for her, I'll just die.*

CHAPTER FIFTY EIGHT

India

The house looked comfortable, welcoming and homey, with a long front porch wrapping around one side. It sat far enough off the road to require a long driveway. A line of pine trees circled the property. In the darkness, India could see a white fence. All the windows were dark.

India could imagine coyotes crying in the night, a possum scurrying, deer gathering close, their gentle dark eyes, snouts bowing low, searching for sustenance beneath the last few patches of snow.

Leaving New York City was easier than India ever dreamed it could be. In fact, the farther she got from the Big Apple, the more she relaxed. The flight back was bumpy, but India had grown used to bumpy when she was returning home.

Yes, home.

She was almost shocked to hear herself say the word. Home.

Well, I'm here. For better or worse.

India waved the cab away, holding her bags and her purse, standing on the cold ground in the middle of the night.

If he won't hear me, I'm stranded.

Picking up her resolve, and her bags, India stumbled to the front porch.

This is his house. Shelby told me so.

She rang the doorbell.

Chime, chime, chime.

After a long minute, a light came on.

India winced, shivering in the cold.

I might have made a mistake but I don't think so.

She could see movement behind the front door with its long windows on either side. India took a deep breath.

The door opened, leaving a breadth of light behind it, illuminating the interior, except for the man, standing in front of the light, a beacon.

"There's no reason you would want me here," India said, feeling unbalanced, off.

He was standing in the doorway, jeans and tee shirt on, bare feet, staring straight at her.

India faltered for a second and then went on.

"Except I am here, and I should not have left, I was wrong, and, well, I love you, and that's all. That's really all I have. I love you."

India stepped back.

This could turn out so terrible.

The man in the doorway shifted, foot to foot.

India stood still in the cold, trying hard not to shiver, trying not to look vulnerable.

"There you are," Paul said, and stepped back, opening the door wide.

India stepped in, dragging her humidity-dampened luggage.

"Paul," India began.

He put his fingers to her lips. "But I have to explain," India said, her eyes fixed on his. "Something. I want to make this right. Make us right."

"I knew when I met you it wasn't going to be easy, loving you," he said. "You have your own stuff, you always have. I know your passion for news, you never hid that from me, It's not a secret."

"But," India interrupted, "I betrayed you for that, that life, my career. Tell me why you would even speak to me now, after I left you when I knew you loved me so much."

Paul eased her coat off her shoulders. India didn't notice it until the coat fell to the floor. "Quit falling on the sword, India. I love you, and I know you love me. It's that simple, India. You wouldn't be here if you didn't know that too. You came back a long way, and you wouldn't do that if you thought it was about nothing."

"My sister, she reamed me out," India said, and watched the grin rise in Paul's eyes.

"Well, that's sisters, right?" he said.

"That's sisters, I guess. I reamed her out quite a bit too."

India felt Paul's strong, sure hands cup her face.

"I love you, India Graham. I have since the first day I saw you. There isn't anyone else for me. Not after you."

"I don't even deserve that," India stammered. "You're so freaking me out right now but, I love you too."

She looked into Paul's eyes, those deep pools of brown and black.

His hand cupped her chin and he leaned in close.

"This could get dangerous tonight, India."

India smiled. He kissed her. India kissed him back.

The pull felt the same as it did the first time he

kissed her, all those months ago, outside the Riverwalk Café, the day they got caught making out in the cave. At that moment, India knew what they had together would never change. She would always want him, and he would always want her.

India smiled.

"I'm all in," she said, sliding her arms around Paul's waist. "I feel I ought to warn you though, I'm feeling dangerous tonight myself."

Paul moaned softly, and India felt herself being picked up, Paul's strong arms carrying her to the stairs. One, two, three, four stair steps, a pause for a kiss, and then up the rest of the steps to the hall, and then to the master bedroom.

India heard the door shut with a soft *click*.

Yes, I'm home. Gwen was right. This is home.

CHAPTER FIFTY NINE

Gwen

She was gliding through cotton white clouds, velvety to the touch. In between the clouds, Gwen could see patches of pale blue sky.

It was peaceful in her space, and most of the pain in her chest and back was gone. She felt buoyant, incandescent, and not numb or nauseous at all. Gwen held her hands out in front of her, turning them left and right, smiling at the beauty she was wrapped in. She knew she was in a dream, and she wasn't worried about waking up. She felt no urgency.

Moving forward, she left her soft blankets and pillows behind her. The fabric trailed away landing on the bed.

The girls would be alright. Quinn would be alright. Even Charles would be alright.

A long way in front of her but yet exactly right in front of her, shadowy figures began emerging from the clouds. Proximity meant nothing. They were far away, but they were close too. Gwen felt safe, content.

A shaft of yellow light, almost white, slid through the clouds, blanketing Gwen's face.

The light expanded with an irresistible allure, becoming all colors at once. She couldn't look away. It looked like a kaleidoscope bursting in the heavens, spewing jewels in all directions.

Gwen felt curious, but unafraid. In fact, she felt enveloped in the beautiful light, as if she was wrapped in a soft, comforting blanket. It was a rapturous feeling.

Hands reached out, voices called in welcome.

Gwen looked around in all directions. The light was carrying her along, as if she was a baby, riding on a gentle, swift river.

The hands kept coming, fingers outstretched.

Gwen was overwhelmed with the welcome and the love pouring out toward her.

One more time, she turned back to her fleeting memories.

Shelby, in her navy blue nurse's garb, throwing her stethoscope over her shoulder.

She's always rushing, and she ain't got no sense whatsoever, but she'll be okay. She's found her center with Ray, whether she knows it or not. But I think she does.

Gwen turned again.

India, glasses slipping down her nose, sipping a glass of wine, working on the news in the dark.

Ah, here's my favorite. That girl better figure out where she belongs, and she will. I'll make sure she does.

Last, Quinn appeared on Gwen's radar.

Oh, my love, my sort-of granddaughter. She'll be fine too, now the boy is back. She will be fine.

The volume of the voices increased as faces of long-ago loved ones began to emerge from the white, some singing, some calling. All wanted her to come to them.

Gwen realized she wasn't in a dream, but everything was alright, just as it should be.

She could see her bed. In fact, she was hovering above it, seeing the comforter dropped and left askew, leaving her shoulders bare, the wrinkles around her head on the pillow, her glasses lying on the nightstand.

I can go now, I can go.

The release was sweet, breathtaking.

"Here I come, wait for me," Gwen called, and let herself drift forward to the light, grasping for the welcoming hands.

CHAPTER SIXTY

Shelby

*F*or *the love of God and a mammoth-size carton of Twinkies*, Shelby thought for probably the thousandth time that morning, *India, can you not keep talking like I'm not even in the room? Hello. Bride here, everything's done, arranged, paid for, in the vault. Come on, this is my wedding, sister. But then again, thank you. Only you could pull this thing off.*

Shelby bet the old stone church in the country hadn't seen this much action in fifty years.

India was arranging things with the photographer, the caterer, the florist, and only God knew what all else. Every servile person involved was gathered around her and awaiting their marching orders. India had them all mesmerized. Shelby could see the Great Plan igniting in their brains, the earnestness India was instilling, the sheer will to carry her orders out mushrooming in their souls.

She's like a terrorist.

Shelby rolled her eyes one more time, making sure India saw it, which caused India to stop and say, "What?" which sent the minions scattering in every direction, intent on fulfilling their respective tasks.

Truly, India wasn't being mean, and Shelby knew it. India was just, well, *busy,* doing what India did best, which was gathering and commanding, while striking the most beatific fear and awe into the ones she was gathering and commanding.

"This is why I wanted to elope, or just go to the courthouse, this very thing here," Shelby uttered.

"Oh, come on, it's not that bad," India responded and then simultaneously shouted to someone outside Shelby's view, suddenly pin wheeling her arms, "Hey, hey, not there! Over there!"

Shelby frowned and sucked in her lip. India whirled back at her, looking her up and down.

"Why are you not dressed? What if Ray sees you before the I-do's? Huh? Oh, by the way, I like your hair. Now, scoot on in there now, the dressing room, and get ready because I think this show is about to begin in, like, twenty seconds. The organist is warming up. Come on, Shelby, move!"

And with that, Shelby retired to the dressing chamber in the old church, and carefully pulled her white strapless wedding gown on. India was too busy arranging things and people outside the chamber to help her dress, so Quinn stepped in.

"My God, she's a nut," Shelby whispered.

"Well, you put her in charge of this shindig, so don't complain," Quinn said, setting her bouquet down on a table. "You should have known better."

"Who else could, you know, get this done? I mean, really."

"Probably no one. Are you happy, Mom?" Quinn asked, zipping up the back of the too-tight dress.

"Yes, I am," Shelby replied. "I am very, very happy right now."

"So, Ray's the right guy for you?"

"I'm surprised you'd ask that after all this time, but yes, Ray is the right guy, the only guy, for me. And he likes you too, so please treat him nice."

Quinn handed Shelby her bouquet, a huge arrangement of white roses, white hydrangeas, and an orchid in the middle.

"If he makes you happy, he makes me happy," Quinn said.

"He makes me happy. He makes me so, so happy." Shelby looked at Quinn and added softly, "I wish Gwen was here. That would have made this day even more perfect."

"I figure she is," Quinn said, quietly.

"You're so smart, my dear," Shelby said.

Shelby gazed at their reflection in the mirror. Quinn was wearing a dress for the first time in a long time, a modest Grecian folded gown with a broad belt and pleats ina deep shade of purple. A simple gold chain adorned her neck, but of course, her eyes were made up, way over done. Shelby smiled. Quinn smiled back.

The organ music was swelling, and Shelby allowed Quinn to escort her to the front of the church.

It wasn't difficult to smile at the man waiting for her at the end of her walk, up close to the altar. Ray looked radiant, dapper and handsome in his black suit.

Shelby saw India standing at the front of the church, next to the minister, holding her bouquet of flowers, dressed in the simple blue gown Shelby asked her to wear. Shelby knew Paul was in attendance somewhere, and for a brief moment, she wondered if the step she and Ray were taking that moment would cause him to hurry up and get him and India married.

And once Paul and India got their act together, she

didn't care who else got married. This was her day, and she was on cue.

Shelby took her first step up the aisle, leaning on Quinn, smiling, walking elegantly to the front of the church to meet the man she was about to be married to.

Ray's cheeks were pinker than usual.

Shelby smiled wide.

I can't wait.

Truth was, Shelby wasn't about to wait. The urge to run to the end of the aisle, to the front of the church, grabbed her. The farther she got down the aisle, the more urgent it seemed.

Without warning, she gathered her skirt in one hand, dropping Quinn's arm out of the other, and kicked her shoes off. She heard Quinn gasp. *They can call me crazy for all time, but I don't care. I'm gonna run.*

And so, she did.

CHAPTER SIXTY ONE

Quinn

Quinn held a four-leaf clover up to Adrian's nose. "I found one! I told you I would," she said.

Just inside the entrance to the cemetery lanes and avenues, Quinn spied the tiny green good luck charm and quickly pulled it up out of the ground.

"Cool! Good luck forever," Adrian straightened up. "Let me see it."

"No," Quinn snatched it out of his vision. "Find your own good luck charm."

Prancing away, she looked back laughing.

"You're not gonna catch me, and my four-leaf clover," she sang.

She heard Adrian's footsteps rush up behind her and in an instant, she felt herself lifted off the ground and whirled around.

"I just did," Adrian laughed, setting her down. "So what do you say now?"

Playfully, they dodged pink and red azalea bushes

and urns of flowers, being careful not to get too close to other peoples' loved ones, giggling and hiding from one another as they made their way down the path.

They finally slowed as Quinn began pointing. "It's over here somewhere," she said, reading names on graves, walking steadily to her left. "I know there's a peony bush my mom planted next to it."

Quinn looked up to see Adrian pointing to a small granite headstone next to the red reedy stalks of a growing peony bush.

"Oh," she said, staring down at the name and dates. Gwendolyn Melva Baker. And the etchings of a beginning and end of a life.

"Are you okay, from Gwen and everything?"

Quinn felt tears coming, starting to burn in the corners of her eyes, remembering the morning she stopped by Gwen's house and Gwen didn't answer the door. Luckily, Quinn knew where the spare key was hidden, and let herself in.

Gwen looked so peaceful, her face was so pretty. Her eyes were closed, and she was lying in her white cotton nightgown, the comforter half off the bed and one leg sticking out.

Quinn sniffled. It wasn't easy to remember it.

The funeral was short, but the Baptist church Gwen attended for years was packed. Charles Perry did not attend, but sent a huge bouquet. *For who?* Quinn wondered at the time. There was no one to give it to after the service was over. Quinn rescued the beautiful white, pink and lavender flowers, keeping them until they turned brown and dropped their blossoms on the nightstand in her room. It was painful to throw the poor brown dregs out.

Gwen was buried on an early spring day, the temperature hovering somewhere between sunny and warm, and sunny and frigid, depending on when the wind decided to kick in.

Standing under the tent where the casket stood on risers, Quinn shivered in the wind and sweated when the wind ebbed. Her mother sobbed, while Ray comforted her, putting one big gloved hand over hers, pulling her close with the other hand. India sniffed and blew her nose over and over again, staring into space. Quinn remembered India standing alone, and then out of nowhere, that Paul guy was there and India was crying quietly into his shoulder.

The argument between the sisters came to Quinn's mind. What would Gwen be buried in? Shelby wanted a formal dress, which Gwen's closet didn't really yield a lot of. India favored something else.

"She didn't wear a lot of dresses, Shelby," Quinn remembered India saying. "Do you really want Gwen to be all stuck up in a dress for all eternity? I mean, she just wore them to church, and sometimes not even then. She'd be more comfortable in a sweat suit, really. I mean, they split the clothes down the back anyway, it's not like she's really dressed. Let's just make her comfortable, okay?"

Comfortable? Is that a word you use about a dead person? Quinn wondered.

In the end, India won the argument about the burial garb, but Quinn knew her mother hated the whole idea, and really wanted Gwen to don some kind of churchy finery for her stay in eternity.

Somehow, Quinn did not cry, or at least did not blubber, during the funeral. The ache she felt brought no tears along with it.

Without Gwen in the world, Quinn wasn't sure if life would be the same again for any of them.

Quinn brought herself back to Adrian's question. "I wish she was here. She meant a lot to me, and I miss her. She was like another mom, or a grandma. Someone I loved, who loved me too, and I didn't know how much I loved her until she was gone."

"I know," Adrian said, in a quiet voice. "She couldn't help it. It was her time to go, and she'd never leave you on purpose."

"I know," Quinn said. "I know."

They lingered for a few minutes, and then mutually turned to walk back down the path to where Adrian's car was parked.

"It's funny how we do things in tandem," Quinn said.

"You turn, I turn," Adrian said. Her hand in his felt warm and secure.

"I'm glad your mom's happy," Adrian said. "Aren't you?"

Quinn sighed. "I'm happy too, and I'm happy Ray married her. I really am. And they lived happily ever after," Quinn said, trailing her fingers through the air in a rolling circle.

"Yeah, let's hope," Adrian said. "But I think they will. He seems serious about making her happy, that's the good news. And you've now got a stepfather, maybe more good news."

"I know," Quinn said. "It's all good, I'm pretty sure. I'm just happy you're here."

"Me too. It's pretty cool working for India. She's taught me a lot about journalism."

"Yeah, I can see that, but you're smart. You didn't graduate second in your class for no reason. My mom told me India and Paul would be married by now, but they're not. I don't know what's holding them up, I really don't. It's like they screw all the time. I mean, come on already. Sometimes he even stays over at our house now that Mom pretty much moved out to Ray's place. They play music and stuff but still. Gross."

"Got earplugs?" Adrian laughed.

"I know, right?" Quinn said. "That's what I'm saying."

"Hey, Quinn, we've never talked about this, but you know, I just want to wait."

Quinn startled. "What for what?"

They were at Adrian's car, and Quinn grasped the door latch and looked over the top of the car at him, ready to pounce.

"You know, wait. For sex."

"I don't want to have sex," Quinn said, staring hard at him.

"Never?"

Quinn twisted. "I mean, no, not *never*. Just not now. I mean," she said, sliding into the passenger seat. "Like, okay, it's so weird how our birthdays are two days apart, and you just turned eighteen and I'm sixteen, and hey, I don't even have a driver's license, you know what I mean? Like, I don't even drive a car, why would I want to do something even more adult when I'm not ready? I never see Ivy anymore, and we're best friends, and she's all hanging out with that Duane guy, the one I don't like, remember?"

Likewise, Adrian slid into the driver's seat and was fingering his keys.

Quinn pulled the seatbelt around her and clicked it. "And when I do get to see her, all she talks about is him, and when I see her in school, she's always with him, and they make out all over the hall, worse than India and Paul, or at least as bad. I don't know, but she's changed, and we don't have fun anymore and I'm like, so *done* with that. Like, I'm over it. Over her."

Adrian looked puzzled but relieved at the same time. "Okay, well, just know I'm not ready, and that doesn't mean I don't love you, because I do, and I don't think you're ready either, and you've been through a lot. So, I'm saying, let's be kids and have fun until we're ready. Okay?"

"Me too. Okay."

Quinn watched Adrian push the keys into the ignition, and turn it over.

"But one thing I know. I'm never leaving you again, Quinn." He looked so earnest with the gentle spring light etching lines on his face.

"I know. And if you tried to, I'd chase you to the end of the earth, you know that, right?"

"I know that. But you won't have to."

"It's settled then," Adrian said.

"It's settled." Quinn said.

CHAPTER SIXTY TWO

India

India looked up over her glasses at the slight frame standing in her office doorway, the sunlight glaring behind her.

India minimized her email on her computer screen. A report came in, not five minutes earlier, regarding an Oak Ridge High School athlete, taken into custody for the rape of a classmate, while the classmate was passed out at a party. The athlete's name was Clayton Carmichael Reston. India's eyes widened, remembering Adrian's long ago message about the bonfire party and rescuing Quinn from a potential rapist. Someone named Clay.

Does she know? Has she heard?

Nothing about Quinn's stance indicated she had any idea of the arrest.

India decided to wait for more information, and relaxed. "Ah, hello there. What brings you to see me?"

Quinn stepped out of the glare, hugging her middle,

long brown bangs falling over her eyes. India warmed to how pretty her niece was wearing her normal, rich brown hair color.

A blast of hot, humid air flowing from the air ducts smacked India's feet and traveled up to her face. "This place is like a pig roast in Hawaii," India said, jumping up to punch buttons on the thermostat. "But of course, it's June, and the weather is crazy now. Come on, sit down, tell me what's going on."

India sat back down.

Quinn stepped forward, closer to her desk.

"Um, well, yeah, hi. I came to see if you would give me a job."

India pulled her glasses off her face and laid them down, remembering that long ago day when she approached Carmen Stauffer in that same building, in the office she now occupied, asking, or maybe begging, for a job, any job ("The obituaries? Seriously?"). She remembered how Carmen turned her down, laughing in her face, insulting her family. At the time, the rejection was a low blow to India, but after she found no happiness in New York, she returned home to march into a new venture with the newspaper and the building. India was ready to let history roll into the past.

She had it all now, or most of it. She had the man, she had the building, and she had the paper. Sort of.

It hadn't been easy.

Carmen negotiated long distance, always from God only knew where, on the sale of the building and the paper. The building sale went through with ease. After all, as India knew, Carmen wanted the money so she could keep traveling the continent in her RV. Negotiations on the paper were a little more difficult and time-consuming, and still weren't finished. Carmen told her lawyer, who told India's lawyer, who told India Carmen wanted her name on the newspaper as a "founder."

"Bullshit," India said. The paper existed over one hundred years before Carmen was born.

"How about manager absentia," Carmen's lawyer suggested to India's lawyer.

"How about done and out," India said to her lawyer, who took it back to Carmen's lawyer. "Don't bring this to me again."

Status quo, limbo, whatever.

No matter. The paper was running every day, thanks to India and her staff. It wasn't big, but it was going, and there was every possibility it would grow so long as India continued working it.

The air conditioning struck "on" with a roar. Bursts of cold air swarmed around India's feet. Quinn seemed lost in a vapor of sudden cold air.

"A job, huh," India mused, stepping around the desk.

"Yeah, I mean, I know I'm not old enough to do a lot of stuff, but I could maybe answer phones or, I don't know, I don't know, maybe this was a bad idea. I mean, I know Adrian works here sometimes, but I don't want to be a reporter or anything, I just want to get to see all this, all this," Quinn said waving her arm around the office. "I want to see how this all works."

India smiled. "Listen, how all this works is kind of complicated sometimes. The newspaper is slow moving, kind of dull, but there are things to do even so. I do my news show from here…"

"Yeah, yeah, I want to see that. I've never seen it," Quinn interrupted.

India paused and went back to her chair. "Well, if you're serious, I can find you something to do. It may not be the most exciting thing in the world, but you'll learn from it. Are you willing to put in the time? Outside of school, because school comes first, okay? And is your mom okay with it?"

Quinn sat straight up, a slight lean forward. "I'm okay with it. I get it. Outside of school, and school comes first. I'll do it. Whatever it is. Mom will come around. She's busy with being married and all."

India smiled. Quinn smiled back.

"Okay," India said. "So long as you talk to your mom and she says okay, you can be my intern. My sorta intern. I will find you something to do. You're hired, girlfriend."

India raised her hand for a high-five, and Quinn responded with a flourish.

"Okay, now, get out of here and do what you teenagers do. We'll be in touch. I got your number," India said, laughing.

"Okay, yeah. Great. Thank you, thank you," Quinn said before disappearing out the frost-kissed front door.

India watched her go. *How funny. I never expected that.*

India leaned back in her chair and smiled, twirling the chair around.

I never expected that.

She picked up her cell phone to call Paul about what to have for dinner. Once she heard his voice say, "Hey baby," she smiled, and began with, "You'll never believe what just happened."

The End

RECIPES

Quiche

10 eggs, mixed with a half cup of half-and-half
Four or five strips of bacon, browned and crumbled
Chopped onion, about a half of one medium-sized onion
Pie crust, store-bought
Gruyere and parmesan cheese, a handful of each
Mushrooms
Kosher salt, pepper, cayenne pepper

Brown the bacon and onion together in a skillet with a little butter. Throw in the mushrooms, and let cool.

Whisk eggs together until yellow and thick; stir in some half-and-half. Add salt, pepper, cayenne pepper. Stir in cheese. Preheat oven at 350 degree.

Line pan with crust. Pour in the egg mixture. Stir in the cooled bacon, mushrooms and onions.

Bake at 350 degrees for 45 minutes.

Accompany with:
Salad of torn romaine, ice berg, carrots, radishes, red onions, feta cheese, roasted pecans, and blueberries. Toss with salad dressing of your choice.

Baked Gnocchi and Italian Sausage

4 oz. baby spinach
2 tbsp. extra virgin olive oil
1 cup diced onion
1 ½ cups chopped peppers, assorted colors
¼ tsp. hot pepper flakes
1 clove garlic, minced
1 pound Italian sausages, casings removed
2 15-oz cans fire-roasted tomatoes
4 tbsp. tomato paste
1 pound gnocchi
½ cup heavy cream
1 ½ cups whole milk ricotta cheese
1 beaten egg
1 cup fresh Italian leaf parsley, chopped
1 tsp. kosher salt
½ tsp. ground black pepper
½ cup fresh basil, chopped
1 cup parmesan cheese, divided
2 cups shredded mozzarella cheese

Bring a pot of salted water to boil, then place a strainer in the water. Add the spinach and boil for one minute, and one minute only. Remove strainer and drain, but leave water on the heat. Squeeze spinach to get out the excess water, place in medium bowl and set aside.

Sauté the oil and throw in the onions, peppers and pepper flakes. After three or four minutes, add the garlic. Cook for only 30 seconds or so because garlic burns easily. Shove the vegetables to the outside edge of the pan and add the cut-up Italian sausage.

Dump in the tomatoes and tomato paste; continue to stir. Once the mixture thickens, move the pan to a cold burner.

Preheat the oven to 375 degrees.

Turn the heat back up under the pot with the cooking water. Dump in the gnocchi. As soon as the gnocchi begins to float, dump them into a strainer, allowing the cooking water to go down the drain. Drop gnocchi into the vegetable mixture, add the cream, stir until the gnocchi absorbs the cream and then remove from heat.

Into a large bowl, dump the spinach, ricotta, egg, parsley, salt, pepper, basil and ¾ cup of parmesan cheese. Stir, stir, stir.

Layer half the meat sauce into a casserole dish, all of the ricotta mixture, and then all of the gnocchi, the rest of the sauce and the remaining parmesan cheese. Toss the mozzarella cheese on top and bake for 30 minutes.

Accompany with:

Artisan bread, baked, arranged nicely on a wooden platter.

Salad of romaine lettuce, radishes, cucumbers, red onion, feta cheese, walnuts, all tossed into a pretty bowl with salad dressing of choice.

Wine, red or white, again, of choice.

Italian Almond Tart

1 rolled-out round of tart dough
8 tbsp. (1 stick) unsalted butter, at room temperature
1/2 lb. almond paste, cut into 1-inch cubes
1/4 cup sugar
2 eggs
1/3 cup unbleached all-purpose flour
1/3 cup raspberry, plum or cherry jam*
1/3 cup sliced almonds

Fold the dough round in half and carefully transfer to a 9 1/2-inch tart pan, preferably with a removable bottom. Unfold and ease the round into the pan, without stretching it, and pat it firmly into the bottom and up the sides of the pan. Trim off any excess dough by gently running a rolling pin across the top of the pan. Press the dough into the sides to extend it slightly above the rim to offset any shrinkage during baking.

Refrigerate or freeze the tart shell until firm, about 30 minutes. Meanwhile, position a rack in the lower third of an oven and preheat to 375°F.

Line the pastry shell with aluminum foil or parchment paper and fill with pie weights or raw short-grain rice. Bake for 20 minutes, then lift an edge of the foil. If the dough looks wet, continue to bake, checking every 5 minutes, until the dough is pale gold, for a total baking time of 25 to 30 minutes. Transfer to a wire rack.

Position a rack in the middle of the oven and reduce the heat to 350°F.

In a bowl, using an electric mixer on medium speed or a whisk, beat the butter until smooth. Add the almond paste, one piece at a time, beating until smooth after each addition. While continuing to beat, sprinkle in the sugar. Add the eggs one at a time, beating well after each addition. Stir in the flour.

Spread the jam evenly over the bottom of the partially baked tart shell. Spoon in the almond paste mixture and spread evenly over the jam. Sprinkle the surface evenly with the sliced almonds.

Bake the tart until the filling is golden and the middle is firm to the touch, 35 to 45 minutes. Transfer to a wire rack and let the tart cool completely. If using a tart pan with a removable bottom, let the sides fall away, then slide the tart onto a serving plate. Serve at room temperature.

Basic Tart Dough

1 egg yolk
2 tbsp. very cold water
1 tsp. vanilla extract
1 1/4 cups unbleached all-purpose flour
1/3 cup sugar
1/4 tsp. salt
8 tbsp. (1 stick) cold unsalted butter, cut into 1/4-inch cubes

In a small bowl, stir together the egg yolk, water and vanilla; set aside.

To make the dough by hand, in a large bowl, stir together the flour, sugar and salt. Using a pastry cutter or 2 knives, cut the butter into the flour mixture until the texture resembles coarse cornmeal, with butter pieces no larger than small peas. Add the egg mixture and mix with a fork just until the dough pulls together.

To make the dough in a stand mixer fitted with the flat beater, stir together the flour, sugar and salt in the mixer bowl. Add the butter and beat on medium-low speed until the texture resembles coarse cornmeal, with butter pieces no larger than small peas. Add the egg mixture and beat just until the dough pulls together.

Transfer the dough to a work surface, pat into a ball and flatten into a disk. Use the dough immediately, or wrap in plastic wrap and refrigerate until well chilled, about 30 minutes.

To roll out the dough, on a lightly floured board, flatten the disk with 6 to 8 gentle taps of the rolling pin. Lift the dough and give it a quarter turn. Lightly dust the top of the dough or the rolling pin with flour as needed, then roll out until the dough is about 1/8 inch thick. Fold gently into pan.

Courtesy of Williams-Sonoma

*For the record, Quinn used a dark cherry preserve. It was delicious.

Family Night Pizza

Basic Pizza Dough:

- 2 cups all-purpose flour
- 2¼ teaspoons (1 package) instant dry yeast
- 1 teaspoon sugar
- ½ teaspoon salt
- ⅔ cup lukewarm water (105-115 F)
- 1 tablespoon extra-virgin olive oil

Combine warm water with olive oil. Set aside. In a large bowl, whisk together flour, yeast, sugar and salt. Make a well in the center, pour in water mixture and mix until all the flour has been incorporated and the mixture pulls together into a dough (If the dough is too sticky, add a little more flour, if it's too dry, add more water, a little at a time).

Place your dough on a lightly floured surface and knead it with your hands until it is smooth, elastic and springs back when pressed (about 7 minutes). Shape the dough into a ball and place in large greased bowl, rolling the dough around the bowl to coat with oil. Cover tightly with plastic wrap and allow to rise in a warm place for about 1 hour, or until it doubles in size.

Punch the dough down to release the air. Turn the dough out onto a lightly floured sheet of parchment paper and shape it into a 12-inch round. Now your pizza dough is ready for your favorite toppings!

Alfredo Sauce:
2 tbsp. butter
3 cloves minced garlic
4 oz. softened cream cheese
1 cup milk

1 cup grated parmesan cheese
Salt and pepper to taste
Nutmeg

Ingredients:
1-2 cups rotisserie chicken, pulled
¾ cups mozzarella cheese
¼ cup parmesan cheese
Basil, if desired
Chopped peppers and onions

Preheat oven to 450 degrees, setting a pizza stone on the bottom rack of the oven.

Melt butter in a medium sauce pan over medium heat, add garlic and cook 30 seconds, stirring constantly. Add cream cheese, cook one minute until mixture is smooth, stirring constantly, gradually add milk and cook three minutes or until thick and bubbly, stirring constantly. Add parmesan cheese, stirring until cheese melts, and sauce reaches velvet consistency, about two minutes. Add a pinch of nutmeg and season with salt and pepper to taste.

Stretch the pizza dough out to a 12-inch round and transfer to a cornmeal dusted pizza parchment paper.

Spread alfredo sauce over the pizza dough, leaving a half-inch border around the edge. Top with chicken, mozzarella and parmesan, and any other vegetables you wish (i.e., onions, eggplant and peppers). Slide the pizza onto the pizza stone and bake for 12-15 minutes, until the bottom is crisp and the cheese bubbles. Let the pizza set for 5 minutes before cutting. Sprinkle with fresh basil before serving.

ABOUT THE AUTHOR

Yvonne Erwin is a women's fiction author, living in Springfield, Missouri. Her first novel, *The Discovery of Joy*, was published in 2015. She loves to connect with readers in person or on the internet, and is active in writing groups in Springfield to encourage and assist other writers in their craft.